The Way
of the
Nameless

By M.M. Bartlett

M.M. Bartlett

First edition

Editing by Alysha Thornton

Cover art by Magdalena Mieszczak

Illustration by Jessie McMurray

M.M. Bartlett

Dedication

This book is dedicated to: My Callan; my husband, Caleb. From day one you have been my knight in shining armor and have continued to be just that. To be with you is to live out my own adventure every day. Without you this story wouldn't have been possible.

I love you most.

M.M. Bartlett

Epigraph

"For every one of us, there's an army

of them. But you'll never fight alone."

"The World is Ugly"- My Chemical Romance

M.M. Bartlett

Author's Note

Thank you for picking up this book and for supporting my dream of being an author. I have always loved stories and I have always loved sharing them even more. Thank you for giving me the opportunity to share one that I have had swimming around in my imagination for as long as I can remember.

Before reading, know that there are topics like–and/or including–abuse, abandonment, death, gore, and trauma. Mental health is of the utmost importance and while reading about fantastical worlds with knights, faeries, thieves, and giants is something I would love for you, the reader, to enjoy, take care of yourself first! Welcome to The Five Realms!

-M.M.B

Contents

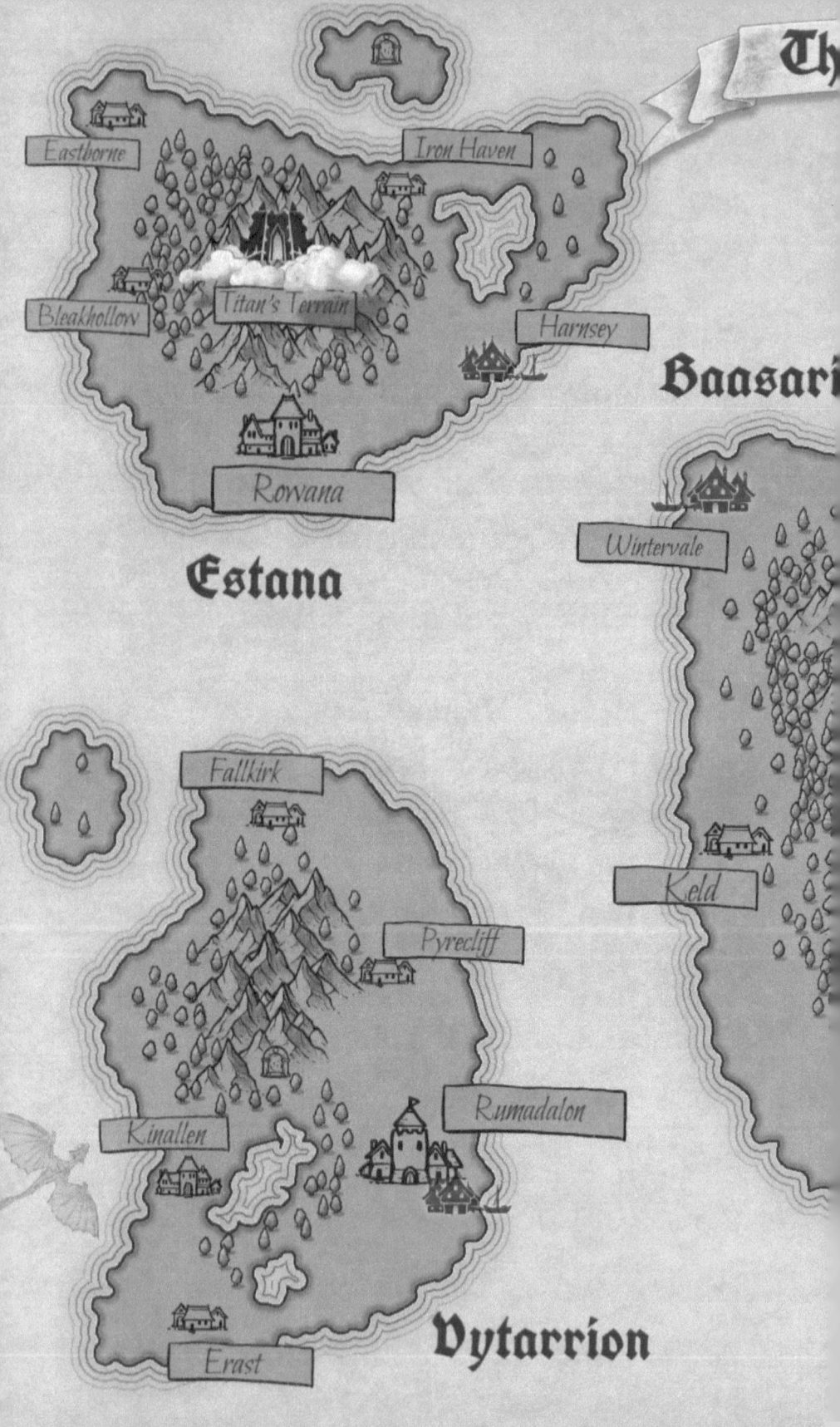

Th

Eastborne

Iron Haven

Baasari

Bleakhollow

Titan's Terrain

Harnsey

Rowana

Wintervale

Estana

Fallkirk

Keld

Pyrecliff

Rumadalon

Kinallen

Erast

Vytarrion

M.M. Bartlett

Prologue

The old man sat in his study, surrounded by the legends and tales he'd collected throughout his time in The Five Realms. As he looked around, he felt comforted by the endless well of knowledge and the security it granted those who sought it out.

Just before he could look back down and continue his latest edition on the history of Baasaris' plant life, his youngest granddaughter peeked around the corner of the door that had been left slightly ajar.

"Come now, Darcy, you know it is nearly impossible to hide when I can sense your essence." The old man had this conversation with the young girl on a regular basis, explaining to her again and again how her gifts were like an alert to him.

He placed his pen on his desk and interlaced his fingers as he propped his bony elbows on the pages he'd been scribbling on. The girl bashfully shuffled across the wood floors that had seen many weary souls take the same steps that she took now. Only, the old man did not see his granddaughter as weary, but as a young girl leaving the stages of being a toddler behind her. She approached his desk with curiosity. A look he hadn't seen in many years.

Across from him sat a large, hand-carved chair that his brother had gifted him long ago. He'd claimed the chair that had previously occupied the spot "didn't complement the rest of the room". The old man shook his head as he thought of the giddy whims of his brother and his endless need to craft and invent.

As Darcy pushed up on the edge of the chair and plopped down in front of him in a chafed manner, she scanned his desk before setting her big blue-green eyes on him.

"What is it that I can do for you this afternoon, young one?"

The girl fidgeted with her hands in her lap before she blew out a frustrated breath. "I know you said that it may be a while before I can use my gift but... I am tired of waiting."

The old man tilted his head to the side and smiled at the girl. He couldn't help but feel sorry for her given that most children with Draoi essence start showing glimpses of their gifts at ages far younger than she. "Darcy, I know it must be difficult to wait, but it may be that your gift is exponentially more special and needs time to grow."

The girl didn't show an ounce of gratitude or relief at his words, she merely folded her arms and turned her head away from him in one quick movement, showing her distaste at his explanation.

The old man leaned back in his chair and stroked his beard in thought, trying to find anything to quell the small child who was filled to the brim with worry over her seemingly endless waiting.

"Darcy, have I ever told you the story of Callan Bram?"

The small shake of her head and confusion in her eyes told him what he already knew. He hadn't told the story of Callan since the first time he wrote it down; on the day his own adventures were over.

"You remind me of Callan Bram. He was forever impatient when it came to waiting for anything. But Callan fought for the answers that he didn't want to wait for. Way back before you were born, and even before your parents were born, knowledge, history, and legends were not so readily available. In fact, if you knew something that you were not meant to know, you were often imprisoned and executed."

His granddaughter turned back slowly to face him, her disgruntled face carrying hints of subtle interest as he spoke.

"There was a time when humans with no godly essence, the Nondraoi, were angry with those who had the gift and afraid that they would be seen as weak if they took no action. Long ago, the five gods gave some of their essences to their mortal subjects as gifts. These gifts brought generations of elemental powers, flying creatures, and misshapen humans with horns, pointed-ears, wings, and tails. Do you know where Grimmstone is?" Darcy nodded silently, waiting for the old man to continue. "Grimmstone was the city run by the Nondraoi. They gathered there in large numbers and built their own weaponry and armies. But they did not directly challenge the Draoi people, the people that you yourself belong to. They instead began what we knew as the raids."

The young girl's face no longer held any trace of anger or frustration. She was fully invested in the old man's story, so much so that she had begun to lean forward in her chair.

"The raidsmen spread throughout the realm of Baasaris, they executed entire families of Draoi people in their sleep–sometimes, even the children–simply because the Nondraoi were *afraid* of the essence of the gods." Darcy shivered at the implication that she could have very well been one of those children.

17

"The raidsmen, led by the Nondraoi leaders in Grimmstone, worked quickly to wipe out most of the Draoi people in Baasaris since it was the largest of The Five Realms and the realm in which their city was the capital. But they did not stop there. They spread out west to Vytarrion and east to Qoohria, the realm that took the hardest hit since it was the smallest of the five. Much of Estana and Phyruh were untouched, largely in part of the uncharted terrain and creatures that dwell in the northern realms. But even they had clans of Nondraoi who would kill for sport."

The old man expected any young child to be terrified by this story, but not his Darcy. She reminded him so much of her grandmother, the woman he missed with every ounce of his soul. Darcy's brow suddenly pinched, "What does all of this have to do with Callan Bram?"

The old man couldn't stop the grin that crept onto his face. "I haven't gotten to that part yet. Remember that this story is supposed to be about learning patience."

Darcy settled back in her seat and gave him a quick nod, eager for him to continue.

"The raids began to occur less and less over time. The Draoi people left were largely in hiding. Some of them had to conceal their gifts or even their physical appearances to hide from those who threatened their livelihoods. Many of the Draoi left alive were children learning to survive without their parents, parents that they watched suffer.

"In a time of secrecy and terror for the Draoi people, rumors spread of a man called The Nameless. He was a mysterious figure who led a group of Draoi who were planning to take back their lives and overthrow the chokehold that Grimmstone and the

Nondraoi had on the realms. The Nameless urged those in hiding to come together during a time when the Nondraoi benefited from Draoi culture, Draoi artifacts, and Draoi history.

"You see, during the raids, any documentation or records of Draoi families were destroyed or locked away so that the Draoi didn't have the knowledge of their own people. Many of the young Draoi children even grew up without a family name. The Nondraoi believed that keeping their histories away from them would keep them weakened and unknowing of the essence in their blood and how to wield it. This was the only way the Nondraoi could hold onto their power over the Draoi people."

"Did the Draoi people join The Nameless?"

The old man was surprised that young Darcy didn't repeat her previous question, yet he almost wished that she had.

"No, they did not. They were afraid to gather in large groups. There were many cities, towns, and villages where you'd likely not hear anyone speak unless they needed something or purchased something from the market. Greetings, unions, and gatherings were slim to none the closer one lived to Grimmstone and in Grimmstone there were no Draoi people permitted entrance, outside of special circumstances.

"There eventually came a time when the raids stopped. It was as if the Nondraoi felt accomplished in their wicked endeavor to rid the realms of the Draoi people. At that time the rumored rebellion of The Nameless was just that, a rumor. A rumor that the Draoi people feared would bring the raids back and a rumor that the Nondraoi feared would result in the resurgence of the essence of the gods.

"Now, Callan was only a child of four, not much younger than you, Darcy, during the year of the last raid. It was many years later, when he was twenty-three years old, that his life changed forever. And it was Callan Bram, a young man whose stubborn, impatient, iron-whimmed soul that would change the course of The Five Realms forever."

The Way of the Nameless

Part One: A Whim of Iron

The Way of the Nameless

Chapter One
Callan

Callan knew only three things in that moment:

One, he was alone in this world (with the exception of Ash).

Two, he would stop at nothing to be the most sought-after White Knight in The Five Realms.

And three, he was about to fall on his ass.

Not so gracefully poised on a taut rope suspended above a small crowd of about thirty Grimmstonites, Callan had an arrow secured in his bow, ready to take the shot.

He was never really fond of heights, but Madame Loch didn't care about this disposition. Callan's training as a performer was strict and it had been that way his entire life. But this was his last performance at The Phenomicron. Madame Loch's contract with Callan stated that at the end of the season before he turned twenty-four, he was free to do as he pleased and make his own decisions about what to do next in his life. Of course, Madame Loch had always hinted at the prospect of just signing a new contract, one that made him a permanent resident at The Phenomicron: *Magical Entertainment Troupe.*

The troupe had been his home as long as Callan could remember and Madame Loch, the headmistress of The

Phenomicron, was his only parental figure, though *parental* was the last word he would use to describe Loch. She built her empire of entertainment on the curiosity of Nondraoi humans who wanted to see the essence that the Draoi people possessed, but to not get close enough to find out what it could do to them.

The Draoi people were predominantly in hiding, worried that another raid would surface and eradicate them. Madame Loch's troupe of Draoi performers were only protected by copious amounts of documents and contracts, secured and collected over many years, stating that they were allowed to utilize their gifts *only* in the confines of the arena.

The last raid was about twenty years ago. Callan was almost four years old during the raid and lost everything. All that was left of his past was a silver ring with a small foggy grayed stone set in the middle. The inside had an inscription that he'd never understood, the image of two hands just out of reach. He wore it on a chain around his neck every day until he was big enough for it to slide onto his index finger; it had remained there ever since.

Madame Loch took Callan in as a child and raised him as a performer. Unlike the other performers, he was just a Nondraoi with no essence or special abilities, so he earned his keep by learning various acts of balance, dexterity, and his favorite, archery. He had become an excellent archer, able to send an arrow flying at such precision he could split a twig from fifty feet away.

Callan locked in on the show's ticket stub that was tacked to the opposite wall standing about sixty feet away from him. The arena was constructed underground, making the outside of The Phenomicron look like any other tavern one would pass in the slums of Atreyu. The spherical room had hundreds of seats, but the

25

largest crowd hardly ever surpassed one hundred, many of the patrons visiting from Grimmstone, the largest city in The Five Realms and capital of Baasaris.

The ticket stub was an easy target for him. The majority of the act was *theoretically* easy for Callan. His arrow, which was covered in an igniting goo, would fly through Ash's beautiful flaming imagery and incinerate the ticket stub. As long as he didn't accidentally drop the slimy arrow or lose his balance and fall onto the egregiously wealthy spectators below him, he would be just fine. He repeated this to himself like a mantra.

Ash gave Callan her signal that she was ready. Of course, summoning flames wasn't arduous for a Pyre Faerie, but crafting an image of flame was a true art for Ash. Callan, having seen her flaming versions of rocky mountains, vast plains, and even blue oceans, knew they were a show all on their own.

Ashlun, who almost only went by Ash, came to The Phenomicron shortly after Callan did. They grew up alongside each other in the troupe that sometimes felt like a family, or at least what Callan pictured a family to be. Many of the performers would help to train Ash and Callan in basic skills like balancing acts, juggling, and acrobatics.

The Phenomicron employed about ten people on average, some had enough Draoi essence to call upon flames, water, wind, or earth while others had the abilities of many creatures throughout The Five Realms. Callan could remember a young woman with the eyes and ears of a wild cat who would dance along tight ropes and climb to vast heights reaching the ceiling of the arena, something he found to be absolutely terrifying when she tried to teach him her ways.

The performers took Ash and Callan in as their own, filling in the empty spaces where mothers, fathers, aunts, uncles, and siblings would usually be. Callan always saw Ash as the sister he was meant to have. She was there for him when no one else was and always would be.

Ash knew she had the flames of a pyre faerie when she came to The Phenomicron, always doing tricks like lighting candles with the tips of her fingers instead of using a match or burning the wrappers of the forbidden candies they smuggled in from the sweets shop down the street.

Ash grew into her powers at the same rate she did her beauty—she almost looked like the very center of a flame herself. Her hair was so fair that it resembled the first snows of Phyruh in the north, and her bright eyes would've blended into her irises if not for the faint presence of silver that shimmered through. She had iridescent wings—she said they reminded her of her father's— that were clipped during the last raid, and that was the affliction that would haunt her at times. Callan would always do what he could to lift her spirit and bring her back to the person he knew her to truly be.

Ash taught herself to harness her flames and manipulate their colors and forms to shape them into imagery and scenes like a painting. Callan would sketch things for Ash to then re-create in flaming form, and she would always expand upon them, her creativity and blazing artistry running wild; if he drew a flower, she made a garden. Even if he illustrated the city of Grimmstone, she would map out the entire realm of Baasaris, leaving his image of Grimmstone looking like a tiny speck.

There were very few performers that came along with the essence of Vytarr, The God of Day. From what Callan knew, there were very few who wielded the gift of flame. Draoi who were bestowed this gift were the first to be targeted when the raids first began. Those who came and went with this essence would try to teach Ash various things, but she would quickly surpass their talents, rendering them useless to Madame Loch. This, of course, would infuriate Loch as she would have to replace them in her elaborate shows with Ash, and in Callan's eyes, she was always more worthy of the spotlight.

Callan shakily turned himself around on the rope, facing away from his target. He knew his mind was looking for any way to distract him from the fact that his feet were too far from the ground where they belonged. He knew he would hit his mark, but the irrational fear caused his fight or flight to engage shaking limbs. With a slight bend in his knee, Callan took one bounce and launched into a backflip, sending his arrow flying through the air. He closed his eyes tightly and prayed to any god who would listen, though he had the feeling that none of them were particularly focused on his petty plea.

To his shock, he landed back on the rope with immaculate footing. He looked at his shaking hands to assure him that he was actually alive and not dreaming for the first time in years. That's when he noticed his ring had a faint glow. The small pulsing glow distracted him long enough that he missed the colorful flames Ash displayed before his arrow ignited and promptly incinerated the ticket stub into a small pile of soot on the ground.

The crowd leaped to their feet and cheered. Ash bowed, fluttering her clipped iridescent wings, casting small glowing embers around her. Callan gave a smile, a half-hearted bow, and a wave before quickly descending the vertical rope to his right that would have his feet back on solid ground.

*****

After their performance, Callan and Ash walked to a local tavern in Atreyu to celebrate their final night working for Madame Loch. Callan found the moment to be bittersweet; Loch always treated them as fairly as any other performer she hired throughout the years, but he was ready for the next chapter in his life, ready to join the White Knights guild.

Atreyu was the town in which many humans resided if they couldn't afford the luxurious homes in Grimmstone along with their Draoi neighbors who were hiding in plain sight in hopes of selling goods to those who strayed from the comfort of the capital.

On every other corner lay a tavern where a weary soul could drink their problems away. There were artisans who crafted useful tools and subtle works of art that were often overlooked as most residents of Atreyu couldn't spend their coin on items that weren't necessary for survival or daily needs. The streets were cobbled and altered by many years of repeated paths and passing travelers. The caked dirt and weathered holes served as reminders of what the people in Atreyu and everywhere outside of Grimmstone were: forgotten, strayed, and unwanted.

The faces of those that Callan and Ash passed were uncaring or sad mostly. There were very rare occasions of laughter or excitement in most of Bassaris' towns and villages. When holidays came and went there would be few smiles and celebrations, many knowing that once they passed, life would return to the mundane and ever-constant fear of the raids returning.

The Rusty Tankard was a modest-sized construction placed at the intersection of the roads that would take travelers north to Grimmstone, west to The Phenomicron, east to the sea, and onwards to the island of Knife's Edge. This particular tavern had the best ale in Atreyu, which was watered down on most days. The mead was subpar and the food, well, the food was sustenance for people who needed to eat something that wasn't bread and cheese for one night.

The barmaid, matching in her establishment's appearance, was the opposite of fair. A woman that no man would dare cross, and if–or when–they made this grave mistake, Claudia, or Claude to most of her patrons, would quickly remove the risktaker's nearest digit with the serrated dagger looped in her belt.

Opening the doors to the tavern brought out the smell of sweat and wheat. The latter from the ale and the former from Claude and her regular customers. As she sluggishly approached the bar, Ash ordered her usual chili with blackberry milk, always getting an odd look or a quizzical brow from Claude, and Callan started with a bowl of Claude's famous potato soup and a glass of mead.

The tavern had its regular groupings of rowdy patrons sitting around enjoying their meals and listening to the lute player's music floating through the room. Along the walls were worn paintings of battles from long ago depicting the gods, Draoi-gifted beings, and the White Knights of Knife's Edge. Posted on the job board just inside the doorway were posters from the rebel group, *The Nameless*, looking for Draoi beings, Xestorals, otherwise known as Nondraoi who could wield the Draoi essence with imbued items, and Draoi artifacts to "take back what is ours". Alongside them were job listings from the locals, postings of common thieves, and more political posters supporting The Nameless in his cause to reestablish the Draoi people in The Five Realms.

Callan noticed how weathered and tattered the posters were—no one ever took one down for inquiry and no one ever spoke of them, though they remained in their place on the board.

Despite the years of dirt and grime coating the bar, it was Callan's favorite place to go after performances. Ash pleaded with him on many occasions to try some other place, one that required less bathing after entering. Even in that moment, Callan could see the faint look of disgust that lingered in her pinched brow and scrunched nose. The only sign that she was going to make it through another meal at The Rusty Tankard was her slight sway to the lute player's soft music.

Ash took a deep breath after finishing her last bite of chili before she finally spoke. "So, we are free of Monster Loch and have all of The Five Realms to explore. What's first?"

Callan only had one plan, and that was to become a White Knight of Knife's Edge. The guild of mercenaries, adventurers, and heroes that traveled throughout the realms to help those in need. Knife's Edge was the name of the guild itself and was on a nearby island of the same name. Callan had often dreamed of the day he would take his first step toward the front gates and be trained as a White Knight.

He was a skilled archer and his performances at the Phenomicron required him to be quick on his feet, strong, and flexible; all things that a White Knight may need to go on missions and quests. He knew, of course, that Ash did not have the slightest bit of interest in being a White Knight herself, and her question

31

was leading into a repeated conversation of seeing the world and exploring places they had never been, ultimately prolonging his dream.

Before Callan could answer, whispers fell over the tavern and the lute player came to a halt. Coming through the door in his iconic black hat, a red feather poised on the side, and a billowing cloak was Captain Edmund Blackwell, the most prestigious White Knight to have ever existed.

"Well, do go on with your meals and merriment," Captain Blackwell nonchalantly stated to the watchful eyes, bowing at the waist in greeting to the tavern folk.

Many of the patrons raised their pints to him out of respect and genuine awe. Callan couldn't believe his luck. He'd never seen the Captain in The Rusty Tankard before and would've pondered why he was there in the first place, but his mind was wiped blank when the Blackwell met his ogling stare.

As Captain Blackwell and his fellow White Knight companion found a stool at the bar and ordered drinks, the lute player picked up a sea-faring tune that he likely knew would make the Captain smile. Callan thought the knight with Blackwell looked familiar, but he couldn't recall his name. In that moment all he could remember was that the man was famed for his brute strength.

"If you really want to be a White Knight, you might as well go and speak to him," Ash teased, drawing Callan's attention back to her.

"I have no idea where to even begin," Callan replied studying his half-glass of mead. Not being the timid type, Callan really wasn't sure why he had never simply gone up to the captain before. He had imagined this scenario in his head a thousand times, yet he couldn't conjure one introduction perfect enough to approach *The* Captain Blackwell.

"He is just a man, same as you." Ash's sage words were the ignition to Callan's flicker of confidence. With a heavy swig from his glass and a swift nod to Ash, Callan rose from their booth and made his way over to the captain.

Callan squared his shoulders and took in a too sharp breath that caused him to choke on his words. The Captain turned to face him, a knowing half-smile painted on his face.

With a stifled cough, Callan made another attempt at speaking. "Captain Blackwell, I am Callan Bram and I wanted to—"

"You are the young archer I have seen at Madame Loch's Phenomicron, no?" Blackwell cut him off.

"Ye-yes, I am," Callan managed to get out, somewhat shocked that Captain Blackwell knew of his existence. The swagger that he had managed to muster was beginning to dwindle, but he shook away the nerves once more. "I wanted to speak with you about becoming a prospective White Knight."

"Ahh, I see. Well, you certainly have the stamina for it, but do you have the heart for it? Being a White Knight takes the utmost courage and compassion for others. To simply be a White Knight is to give up your life as it is, to become a new man, or woman, in the name of righteousness."

Callan was fixated on how the Captain knew of him. Had he come to The Phenomicron? Had he seen him perform? Callan truly had no recollection of the Captain attending any performances, though if he was on a tightrope at any given performance, Callan had the tendency not to look down.

"Well, to speak truthfully with you, Captain, I haven't found much purpose in my life as a performer and I believe that helping the people of The Five Realms is where I am truly meant to be." He was proud of himself for that line.

His flame of confidence began to waver in stale air of the tavern. The Captain took a long drink from his ale as he looked Callan over. Little did he know that Callan was actively sweating beneath his tunic.

The lute player's sea shanty was the only thing he could hear outside of his racing mind and the voice of rejection that had begun screaming. Blackwell's companion didn't seem to even notice Callan was there as he bobbed his head side to side in time with the music.

Blackwell leaned to his left to peer over Callan's shoulder, looking in the direction he had come from, likely at Ash who he knew would be staring the Captain down. She had a knack for looking a lot scarier than one might think her capable. Callan always told her she was overprotective to which she would respond by calling him a hypocrite.

Blackwell jarred Callan from his thoughts, cheerfully saying, "Come to Knife's Edge tomorrow morning, Mr. Bram. I have, let's say… a challenge, for you!"

With overwhelming excitement Callan nodded his head and bowed, thanking Blackwell for his generosity and turning on his heels before the Captain could change his mind.

His mind was reeling. In the short walk back to his seat, Callan could hardly wrap his mind around what the Captain meant by "a challenge", but he didn't care. In a matter of seconds he was one step closer to what he had been preparing for; one step closer to that white armor trimmed in gold; one step closer to someone looking up to *him* one day as their hero.

Once Callan returned to his seat across from Ash, he told her of his conversation with Blackwell as he hurriedly finished his soup and the last of his drink.

Ash solemnly began, "Well, I guess there will be no traveling before—"

Callan cut off her sentence, "Will you come with me tomorrow?"

Ash gave him a look of surprise. "Come with you? What am I going to do?"

"Captain Blackwell may have seen your gifts at Phenom too! You could become a White Knight, and then we could travel throughout all of the realms together."

A moment of silence lingered over their table. Ash, still wide-eyed, said, "This is your dream, *Callie*, no one is going to want a faerie White Knight."

Callan rolled his eyes. "You have got to stop calling me that. And since when do you care what anyone thinks? Anyone would be more than thankful if you incinerated their *problems*." Callan gave her a mischievous smile and Ash couldn't help but laugh at him.

With excitement, nerves, and mead bundling together in Callan's stomach, they paid Claude their tab and left The Rusty Tankard, heading back to their rooms at the Phenomicron.

Chapter Two

Ash

The next morning, Callan was all too eager to get going. Ash was still sprawled in her bed when Callan came bursting into the room. "Why aren't you up? This is the day our adventure begins!"

Callan's room was next to hers, as it had always been. Ash was awake already, having heard his frantic rummaging, she knew he was in search of his nice clothes that rarely saw Vytarr's light.

The earliest rays of sunlight poured into her room, casting shadows over her bookshelves and vanity which was covered in letters she would write and never send to her father.

Her father, Kaster, had taken her to The Phenomicron abruptly when she was almost six years old. Ash's mother, Reya, was executed for trying to protect her from being clipped, but her efforts were fruitless. Kaster had just returned from meeting with the now disbanded peacekeepers union, in an attempt to stop another raid from taking place. He was too late. Ash truly couldn't imagine finding her only child, her wings mutilated, cradling her mother's cold body.

Ash's grandfather had come to their once loving, peaceful home as soon as he heard the news of Reya's passing. He'd told

Ash of her mother's gifts, the ones that she herself would one day possess. Ash–being a young child–didn't quite comprehend the information that her grandfather was giving her and hardly remembered what he rushed to say in those horrific moments, but even then she knew that it was his only opportunity to tell her what she would one day need to know. She often found herself trying to recall his frantic words but could only hear the wailing of her heart-broken father.

She toyed with the ring on her finger, the golden petals of a flower she remembered from her home shimmered in the light of dawn. The ring was the last gift she was given by her grandfather, promising with it the protection she needed to fulfill her predestined future. Ash remembered the very moment he slipped the ring from her mother's lifeless hand and brought it to her.

Kaster had flown Ash across the sea east from Vytarrion to Baasaris, carrying her in his arms for the last time. Ash would often dream of her father's wings, the wings that brought her to a safe place. She could still smell the embers and sandalwood scent that followed him.

Kaster placed her in the care of Madame Loch and fled. He told Ash that she was not to tell anyone who she was and that for her safety, she could not contact him until the raids were officially stopped, once and for all. That was the last time she saw her father.

Twenty years, no raids, and still no word from him.

Breaking from her fleeting thoughts, she looked to Callan who was all dressed and ready, nervously picking at a frayed thread on his tunic in her mirror. She watched him for a few moments and reminded herself that she wouldn't have Callan if her life had been different.

"We can't have coffee before our *adventure* begins?" Ash groggily slurred. She reached for her housecoat to cover herself, not really concerned about Callan being in the room since he had always been a little brother to her, annoyances and all.

Ash moved toward her wardrobe and lazily dressed into an off-white cotton dress, her belt, and her worn out boots with small burn marks freckled on the toes.

When she reached for her hairbrush, the weight that once held an open book hanging off the side of her vanity fell to the floor with a thud. A groan came in response from her downstairs neighbor, Ivan, whose features resembled that of a giant. He performed acts of strength in various acts and Ash knew he was not one to provoke. Fearing his retaliation, she yelped out an apology that certainly did not reach his ears. Ash knew this because the typical response she received was a string of harsh language.

Ash and Callan's rooms were on the top floor of The Phenomicron. Down the staircase were the third and second floors of bedrooms for performers and on the first floor was the entrance.

When the doors of The Phenomicron were opened by patrons seeking the taboo nature of the Draoi, they were first greeted by elaborate posters and artworks of the performers showcasing their acts. Many of the works had been rendered by Callan, his hobby of sketches creating the illusion of mystical experiences that would entice the patrons of The Phenomicron to enter the arena that waited below. The posters were plastered on a wall that separated the foyer and lavish downward staircase from the office of Madame Loch and her bedchamber which had always been off limits to everyone.

Ash could remember times when Callan would convince her to peek through the keyhole of Loch's office to see what "monster loch" was hiding in her "lair of secrets". He always had a knack for convincing her to do the most idiotic things. When Madame Loch inevitably rounded the corner and saw her snooping, Ash would be sentenced to a week of no performing, no reading, and no time with Callan. Loch was always far smarter than they gave her credit for as she sentenced Callan to the same fate and they would talk through their shared wall until they were once more free to roam the grounds.

"You really want me to go with you?" Ash brushed the sleep tangles from her long blonde hair that fell to her lower back.

"Yes, for the thousandth time, I want you to go with me. If you will not recognize that you would make an excellent White Knight, then I at least need the support of my friend," Callan expressed.

"Your *best* friend?" Ash prodded.

"Yes. My *best* friend in *all* of The Five Realms," Callan boasted as if he were delivering a monologue to an audience, "my best friend who if I didn't have life would be dreadfully boring and sad!"

Ash giggled and shushed him before partly whispering, "Fine! Be quiet before Ivan decides to strangle us both."

*****

The white towers of Knife's Edge were almost blinding to look upon in the bright morning sun. It was clear to see that the guild was built with The God of Day in mind, Vytarr being all things in the light and all things good and righteous in the realms. Ash's home in Vytarrion, the realm of The God of Day, was always bright and beautiful during the day. She loved the feel of the sun on her skin, of feeling like a flame herself both inside and out.

Ash thought that the long walk to the guild wasn't so bad. In fact, she relished a bit in Callan's discomfort seeing that he'd spent most of the walk shielding his eyes from the blazing sun between buildings that briefly cast shade.

The island of Knife's Edge was connected by a bridge to the mainland of Baasaris, the realm that was known for its worship of The Goddess of the Hunt, Baasis. Ash thought that the island didn't quite fit the image of Baasaris' lush plant life outside of its capital city.

Knife's Edge was surrounded by ships of all sizes, had very little trees, land, or living creatures other than the White Knights who inhabited it and the visitors who sought out the help of the guild. The island was practically made up of only cobblestone streets that were just as dirty and unkempt as Atreyu's, and the massive towers of the guild made them look even worse. The glistening white ivory of the guild's base was reflected by the waters it was surrounded by, making the guild look like a place the gods would live instead of the White Knights who were righteous in their duties but not holy in the slightest.

The large iron doors loomed over Callan and Ash. Ash knew this was Callan's dream. He had told her time and time again how he would step up to these very doors and present himself as "the knight they have been waiting for".

Ash rolled her eyes to herself, but even she could admit that Callan did look like a knight today. He didn't don any armor like the knights, but he was in his cleanest tunic, one with gold thread that used to shine against the deep greens of the fabric, but it now looked like simple threaded patterns on a faded sage green. She noticed that he even brushed his deep brown hair back and trimmed the scruff on his face; she had only seen him do this when they were in their early performances at The Phenomicron. His tranquil green eyes were on full display, shining with hope and excitement, ready for his most important performance she thought.

Ash stood by his side as Callan took in a deep breath as they reached the grand door of the guild. Before he could reach the golden rapper in the shape of a ship, the doors opened on their own. The entry hall to the guild was festively decorated in various shades of reds and golds, a stark contrast to the dark and earthy tones seen throughout Grimmstone and Atreyu. A grand staircase was the focal point of the large entry room that spiraled up to the highest towers.

Captain Blackwell's voice echoed through the foyer. "Welcome Callan Bram! I see you brought your incandescent friend along." Blackwell was dressed in the deepest shades of purple, billowing white sleeves covering his open, welcoming arms as he glided down the stairs. His long chestnut hair was tied back, some stray pieces floating about as he made the last few strides to them. She'd never been close enough to him to notice that he couldn't be much older than she was.

Callan and Ash bowed to Blackwell in greeting. "This is my friend Ashlun," Callan stated in a proud fashion, giving Ash a sly smile as he clasped forearms with Captain Blackwell.

The Captain bowed deeply to her, taking her hand and placing a light kiss to her knuckles, "Lady, welcome to Knife's Edge."

Ash couldn't stop the blush that creeped onto her cheeks, and she quickly said, "Please, call me Ash. I appreciate you allowing me to be here in support of my friend."

"You have no dreams of being in the guild? The knights would greatly benefit from having a knight with your gift of flames, a beautiful knight at that." Blackwell purred.

Ash had never received this kind of praise in her life. She felt like a fish on dry land, not knowing how to react to someone who didn't turn their nose up at her; to someone who didn't throw rocks as she passed; to someone who saw her as beautiful and not wretched.

Madame Loch had trained her to wrap her wings, to keep them as minimized as possible when she was away from The Phenomicron. Ash always had long hair to cover her pointed ears, and she never wore clothing that would draw attention from those who would bring her harm. She knew the Nondraoi were afraid of her, of her gifts. But she never understood why they *hated* her. She had done nothing to them. She merely *existed* and for that alone she was blamed and persecuted. It was as if her desecrated wings were not sign enough that they had already won.

She finally decided to incline her head and say, "While it would be an honor, I am not currently looking to join your establishment."

"Then perhaps, we can change your mind someday," Blackwell added with a wink. Ash couldn't help but notice the somber look that Blackwell yielded when his sea-green eyes passed over her wings. She felt at that moment that he somehow understood her loss.

Seemingly shaking off his distant thoughts, Blackwell addressed Callan, "Mr. Bram, I spoke to you of a challenge yesterday, it requires you to collect some information. Come, join me in my quarters and I can tell you more about your quest."

As Captain Blackwell led them up the staircase, Callan quickly looked over to Ash with the grin of a child having his first taste of sweets. Ash could only shake her head at him with a small smile.

Captain Blackwell's quarters in the guild were just as festively colored as the foyer, but the rooms were modestly furnished. The main room had a well-worn red velvet couch and matching chairs next to a fireplace, a used piano in the far corner with sea shanties written over an array of sheet music, and next to the large open windows sat a plain wooden desk with two red fabric chairs. Blackwell motioned for them to take a seat as he sat across the desk from them.

"So, the guild has been closely following rumors about The Nameless, have you heard any of them?" Blackwell led.

Unsure what to say, Ash looked to Callan who also had a quizzical look on his face. Callan replied, "We have heard that The Nameless are trying to rally Draoi beings and items to start a war against the Nondraoi. But I assume it's a lost cause since no one seems very worried about the prospects of a war."

"Ah, yes, but did you stop to think that maybe no one is worried because it is unknown what The Nameless may already have planned?" Blackwell asked. Callan sheepishly shook his head. The Captain continued, "Let this be White Knight lesson number one: you cannot dismiss a claim if you do not have the evidence against it. The Nameless may indeed be a hoax that city dwellers use to spread gossip in tea houses, but it could also be a veritable danger to the realms if they are found to be a real threat.

"With that being said, the knights have gathered very little information on an item known as the Draoi War Cuff. It is said that the cuff was forged for the celestial of Vytarr to control Nondraoi in a war of the gods." Blackwell leaned back in his chair and placed his boots on the desk in a relaxed manner and pulled a pipe from his breast pocket, "Of course, this item is that of children's stories and legends, as is the war of the gods. But, as I said before, if no one knows for sure, they cannot dismiss the claim."

"I'm sorry, but what is a celestial?" Ash couldn't help but interrupt, she thought the term felt familiar to her, but she couldn't place it in her memory.

"The celestials were very mysterious beings; some believe that they didn't even exist." Blackwell spoke nonchalantly as he lit his pipe and blew three smoke rings before continuing, "Legends claim them as the right-hand of their respective gods, each of them having their own celestial to do their bidding in the realms. You can perhaps learn more about them while you complete this task."

Blackwell gestured to Callan with his pipe, "What I would like for you to do is visit Nikolai and Percyful Cromwell in the village of Keld, a few days' travel from here. They are engineers by day, but the brothers have a vast knowledge of Draoi essence and items. They have been helpful to the White Knights in the past. Speak with them and bring back any information you find. Lady Ashlun–my apologies, Lady Ash–is welcome to be your travel companion but speak to no one about what you are inquiring."

The Captain rose from his seat prompting Callan and Ash to do the same. With his pipe placed between his teeth and his hands in his waist-coat pockets he began walking to the door. Had Ash missed the ending of the conversation? Had they agreed to travel on *his* behalf without the slightest idea of who these *Cromwell* people were, how to find them, or even how they would get there?

Ash felt her flames heating with anger beneath her skin. Before she could get a word out, Callan broke the silence first. "Why haven't the knights already spoken to the Cromwells about this war cuff?" His voice carried a hint of irritation that Ash knew he was keeping at a bare minimum to his real-life hero.

The Captain smoothly turned on his booted heel and faced them. He studied Callan and Ash and looked as if he were unsure of what more they needed from him. He took his pipe from his mouth and rocked back and forth on his feet before saying, "This is somewhat of a new investigation for the White Knights. I thought this would be a simple task for you to complete as a prospective knight. A test of your competence, secrecy, and speed in retrieving detailed information about the Draoi War Cuff from our trusted intelligence. This is information that we cannot simply transpose in writing. Remember, it is only a rumor until you have the evidence. Lesson number two: you cannot let that evidence get into the wrong hands."

With that, Captain Blackwell escorted Callan and Ash back to the grand foyer. He smiled deeply and said, "I will procure two horses for your travel and some basic traveling necessities. It is best to ride out first thing in the morning so that you can make it to Keld in about three days' time. I wish you luck with your travels." He told them he would provide them with a map and directions to Keld, reassuring them it was a straight path and that they couldn't be easily strayed. With a bow and a wave, Blackwell shut the doors to the guild and Callan and Ash began their walk back to The Phenomicron.

Ash couldn't help but feel as if the Captain was withholding information about this task. When she asked about the celestials Blackwell was quick to cut their conversation short. He was warm and friendly, she thought. Why did she feel as if he wanted them to fail and succeed all in the same breath? Why tell them next to nothing about this item that was rumored to start a war? Why not send a more experienced knight to procure this *secret* information?

When Ash confronted Callan with her endless questions, he seemed too focused on his path to becoming a White Knight to heed her worrying tone. He told her that the Captain could only give little information because that was all he knew of the cuff and that was why he was being sent on this quest in the first place. Callan reassured her that Blackwell was the very image of righteousness and would never put his people in harm's way.

She desperately fought the urge to tell Callan that he couldn't go on this "quest", but she wouldn't put a stop to his dream. Ash also knew that Callan wouldn't accept her reasoning, he would go with or without her. He would of course beg her to go until she conceded, but she knew that even she could not stand between him and his future.

Upon their return, Ash lingered at her bedroom door for a breath before entering. She felt like this was the end of a very long chapter in her life; she was leaving her home away from home and she didn't know when she would be back. The Phenomicron never really felt like a true home to her. She had been filled with a sense of longing since her father brought her there after the last raid. Although she struggled to remember at times, Ash longed for the Vytarrian heat, for the endless fields of yellow flowers, and for the open night skies full of stars she could reach.

She could only remember the overwhelming feeling of sadness. She lost both of her parents and grandfather in a matter of hours and was dropped off into the hands of a stranger and forced to hide herself from everyone. She was grateful that the tragedy brought her to Callan, but she still remembered the pain. She still *felt* the pain.

Ash looked down at her mother's ring, she remembered the last time she felt as if she were losing something forever.

With a deep sigh, she began to pack what little she owned. A few clothes, her favorite book that Callan gifted to her, and the sketch that came with the book that Callan drew for her. The drawing was of their first performance together. To anyone else they would seem insignificant. To Ash, Callan's small gifts reminded her that she wasn't alone in this world.

Looking into her vanity mirror, she contemplated what was to come next. She asked for an adventure and her best friend had procured one for her.

Chapter Three

Ori

The streets were damp with the afternoon's rain. A well-dressed man and his lady, also dressed in the highest of fashions, walked by. Her black dress glided along the cobblestone street and her obnoxiously large hat covered little to none of her hair that had been pinned in very particular places. The lady was clearly in distress over her hair getting wet. Her breaths were clipped, and she took gasping breaths between each complaint, though this was likely the doing of her corseted waist more than her anxious chatter.

Her bickering was cut short when she slipped on a stone that her dainty shoes were not meant to jaunt. The gentleman escorting her stopped to make sure she was alright, and while he was distracted a cloaked nobody bumped into him. He didn't pay the annoyance any mind, for the lady was all that he worried for in that moment. That was his second mistake.

Ori always preferred moving about in the night, her shadows cloaking her appearance to others. It made it far easier to pick the pockets of unknowing Grimmstonites when they were doting on a melodramatic female in desperate need of attention. It was even easier when they decided not to walk in the glow of the gas streetlamps; their first mistake.

Flipping through the man's wallet, Ori found a punched ticket stub for the previous night's Phenomicron performance, a few coins, and a picture of an older woman. "Looks like we have a mama's boy on our hands," saying this to herself, Ori pocketed the coins and tossed the wallet into a nearby puddle. Grimmstone residents were those who lived lavishly in the capital city of The Five Realms. The fancy man's wallet was likely full when the night began.

The Grimm family had been the instrumental factor in the Nondraoi rising to the tops of society. The Grimms, being the aristocratic heads of Baasaris, gathered large armies of Nondraoi to continue the raids that had begun decades ago, only with more force. The Grimm family was composed of vicious opinions on the Draoi people. Mainly that they were not worthy of a happy life, or- Ori contested–not worthy of life at all.

Arthur Grimm was the man in charge of not only Grimmstone but its armies, banks, homes, and everything he could get his greedy hands on. While only being the *aristocratic* leader of Grimmstone, the majority of The Five Realms feared the Grimm family's collective power. Many of the villages and towns lacked the numbers needed to surpass them in their ranks and riches.

The Grimmstonites called Arthur Grimm 'Art' and praised him for keeping them "safe" for generations—their *precious* Art whose predecessors were responsible for mass murders. The political reign of the Grimm family was one that would not be voted out or ended any time soon. The only rival to the Grimm throne was The Nameless.

Only rumors of the man circled around The Five Realms. A man who despised the rule of the Grimms and wanted to reinstate the Draoi people as the ones in power. This inspired hope for a few and fear for others at the possibility of another raid.

There were posters everywhere outside of Grimmstone with the agenda of The Nameless. Ori saw them as sad attempts to rally those who were in hiding and afraid to come together with other Draoi people in fear of being maimed or executed for their essence or even simply their appearance.

Draoi people with animalistic features were known as Corpoi. Ori and her mother both had traits similar to the arctic foxes that roamed her home realm. Ori had never met anyone else with the same features. These particular physical traits came with the bonus of better hearing from her slightly pointed ears, smell, vision, and agility. Ori could sometimes still feel the ghost limb where her white tail should have been above her tailbone.

When Ori was a child, her mother was executed in front of her by an attacker in the night. The man was cloaked in all black. A large hood, a black cloth covering the lower half of his face, and dark glasses over his eyes masked his features. Her mother told her to run, run until she could run no further. The only thing she was more afraid of than the man in black was her mother's own fear, so she ran. She ran to the coast and waited for what felt like hours.

When the sun began to rise, she ran back home, praying to all of the gods that her mother would still be there.

It was the same that day she stopped calling on the gods for anything.

Her mother was nowhere to be found in their once-quiet home. The unfamiliar quiet that now seeped from the walls reeked of death. Ori fell to her knees and cried, screaming silently for her mother who would never come to her.

When she had cried the last of her tears, a gruff voice whispered into her ear, "Your mother has kept you from him for far too long."

She didn't hear him approach, she'd thought he was long gone. Before she could scream the man in black placed his hand over her mouth, effectively cutting off her air supply. He dragged a knife along her cheek, a line of blood dripping down to her neck.

The man paused his torture. He muttered something under his breath in a language Ori did not know as he went from menacing to angry. He took her tail in one hand and savagely cut it from her back. The pain was too great to bring out any sound of misery.

Ori blacked out.

When she awoke, the man was gone, her mother had still not returned, and she lay on the floor maimed.

Alone in the world, she was forced to steal to live. When she was fifteen and old enough to travel by ship alone, she made her way south from her cold and unforgiving hometown of Coulteron in Phyruh to Baasaris. She thought then that Baasaris would be the land of promise and new beginnings. She made the trek to the big city of Grimmstone, more people meant more pockets to thieve from. More importantly it meant a better chance at survival on her own without the cold winters and unforgiving nature of Coulteron's residents. In her favor–though Ori viewed it as a curse most nights–she had a gift that allowed her to maneuver shadows. A gift she knew came from her father.

Ori had gone through most of her young life as a common thief. She had been sneaking around Grimmstone and its surrounding towns for three long, lonely years before she was approached by another Corpoi woman.

The mysterious figure was cloaked from head to toe. She spoke softly, "We are the same," and as she said this, she shifted her hood down to reveal a pointed ear, not so different from her own. Ori watched the kind stranger with trepidation as she turned and pulled her cloak aside to reveal iridescent wings wrapped neatly on her back.

Corpoi beings did not show their true selves to just anyone. It was rare that one would casually see horns, wings, or tails on people walking the streets. If they weren't hidden in some way, they had often been removed altogether. Ori felt that she had no reason not to trust her, the woman was brave enough to not only reveal herself to Ori but to also trail her long enough to learn that she too was different. Showing the broken parts of oneself was the ultimate form of self-sacrifice when revealing them almost guaranteed death in *perfect* Grimmstone.

Lyra was her name. She brought Ori into the world of the Celerity Channel and showed her how to put her skills to use as a *hired* thief. The Celerity Channel was a secret underground organization of thieves that operated through a tunnel system under Grimmstone. They were often tasked with *collecting* items and information that might bring the organization and its members considerable amounts of wealth, unbeknownst to the rest of the realm.

Lyra was a Lumi Faerie. Her eyes were the silver of the moon, and her dark hair would cast hints of purples and blues under the night sky. The Lumi Faeries were thought to have gotten their essence from The Goddess of Night, Qoohr. Lyra's wings were iridescent like most faeries, although it was rare to meet a faerie that still had any wings left at all.

One of Lyra's wings was whole while the other was horribly scarred restricting her from flying more than a few feet, but they were still beautiful. Ori would catch herself staring at them when they were in the channel and free to show their true natures. Lights from lamps and candles showed the sparkling shades of blue, green, purple, and silver that would make them glow on certain nights more than others. Lyra had always said that the fullest of moons would make them glow, longing for their return to the ocean.

In a village by the sea, Lyra grew up in Qoohria, the realm to the southeast of Baasaris. Her parents told her of their heritage as much as they could, a rare thing to have being a child born during the raids, but there were very few stories that Lyra shared with Ori. One story in particular that Ori remembered was a tale Lyra told her one night after Ori had awoken from a nightmare of her past life.

"Once upon a time, there was a world where Lumi Faeries ruled the seas. When the night goddess called upon the Lumi Faeries, they would shift into their true forms of seadragons and patrol the darkest waters of The Five Realms for enemies of Qoohr..."

The tale was that of legend according to Lyra, one that her parents told her too when she was young. Lyra's parents were taken from her by the raids. She had come home from visiting her friend in the neighboring village, to find her parents' lives stolen from them.

When she tried to run and tell someone, anyone of what had happened, she was captured by a lone raidsmen who had stayed behind in search of her. Before she could get away, he mangled her now dysfunctional right wing. Lyra told Ori then that she often pondered what could have happened that day if she hadn't managed to escape his clutches. Ori knew the feeling.

Lyra was the one person Ori looked up to in this world of darkness. Lyra taught her the ways of the Celerity Channel and how to utilize her gifts in their line of work. Ori was often tasked with simple jobs where she would lurk in dark corners and listen for information about The Nameless. The Celerity Channel had been interested in The Nameless' efforts of bringing the Draoi people back to the forefront of The Five Realms. Ori dismissed the majority of the claims she would hear whispered in tea houses or outside of taverns. She knew there would never be hope like what The Nameless promised.

Aside from the fancy man's wallet, Ori hadn't found much of the night to be fruitful and had begun her walk back to the buried haven of thieves where she would add her new coins to her stash and open the bottle of blackberry mead that she swiped from a showcase window. She always thought it was rather silly of them to leave bottles out for people to taste. Ori figured she could just *taste* the whole bottle–since they were offering.

When Ori neared the corner of the museum, which held only stolen artifacts of the Draoi and the history of the Grimm empire, she heard someone whispering. She cursed under her breath. This *would* be the alleyway someone chose to occupy as it was the nearest to her with an entrance to the channel.

Cloaking herself in her shadows, Ori slowly rounded the corner and found not one familiar silhouette, but two. Lyra was dressed in her black leathers from head to toe, her hood pulled over her face. The only reason Ori knew it was Lyra was the dagger strapped to her left thigh, a Qoohrian blade with three opals embedded in the hilt. Lyra had gifted her the twin blade on her past birthday.

The second figure took no attempt at masking himself. His black, red feathered hat would have given him away anywhere in Baasaris. Captain Blackwell of Knife's Edge was poised, leaning against the brick wall of the museum. He was patiently listening to Lyra, who seemed to be rather upset by their conversation.

Ori honed in her auditory range, "Do you have any idea how dangerous this is? Sending two ill-prepared *children* to look for one of the most formidable weapons in the history of The Five Realms?" Lyra placed her forehead in her hand and crossed her other arm over in clear frustration.

Blackwell's smoky voice was hushed when he replied. "What reason do we have to believe that this supposed weapon is *real* at all? The last celestial to Vytarr died two decades ago and the legend of the war cuff with them. Who's to say that the war cuff even existed in the first place? This is the only way. We had to send her. She is the only one who can wield it anyway if it is more than a rumor."

Blackwell pushed off the wall, towering over Lyra by almost a foot. That's not to say that Lyra was short, the Captain was just very tall, reaching probably above 6 foot 4 without the hat and feather. He took the hand that was placed over her face and held it between his own hands. "Lyra, I know you and everyone else in The Five Realms have been hoping for this retribution on the Nondraoi, but I truly do not believe it will come as soon as you would like. Let us nullify some of the rumors or at the very least, gather more information before we jump into a war we are not prepared to fight in or for."

Lyra pulled her hand away from Blackwell with an expression Ori could only see as hurt.

"I will always be ready and willing to fight this particular war. My people have been in hiding for too long for crimes that were never committed. For crimes of which they were blamed. I have no family outside of the one I have made on my own and I will protect them with my own life." Lyra stepped back a pace, just out of arm's reach.

"I hope you are right about that cuff. I hope that it isn't as dangerous as the legends have taught. But I still hope that it could be the remedy to what I have been searching for my entire life. Peace. I hope that she is the answer we have been waiting for." Lyra turned and solemnly walked through the channel entrance leaving the Captain alone. Blackwell waited in the darkness of the alley for all of ten agonizing minutes before he turned back towards the way of the guild.

*****

Ori's mind swam with the information. What the hell was this cuff they spoke about? What the hell was this about a war? And what the hell was Lyra doing even speaking to the captain of the White Knights? Lyra was putting not only herself but the Celerity Channel in danger by even being associated with Blackwell. And they seemed... *close*. *Intimate* even, Ori thought.

The channel entrance was a small opening in the back of the alley that most passersby wouldn't take notice of. When no one was around–finally–Ori slipped through and began the long spiral down to her room. The tunnel system slowly turned less structured the further one walked, the walls of brick and stone smoothed out into a cave-like structure. Once the city overhead was long behind, the cave ceilings opened up to the night sky. The base of the Celerity Channel was perched beneath the Baasarian mountains, pools of shimmering waters were spread throughout the channel, and embedded in the halls were dozens of rooms for each of its members.

Ori's room was near the end of one of the many tunnels. Ori's room had a simple cot, a desk cluttered with various jobs current and passed, and an armoire filled with black leathers and various weapons. She had few belongings, many of them *collected* through her time in Baasaris.

The walls were bare with the exception of one painting hanging above her cot. After her first year in the channel, Ori was walking the streets of Atreyu when she saw the painting in an artisan shop. The woman she bought the painting from was overjoyed by the purchase—Ori had never purchased anything in her life and hadn't since.

The painting depicted the mountains of her home in Coulteron. The small houses painted in detail were covered by a fresh, untouched snow, the only light coming from the soft glow of candles in the windows which were lit in remembrance of those lost in the raids. Only the Draoi people knew of the candles and their meaning.

Ori popped the cork from her mead bottle, taking a large gulp as she placed her belts and pouch of collected coins from the night on her desk before changing into her nightgown. She sat at her desk and dismantled her braids before running her fingers through her dark, red hair that almost reached the small of her back when it was down.

There was no mirror for her to look into, she had no desire to look at the face of her mother in her own reflection. The face framed by the red hair she knew came from someone else. The face that she only remembered as frozen in fear. The face that bore the mark of her father, the thin white scar that ran along her cheek.

When Ori lay down, she stared at the cracked ceiling. The ceiling that was now spinning from her heavy consumption of alcohol. Running through Lyra and Blackwell's vague discussion, she thought about what stood out to her. *A war cuff. Ill-prepared children. War. Nondraoi.* That last word stuck out in her mind. She knew it to be a slang term for humans without godly essence, but she hadn't heard anyone dare speak it near Grimmstone until it came from Blackwell's mouth. Nondraoi was a slight to those without gifts–of curses, rather– from the gods. As far as Ori was concerned, she would have preferred being called Nondraoi over feeling like an *abomination* most days.

What would provoke Blackwell to speak this way about his own people? He clearly seemed to be fixated on Lyra and what she wanted, trying to make her feel better about a decision that *he* seemed to have made without her. Was Lyra in trouble?

Thoughts raced through her mind as her eyes grew heavier. She drifted into a dreamless sleep aided by the aged blackberry and honey concoction. She longed for these nights when her mind didn't roam into the dark corners she tried to avoid. It was nightmares that plagued her most nights.

M.M. Bartlett

*****

When she awoke, Ori dressed in her leathers, pinned her hair in braids, and exited the channel before anyone else would notice her absence. She'd made the decision upon waking to find out exactly what Captain Blackwell's plan was to "help" Lyra.

The few hours it took her to make it to Knife's Edge paid off greatly. Ori was able to *collect* various supplies and snacks for travel in the event she was gone for a couple of days. When she was mere feet away from the guild towers, she leaned against one of the few trees on the island and made herself look busy. Busy for Ori, in this case, meant cleaning the underside of her fingernails with her dagger.

She had a plan and this was the only way for her to learn what Lyra was keeping from her. The only way to find out what she was doing that could put herself in danger and what Blackwell was doing to aid in that danger. Lyra didn't keep things like this from Ori. Something had to be immensely wrong.

It was only minutes later that she saw a young man with dark hair and a look of arrogance riding away from the guild on a horse weighed down with traveling necessities. He had a bow and quiver strapped to his back; an archer then. He sat tall and didn't make a single effort to look at any point other than the one leading to his destination. She might've thought he was older seeing his neatly trimmed beard, but his sparkling eyes gave away his youth. A sparkle that she found herself jealous of.

His companion rode behind him, a woman whose long locks of hair seemed to glow in the light of day. Her expression was that of worry and hope intertwined.

Then Ori saw the woman's wings.

They were wrapped in the same way Lyra had always wrapped hers. Small leather straps to contain what wings remained, Ori struggled to hold back her shock. Corpoi *never* show their features for everyone to see. Did she know how reckless this was? How easily she could be harmed?

The woman met her stare and gave a soft smile. Ori reigned in her focus, these had to be the two *ill-prepared children* that Lyra spoke of to the captain. Though, she knew they couldn't be younger than she.

*****

Ori trailed the pair for an entire day, keeping a far enough distance that they wouldn't notice her pursuit. She knew they were heading west but this told her nothing yet of their final destination.

The only things they talked about were stories in their books and of people that Ori did not know, but she assumed those they spoke of were either friends or relatives by the inflection of fondness in their voices. She did however pick up on the notion that the pair were performers of some sort. Did they work at The Phenomicron? Ori figured that was why the Corpoi woman didn't seem bothered that her wings were unconcealed. Performers at The

Phenomicron were *allowed* to be themselves, at least within the confines of their area. Ori supposed she knew how that felt to a certain extent. Like a caged animal, only these performers were expected to dance in their cages.

When the travelers stopped outside of a small village to set up camp, Ori scaled a nearby tree to remain out of sight. Once the pair laid out their bed rolls, the Corpoi woman with iridescent wings so much like Lyra's knelt a few feet away. She began setting aside a few sticks and leaves to start a fire. Instead of lighting a match, the woman placed her hand over the brush and conjured flames from her fingertips.

She was a Pyre Faerie.

Lyra had told her there were other faeries in The Five Realms but she hadn't imagined this. The last of the Pyre Faeries were thought long gone, but there one sat delicately in the grass below her. Distracted by her sheer admiration of the woman's gift of flame, Ori was too slow to notice that her bag she'd placed in her lap had begun to shift. A single stolen apple fell from her high perch to the ground with a thud.

The young man was quick to secure an arrow in his bow, aimed directly at her. She didn't even see him, he moved so quickly that Ori had no choice but to stay as still as possible. Like prey caught in a trap.

"I told you we were being followed," the archer nonchalantly called over his shoulder to the Pyre Faerie. His green eyes burned through her very soul.

Chapter Four

Callan

He had never seen eyes like hers. She sat crouched in the tree above their campsite, her golden eyes were a beacon in the setting sun. Those very eyes were on patrol of every movement, every breath. Callan wasn't sure if *she* was even breathing, she was so still.

"Who are you and why are you following us?" He kept his arrow nocked, his eyes on the golden-eyed woman, and Ash in his peripheral vision. The woman took a long time to formulate an answer. She studied him and then Ash. The woman's eyes seemed to soften ever so slightly when she looked at Ash, her gilded focus lingering on her wings.

"You're a Pyre Faerie." The woman stated this with curiosity. Callan darted his eyes to Ash who stood with the same curious look on her face, mirroring the strange creature perched in the tree. He was losing what little patience he had. He had been on edge the entire day, he swore he felt her presence from the moment they'd left the guild that morning. Ash would only dismiss his intuition as nerves about the journey they were taking. He filed away his "I told you so" for later.

"Look,"--he drew her attention to him once more–"I have half a mind to let this arrow fly, and believe me, I do not miss what I intend to hit. Tell me who you are and why you are here." Callan felt irritated and intrigued all at the same time, leaving his stomach in knots. She glared at him with the same expressions twisted on her own face, her eyes narrowed.

The woman took in a deep breath, looked between the two of them again, and finally conceded, "My name is Ori." She looked away, back towards the direction from which they came. Ori hesitated before she said, "I believe my friend may be in danger. I heard her speaking about an item that the two of you may be looking for and I followed you in hopes of finding a way to protect her from whatever she has gotten herself into."

Callan could sense Ori wasn't telling the whole truth, but when she spoke of her friend, he could feel the worry in her words. The same trepidation he had heard in Ash's voice when she would fret over him.

He fixed his bow to his back once more and put his arrow in the quiver, keeping them at an easily accessible distance. He watched as Ori descended from her branch. Callan didn't miss the ease in which she climbed, as if she were someone used to sneaking about. She was dressed in black leathers from head to toe, she was no lady, and she was not on a leisurely stroll. Ori turned and addressed Ash directly. Even though Ori approached with caution, Callan felt himself stepping closer to Ash. "My friend is a faerie too, although she calls herself a Lumi Faerie. Where you have flame, she has water."

"My father once told me of Lumi Faeries, but I have not met one myself. I haven't met *any* other faeries for that matter." Ash gave Ori a tentative smile which was returned with a brittle grin. "You said your friend mentioned the item we are looking for, do you know what it is?"

Callan knew Ash was trying to sort out if Ori was someone they could trust or someone to keep in the dark. Before they left Knife's Edge, Captain Blackwell reminded them not to tell anyone of what they were searching for other than the Cromwell brothers. Ash thought Callan was taking his mission far too seriously, but he wouldn't jeopardize his opportunity to join the most prestigious guild in The Five Realms. And he surely wasn't going to let Ori be the deciding factor of his admittance.

"Truthfully, I do not know what it is or what it does. All I know is that it is dangerous and powerful, if it even exists. I overheard my friend speaking with Captain Blackwell and that's how I learned that there would be two people heading out to find information. All I ask is that I accompany you so that I can know if there is a threat to my friend. I don't need details, just reassurance." Ori's words still felt twisted. Part lie and part truth.

Callan was preparing to tell her to get lost, but Ash spoke first, "Would you mind if Callan and I talk privately for a moment?" Ori shook her head in confirmation, and she moved a short distance from them. Callan was quick to notice that she wouldn't be taking her eyes off them while they spoke "privately", as if *they* were the threat here.

Ash stayed silent for a moment, and Callan not-so-patiently waited while she processed her thoughts carefully. He had the sneaking suspicion that Ash was going to offer for this complete stranger to join them.

"I can see that she does have true concern for her friend. You may not know this, but Corpoi people typically don't show others their true appearances. I was different because I was in Phenom and had the protection of Madame Loch as a performer. The fact that she openly shared that her friend is a faerie tells me she is willing to give that information freely for us to trust her, at least enough to let her tag along." So much for that *sneaking* suspicion, he thought.

Callan removed his eyes from Ori long enough to roll them as dramatically as he could. "We have *no* idea who *she* is," he whisper-shouted, "she could be a *murderer* for all we know! She could work for The Nameless!"

Ash slapped Callan's upper arm, the sting made him break his hard demeanor more than he would've liked. He looked back to Ori again as he rubbed the phantom handprint on his bicep. He could've sworn he caught the corner of her lip curve upward.

"If she wanted to kill us, don't you think she would've done that already? She's had multiple opportunities to throw that huge dagger through the back of your all-too-large head. If she worked for The Nameless, I doubt she would have given us her name or the information about Blackwell. I am sure she is hiding things, but so are we. We will let her know the minimum of what she needs and I'm sure she will tell us the minimum of what we need." Ash then turned on her heels and walked directly to Ori.

Callan was stunned, frozen in place by the metaphorical fire that laced Ash's words. He couldn't help but feel like Ash was connected to her story only for the simple knowledge of her Corpoi features–Callan saw that Ori had pushed her carefully braided hair back enough to show her *slightly* pointed ear–and the mention of her "friend". Every possible negative outcome roiled in his head as Ash approached Ori. How did she know any of her claims were the truth? Did Corpoi have some deep connection he knew nothing about? All he did know in that moment was Ash wouldn't budge on her choice, so he chose to trust his friend's instinct over his conflicted one.

"Ori, you are welcome to join us, we of course can't give you all of the details that you'd probably like, but if you feel that your friend is in danger I completely understand the need to seek out what information you can." Ash offered her hand to Ori, "You can call me Ash. My *scary* friend here is Callie."

As Ori reached for Ash's hand in greeting, Callan was quick to address Ash's poor attempt at being funny, "For the love of the gods, don't call me that." he turned to address Ori, "My name is Callan. Just Callan."

Ash rolled her eyes and giggled. "Callie here is just a little jealous that my attention isn't only on him for once." Callan felt his cheeks flush.

Before he could see Ori's reaction to this slight from Ash, he promptly removed himself from the conversation, throwing up a not-so-delicate hand gesture to the women. To Ash in particular.

*****

That night around Ash's fire, Ori and Ash shared stories about faeries they knew from legends. While they each only had a few, they compared the vast differences and discussed the other faeries from legends long forgotten.

Ori only solidified Ash's trust more by sharing that she too really was a Corpoi, having the features of a fox. This of course being her honey-gold eyes and the delicate points of her ears. She even ventured to share that when she was a small child a raidsman cut off her tail, leaving a large scar down her lower back. She told them that while it was a traumatic memory, not having her tail meant that she didn't have to hide it.

Callan had always wondered about the raids and their horrors. All he knew was the constant feeling of oppression from the Nondraoi, the people that he himself belonged to. He wasn't certain but he had always thought his true family fell victim to the last raid when he was a child.

Madame Loch would only ever disclose that it was his mother who brought him to The Phenomicron in hopes of his protection, but she wouldn't tell him what he needed protecting from. He always assumed it was from the raids, but he was Nondraoi, what would they have wanted with a babe born with no essence? Madame Loch wouldn't even tell him who his mother and father were or if they were still alive.

Callan was left to assume what had become of them since he had never known anything to make him believe they wanted him back or, at the very least, were alive. Madame Loch had always found trifling excuses to turn him away from asking about his past; she always said it was for his "protection". Callan had grown tired of the word. He had grown tired of the excuse. He couldn't remember a time when Madame Loch had attempted to come up with a different answer to his persistent question.

Callan could however remember one long-ago dream of a woman with dark hair and violet eyes. Even though his own eyes were a vibrant green, he knew in his heart he had dreamt of his mother. He hadn't had any more dreams in the years since he saw the violet-eyed lady behind his eyes. He thought about all the times he would wake in frustration having not been blessed with one more dream, one more time to see her. He learned then that dreams were for children.

This was one of those nights he wished he could dream. He wished he could just sleep for that matter, but he was constantly watching Ori, waiting for her to reveal her true intentions or unsheathe the blade at her thigh. She lay curled up next to the fire, seemingly not in a deep sleep herself for the past couple of hours.

Callan found himself consumed by Ori. He couldn't begin to understand why, but he *wanted* to trust in her the way Ash easily had. She reminded him of a feeling he couldn't quite place. Relaxed? Warm?

Her auburn hair once neatly braided had begun to unravel in various places. It reminded him of the autumn trees in the Baasarian mountains. Her face was that of simple beauty, with the exception of the scar that began at her right cheekbone and ended just below her slender jaw. His eyes traced that scar as if he were sketching it on her himself.

He noticed that Ori didn't seem peaceful in her sleep, she would twitch from time to time and readjust her lithe body in a restless pattern. Callan wondered if she truly slept at all or if she too was far too restless to truly sleep.

Ash seemed to also be in the land of nightmares. She would whimper when a gust of wind blew through the trees and dampen her fire that didn't need stoking to maintain its warmth over the three of them.

Callan found his only comfort in the night sky. He would find the few constellations that he could make out and then he would trace his own imaginings among the stars. The night was clear and the small group of trees in which they established their campsite were mostly calm throughout the night with the occasional breeze slithering through.

Lost in thought, he looked down at his right hand to the silver ring that he wore on his pointer finger. This one piece of jewelry was all he had of the past he yearned to know. The ring had a smooth surface with the exception of an engraving on the inside that depicted two hands reaching for each other. The small stone set in the ring usually appeared as an empty gray color, but Callan swore he would catch the stone in the light appearing in a shade of purple at times.

Callan had visited many jewelers throughout Grimmstone and Atreyu, asking if they had ever seen the ring or one like it. He even searched records for his last name Bram and came up with nothing. His efforts were fruitless when it came to finding his family. The majority of historical records were destroyed during the raids, eliminating any legends and records of the Draoi people, much of the records involving Nondraoi were also destroyed in the process. The only clue he had was this keepsake and he had no idea how to cipher its meaning if it even had one.

Dreamless sleep found him eventually as he leaned against a sturdy oak. The thoughts running through his mind were the closest thing he had to dreams. The violet-eyed woman often made appearances, her soft face set in a still image. This night he was plagued with the face of a golden-eyed woman instead.

*****

It wasn't until the next morning that Callan spoke to either Ash or Ori, both of them looking a little worse for wear. "Well, you two don't look like sleep came easy." This comment warranted hostile looks from them both. Callan couldn't help the thin smile that spread across his face.

"The bags under your eyes tell us that you probably didn't sleep at all. Plus, it's not like these bedrolls resemble any bed that I've ever slept on." Ash looked to Ori for support in her argument.

Ori shrugged. "I've slept in worse conditions."

Callan's malicious grin turned to one of surprise at Ori's nonchalant reply. He quickly shook it off by clearing his throat and returned to packing up their camp.

With that, the three of them packed up the horses and prepared for the next day of travel. Ash offered to let Ori ride on her horse with her. Of course, Ash had to sit on the back so that her unwrapped wings weren't constantly in Ori's face.

Ash had always hated wrapping her wings. In her defense she wasn't really used to wrapping them, having spent most of her time in Phenom where she was free to do as she pleased for the most part. Callan remembered the day that Madame Loch first scolded Ash for leaving the arena without wrapping her wings. It was something that always perplexed Callan, but he had no true understanding of what it was like for Ash. Or what it was like for any Corpoi.

Ori seemed to be perfectly content to not be subjected to walking for another day in its entirety, she swung up onto the horse and held out a gallant hand for Ash.

And just like that, a soon-to-be knight, his fiery best friend, and a beautiful stranger set off on the next leg of their unknown journey.

Chapter Five

Asvin

The sky was clear. A cool breeze slid through the trees and flowed through his silver hair.

"Help me." The soft voice echoed through the cave entrance. It was the voice of something ethereal. He looked into the dark passage, not able to see anything further than a few feet.

"Please, help me. I'm lost." The voice didn't sound fearful, it sounded like someone full of heartache, longing. He took a few steps more, standing now at the entrance of the cave, unable to see anyone in trouble.

As he turned to walk away the voice cried out in horrendous pain. He ran into the cave, darkness surrounding him, the voice echoing off the cave walls as he threw all caution to the wind...

Waking with a gasping breath, Asvin abruptly sat up, chest heaving to catch his breath. He wiped the sweat from his brow, steadying his breaths. When he looked to the horizon, the sun hadn't even begun its ascent over the calm blue waters. He'd had those dreams before, always in the same pattern. When he would run into the cave to save the screaming woman he would wake up before he lay eyes upon her.

Asvin stood, stretching his gray feathered wings, feeling the sore muscles in his back from the previous day's flight. He had the first dream three nights ago, and the next morning he began to fly, feeling a pull to the south. He had been following the same pull every day since.

Asvin had no duty to anyone other than himself, and he had been that way since birth. He was the son of a royal family, banned from entering their domain, Titan's Terrain. Asvin's mother, Bronte Falak, was a Cloud Giant, a race of Corpoi people with wings gifted to them by Estus, The God of Stars and Sky. Asvin knew his father to be just a simple Nondraoi man in love. He'd convinced Bronte to run away with him. When the Falak dynasty was told of their whereabouts, his parents were tracked down. His father was slain under Titan law for kidnapping Bronte. When the royal family found that Bronte was pregnant, they convinced her that the baby was cursed. Asvin was tagged, a form of branding to signify his banishment from Titan's Terrain wherein the top of his left wing was given a small triangular cut. He was abandoned on the steps of a village family in Bleakhollow, one day west of Titan's Terrain ground entrance.

The village family raised him as one of their own until he was eight years old. Their names and faces grew more distant from his memory as he aged. It had been seventeen years since he last saw them.

The raids that plagued the rest of The Five Realms did not reach Estana in the north, but there were heretical Nondraoi clans that targeted families of Draoi descent and still did from time to time. Many families, including the one that harbored Asvin, were executed unlawfully in their sleep. One fateful night, Asvin heard the heretics enter the home. He escaped out of his window and into the skies before the home was set aflame. He watched the only home he'd ever known burn before his eyes.

It was his hatred for those who would inflict useless pain on people and kill for sport that pushed him to learn everything that he could about his past, to know why the monsters in Titan's Terrain could let this happen. He scowled at the very thought of being associated with his blood relations.

Titan's Terrain, known by the locals as the castle in the sky, was suspended in the skies above the highest mountains in Estana and was untouched by the chaos below. Some villagers said that Estus himself made the floating city to keep his precious Cloud Giants safe from harm, to live in the skies near him. While some treated Asvin like a god himself, others looked upon him with disgrace. The Cloud Giants were The God of Stars and Sky's most prized creation.

Being only half-Cloud Giant made Asvin more approachable at times, but he still had an effect of terror in some places he visited. Most Cloud Giants stood about eight feet tall, with varying stone-like skin, and large feathered wings that allowed them the gift of flight. Asvin stood at only six foot eight and his skin was chiseled like stone but lacked the stone-like qualities of his mother's family. His wings were the only thing, mostly, whole about him, stretching past the length of his arm span by a foot.

His young adult life had mostly consisted of travel, longing to find where he belonged in the world, but finding less and less hope that he ever would. Asvin traveled throughout the entirety of The Five Realms, but always found himself back in Estana, back where he wished he was wanted. He was able to learn about the child who was banished from Titan's Terrain many years ago, never to return, from various storytellers in Estana. He learned that it was not often a Cloud Giant child was seen outside of Titan's Terrain and gathered that he was the rumored child of Queen Falak. He wasn't certain of this, but he had no other explanations for his existence. He had also never known of or seen a half-Cloud Giant like himself. Who else could he be but the long-forgotten princeling born with Nondraoi blood?

Asvin's solitary nomadic life brought him the comforts he needed to continue moving, never staying in one place longer than a night. He worked odd jobs for those who would offer him coin, food, clothing, or tools. These jobs often included ridding villagers of pests and animals that would ruin their crops, helping to repair their homes after the spring and summer storms, or hunting food for the families who could not hunt for themselves or otherwise afford to pay for food and other goods. Asvin had become like a hero to some in the villages in Estana. Some had even crafted stories about him defeating dragons and other beasts throughout the realms. Asvin had never laid eyes on a dragon, but he had taken down his fair share of beasts throughout his travels, both creature and human when the time called for it.

As the sun started its daily rising, Asvin began his morning ritual. His stretches and training maneuvers would wake his tired body. The morning sun warmed his skin, but not enough to make him break a sweat. He worked on hand-to-hand combat, dagger throwing, and sword practice to keep his skills sharp every morning rain or shine. He then would find food for that day of travel, suit up into his leathers, sheath his sword in the middle of his back so as not to impede his wings mid-flight, and store his daggers in various sheaths over his body.

Preparing for a day of flight wasn't a terrible feat for Asvin, but it wasn't completely comfortable either. Most days he would only fly from village to village, but ever since his dreams of the haunted, faceless voice began, he had been flying for twelve hours or more a day before stopping to rest. This was the day that he would fly all the way to Baasaris. He would cross the southeastern shores of his home realm and into territory that he knew he was less than welcome to visit.

The last time Asvin was in Baasaris, he had met with a well-known captain who requested his help in locating a beast of the seas. The captain was more than grateful for his assistance and protected him during his visit even though the search was unsuccessful at the time. Upon leaving the captain's ship, the city folk in the district gave Asvin nasty looks and told him that he didn't belong. Some even raised complaints that his wings were not clipped, hearing this, Asvin hadn't set foot back in Baasaris and hadn't dared to.

Until now.

Feeling the strange bond tied to him, Asvin took flight among the clouds and over the blue sea. He knew he was following something big, something that had been calling to him, *for* him. He just didn't know what would be waiting on the other side.

Chapter Six
Callan

The village of Keld was almost a mirror reflection of Atreyu, Callan thought. Many of the buildings were just as run down, but instead of the rain-slick cobblestone Atreyu often bore, dry dirt roads were the pathways that Callan, Ash, and Ori now pulled their horses along.

Everything and everyone in Keld looked like they needed a drink of water—the homes and businesses were covered in a thick layer of dust, and the wind offered no moisture even though they were less than a day's ride from the Vytarrion seas. Callan conjectured that Keld being the westernmost village in Baasaris meant that it was also unequivocally the hottest village in this realm. The closer one was to Vytarrion, the warmer their days would be. He pushed up his sleeves and wiped the beading sweat off his forehead as they walked deeper into the bustling streets.

Ash was traversing from local to local asking if they knew where to find the Cromwell brothers, Nikolai and Percyful. Most of the villagers were nice and would point in general directions or pass along information about where the older brother, Nikolai, may be. Others would shrug and move along, not willing to speak to outsiders. Callan ruminated on the idea that Ash being a Pyre-Faerie might have something to do with the cold shoulders in Keld. Then again, Ash was far more pleasant than he or their new companion would be, so he let Ash continue her efforts.

The Way of the Nameless

Ori kept a watchful eye on everyone and everything, whether it moved or not. Her honey eyes mulled over their surroundings like a seasoned critic taking in every tiny detail of a painting. Each brush stroke and highlight that the normal eye would glance over, hers did not miss. Her unwavering focus made way for an unintentional scowl.

He noticed that since she was pulling Ash's horse along with her right hand in the straps, Ori's left was poised over a sheathed dagger with three glittering opals embedded in the hilt at her thigh. Callan still wasn't able to let himself fully trust her, but she had become Ash's new *female* confidant over the last day, and he didn't want to ruin that for Ash. After all, he was the only true friend she'd had over the last twenty years, and he was not built for the lengthy conversations about the romance novels she read all the time. Ori didn't seem to mind the conversation even though she admitted she didn't have much time to read herself.

"The last person who would speak to me said that Nikolai is just two buildings over in the metals shop." Ash nodded her head in the referenced direction as she made her way back and resumed her place between Callan and Ori.

The metals shop seemed to have various scrap metals, barrels of nails and bolts, and any metalworking tools one could possibly think of. "I think that's him over there. I'm going to go speak to him." Ash left them in the street once more as she pushed through the semi-crowded storefront.

Ash walked up to a tall, burly man with light brown hair which was mostly covered by the gray, oil-stained paperboy cap he wore. He practically towered over Ash as she reached him, rising on the platforms of her boots to tap him on the shoulder.

Granted, most people were taller than Ash by at least a foot or more.

When he turned, the man had a genuine grin on his face, shadowed by the large mustache that also looked to be smiling. His rose-tinted glasses were perched on his high cheekbones, and he wore a leather tunic with no sleeves. His features were tanned enough so that he could blend in with the dusty streets if he walked outside. Callan wasn't certain why he had pictured the brothers in his mind as scrawny bookkeepers. Clearly this man labored in more than just information. Just over Nikolai's shoulder, Callan noticed the woman who stood behind him, long dark hair around a tanned round face who also shared a smile while Ash spoke.

When their brief conversation was finished, Ash led the couple out to meet Callan and Ori. Callan's perception did not fail him, Nikolai was tall, but only a few inches separated them. The long-haired woman placed a wide-brimmed black hat on her head when she walked into the uncovered afternoon sun. She had a very natural beauty, and her smile was bright as Ash introduced them. "This is Callan and Ori. Meet Nikolai and Jo." Ash gestured to each respective party.

"Nice to meet you both. Nikolai, I'm sure Ash has summarized what we have journeyed to Keld for?" Callan shook Nikolai's hand and then inclined his head slightly to Jo.

"Please, call me Nik. And yes, I am more than happy to speak with friends of Captain Blackwell. If you'll follow me, I'll take you to my brother, he doesn't get out much these days."

"Are you sure Percy will be up for a visit?" Jo's voice was smooth and carried a calming aura reminding Callan of someone he could not place.

"Ahh, he will be fine. Besides, serves him right for kicking us out this morning."

Callan and Ori shared confused looks but hesitantly nodded and followed Nik's lead. The trio followed behind Nik and Jo as the couple shared a quiet chuckle, their inside joke not loud enough for Callan to hear. He, however, didn't miss the sheepish grin on Ori's face as if she heard the couple's entire conversation. Her smile faded when she noticed Callan's quizzical stare. He recalled then that Ori mentioned something about her extended auditory range. He wondered how often she used that gift to spy on others.

When they rounded a corner off the main dirt path, Jo kissed Nik's cheek before parting ways with the group, saying once more that it was nice to meet them all. They only walked a few streets down before stopping at their final destination.

Nik and the so-far mysterious Percyful's house was a shop front with sleeping quarters in the upper levels. Nik showed them where to tie up their horses in the back and gave the tired creatures all the hay and water they could manage.

The entrance to the shop had gadgets and inventions on display that Nik pointed out as they walked to the staircase in the back. One of the contraptions had the spindly shape of a spider though it was about ten times larger. Its body had a container meant for seeds and the legs had cone-like tips where the seeds would fall through individually into the ground. This contraption would be pulled along behind its user, planting the owners' fields without the risk of throwing their back out after days of endless farming. Nik told the trio that he and his brother built many different inventions for the villagers of Keld, making their day-to-day lives easier. Nik seemed proud of their engineering capabilities.

As they climbed the stairs the second floor opened up to a foyer covered in bookshelves and unfinished inventions. There were two open doors to the right of the hall. Each held a bedchamber with beds and armoires that Callan deduced were for the brothers. One room was neatly organized—bed made, tidy floors, and curtains pulled back. The other had what Callan thought organized chaos would look like. The beds blanket and pillow hanging off the sides of the wooden frame, books open and closed strewn about every surface, and a few unkempt plants starved for water and sunlight.

To the left of the hall, Nik rapped on a door twice before cracking it open. When a frail voice spoke to enter, Callan, Ash, and Ori followed Nik through the threshold. They were greeted by a room full of books, scrolls, inventions in the works, bubbling potions, and magical appliances floating around the room overhead. The room had more personality than most inhabitants in Grimmstone, Callan had a difficult time focusing in the room of wonder.

Nik placed three ornate wooden chairs for them to take a seat. Callan noted the intricate details carved into the wood and imagined that Nik was the one who put them there. Callan thought of his bow he'd left downstairs and the many swirls and stars he etched in his downtime. He gave a tight nod of appreciation towards the craftsmanship to which Nik grinned brightly in return.

It was then that Callan first laid eyes on the old man sitting in the corner of the room. He was hunched over the largest book Callan had ever seen, his bony fingers scanning the pages, lost deep in thought. He wore faded robes of blue, and his chest and shoulders were mostly covered in long scraggly white hair, his long beard lying on the book in front of him. When he got to a line at the bottom of the page he flicked his beard over his shoulder in a hasty movement.

"Percy, these are the friends Captain Blackwell wrote to us about. They are here to discuss the war cuff. Callan, Ash, and their additional traveling companion, Ori."

This was Percyful? Callan assumed that this man was the Cromwell's grandfather by the wrinkles around his eyes and the age spots that littered his pale hands. Learning that Nik was the oldest, Callan had anticipated his brother to be a man in his mid-twenties, not mid-seventies.

Catching Callan's bewildered look, Nik became aware of the minor detail he'd left out and explained, "Ahh, yes, one thing I asked Blackwell not to mention was my brother's current state. Percy here is a Xestoral, he wields Draoi essence through imbued tokens. I don't really consider myself a Xestoral, but I do assist him in his endeavors when it comes to crafting items for him to imbue with essence.

"He has been learning various spell work and cantrips over the years, one of which aged him on the outside, but he is still my little brother on the inside." Nik said this with a sarcastic smile that stretched from ear to ear. It reminded Callan of the haughty grins he often gave Ash.

Percy raised his head to look at his brother menacingly. The room came to a halt, no more pens, pencils, or potions flew around the room. The very air was sucked out of the room. Callan, Ori, and Ash hardly breathed.

Percy sharpened his stare to a deadly focus. His aged voice began at a low volume, "One thing to get straight is that I am *very* powerful and *very* knowledgeable when it comes to the Draoi, be it their people or the very essence that makes them the almighty beings they are," he turned his hunched form to face Nik fully and pulled in a large breath to yell, "I missed ONE WORD! ONE!"

Percy looked down to his book again and took a few moments to catch his breath. The only sounds were the bubbling potions that had begun to boil in Percy's outburst and the light tap of Nik's booted toe on the hardwood floor.

"I am sorry. It is rude of me to yell in front of people who do not understand the ways of the Draoi." Percy spoke softly, still not looking at his stunned guests, "I have researched the Draoi most of my life and I began dabbling in my own collected essence only to end up like this. I was merely scarred before messing around with one too many cantrips. I have been searching endlessly for the spell that will reverse this… hindrance I've created."

Ash slowly rose from her seat; her face was filled with a painful understanding of Percy's situation. Callan even saw a similar, yet more concealed look on Ori's face. They were the ones who truly understood what it meant to be deformed in the eyes of those who always managed to make them feel less than.

When Ash reached the opposite side of Percy's desk, he met her eyes as she brought a small dancing flame to the tip of her finger and lit the burned-out candle sitting to the side of his tome. Percy's eyes grew wide with recognition of Ash, her flames, and–finally–her wings.

Percy glanced over Callan and quickly darted his gaze to Ori, who had tucked her auburn hair behind her pointed ear. Callan figured this was to subtly show Percy that she too understood the Draoi, more than the old–young?–man likely did himself.

This was something Callan would likely never comprehend, never relate to. Being a Nondraoi surrounded by Draoi people was normal to him and he accepted everyone for who they were, regardless of their appearance or gifts. It wasn't until he and Ash first visited Grimmstone as rebellious teenagers that he saw how she was treated. People threw trash at her and splashed rain puddles in her direction. They targeted her with slurs without even knowing who she was outside of her clipped wings, barely visible when they were neatly wrapped behind her. If only they had known that Ash was most definitely capable of burning the very flesh from their bones. He shook the disgusting thought of *that* away.

Callan had always believed that everyone should have the same opportunities as the next, there was no need to judge those who hadn't passed judgment on him. He paused when that thought brought him back to the way he treated Ori just yesterday. How quick he had been to judge her without giving her a chance.

"We understand." Ash's words were soft as they broke through the spiral Callan was slowly slipping down into.

Percy bowed his head in thanks and clear shame. "Forgive me, it is not often that Draoi people show their true selves to others. I haven't left the shop in months and when I do, I pretend to be Nik's grandfather which is as belittling as it sounds given *he* is the older sibling." Percy's last words were directed at Nik who returned his words with an eye roll and a smile that raised his round frames.

Callan intercepted the silence that lingered, "Captain Blackwell told us that the two of you know much about the forgotten history of The Five Realms and may have some information about the war cuff?"

"Yes, I pulled some specific literature about items and tokens crafted by the gods." Percy said this with the same inflection as one would talk about how nice the weather was, seemingly in an attempt to rid the air of the rage that still occupied the room.

Callan, Ash, and Ori shared the same wide-eyed look before Ori spoke. "Did you say the war cuff was crafted by the Gods?" Ash filled Ori in about the item they were sent to gather information on during the remaining ride to Keld, much to Callan's chagrin. But Ash left out the concept of this glorified bracelet being god-formed. A notion that he could hardly wrap his mind around.

"The gods have crafted very few weapons over the centuries. Many of them were gifted to their celestials." Percy looked around the room, but he was only met with more confused stares. "Well, I suppose that Grimmstone and its surrounding towns and villages probably don't speak about the celestials or anything of note when it comes to history." Percy paused. Callan wasn't sure if Percy was merely making a statement or trying to make a joke. He deduced it was the latter given Percy's half-grin.

Percy shook off the attempt at being light-hearted and continued, "Celestials are the wielders of the gods. Legend tells us that each god had a mortal subject gifted with a higher concentration of their essence to act as their worldly counterparts. These beings could channel various gifts that the gods themselves had, this aided in their goal of convincing mortals to join them in ranks of support behind their god or goddess.

"Of course, in the last century, Draoi people were not able to gather in any fashion, thus the celestials had no purpose. From what I gather, the last celestial–Baasis' celestial–died about twenty years ago. If there are celestials alive now, usually the children of the previous bearers of the gift, they are in hiding or they do not yet know what they are. They are very, very powerful beings. Though, I suppose it is possible that with essence being very thinly spread throughout The Five Realms, the celestials may be weakened to the point of non-existence. Come to think of it, I am not sure how the godly essence passes from generation to generation of celestials."

Callan felt a small vibration at his hand. When he looked down, the stone in his ring had a faint purple glow. His curiosity was cut short when Ori chimed in. "If the celestials were so powerful then what need did they have for this war cuff?" she asked this with a hint of brashness that made the corner of Callan's mouth lift. He supposed she had a way with words.

Percy paused, his brows scrunching in thought. "That would be because the celestials did not have the power to *control* others outside of their goodwill, or threats when it came down to drafting people for their respective god. The war cuff, based on my readings and general knowledge, was created by Vytarr for his celestial. The war cuff has the power to wield others. When the wearer gives a direct order to those within earshot, it is followed blindly. Instant mind control."

There was another dreadful silence that filled the room. Callan was sure that, like himself, everyone else was trying to piece together why the cuff was created in the first place. Why did the gods need mind-controlled mortals? And why The God of Day? Of all the gods and goddesses, Callan had always pictured Vytar as the most righteous of them all; at least according to Ash.

What he did know was that everyone in that room understood why The Nameless wanted the war cuff. Likely to control the will of the Draoi people in his ever-growing need to vanquish all Nondraoi.

Callan had never truly given The Nameless a spare thought on most days. Most rumors that circulated around The Nameless were about *someone* finally standing up for the Draoi people. Other rumors that Callan heard when in Grimmstone were that of the Nondraoi being slaughtered and enslaved by the Draoi if The Nameless was successful. While he didn't agree with the mistreatment of the Draoi, being enslaved or dead as a Nondraoi himself also didn't sound like the life–or lack thereof–he wanted. He felt perplexed trying to decipher what could be real and what was truly just a rumor.

"You said the celestials were *drafting* other mortals...why?" Ash whispered her question. Callan hadn't even caught on to that specific detail in Percy's explanation of the celestials. Draft was too distinct a word to be missed by Ash.

Percy fidgeted with a small tear in the arm of his robes before answering. "That, I do not know. Once the raids began, the followers of the gods became nothing more than simple religious practitioners. Some may argue this, but the gods haven't been very present in the last century or so and everyone is still too afraid to talk about the history of the realms. So, the questions remain unanswered."

Becoming a routine that felt practiced, the room filled with silence once more.

A few moments passed before Nik sighed, "I am sure that the three—" he shifted a glance towards Percy, "make that *four* of you, are hungry. How about I make us some soup and open the bottle of port wine I've been saving for dinner with guests? I'm sure it's needed considering the gravity of this meeting."

No one objected to the offer of food and a stiff drink, Callan, most of all, wanted to clear his mind of the never-ending rotation of thoughts. From The Nameless to the celestials to his ring and the information his mind was already too full to comprehend. He hoped a full stomach and a wine-aided sleep would ease the looming tension of their quest.

Chapter Seven

Ori

The small cot was warm, cozy even. Ori's eyes fluttered open as the early morning light began to slide from behind the curtain. The hefty amount of mead she consumed the night prior helped her to sleep the dreamless sleep she had come to covet in the years since she was orphaned. Nik was more than happy to prove that he could outdrink her. Turns out he was wrong, he was a big guy, but Ori was well-versed in the honey concoction of choice. Her winning their half-hearted drinking contest also meant that she had no recollection of getting into a bed last night at all or how she had managed to make it up the stairs.

After their predominantly liquid dinner and late-night conversations, Ori found herself with a lingering headache as she rubbed the sleep from her eyes. The room on the top floor of the Cromwell storefront held four cots, a desk, and one old trunk for storing belongings. Nik told them that they often housed travelers who passed through Keld seeking a place of rest for a night or two.

During dinner, the five of them had continued discussions about the war cuff, the celestials, and The Nameless; piecing what information they each had together. Based on Percy's research, the last known location of the war cuff was in the heart of Qoohria. The realm was named after The Goddess of Night, Qoohr, and lay just southeast of Baasaris. All Ori could think of was Lyra and the stories she would tell of The Goddess. Lyra said that Qoohr loved all her people so dearly that she would often walk among them herself.

Ori, Ash, and Percy were all in agreement that if The Nameless had the war cuff already it may be too late to stop him from whatever his plans may be. Callan remained quiet throughout the night, but Ori saw the unspoken thoughts that he kept to himself. Behind his eyes lay confusion, worry, and an endless stream of emotions that she couldn't quite untangle without his input.

By the time their dinner had been thoroughly picked through and drinks consumed, Nik and Percy asked to join in their search. Percy had more knowledge than the three of them combined and Nik, well, Nik was roughly the shape of a human bear. Not that Ori couldn't handle herself, or that Callan couldn't send a deadly arrow with precision, or that Ash couldn't incinerate someone instantly, *but* having another strong hand couldn't hurt.

There was only mild hesitation from Callan and Ash. The former worrying about the "sanctity of the mission" and the latter worried for Percy's health. Both of which were valid but also very quickly dismissed by the brothers. First, Percy *unintentionally* scolded everyone at the table–very much like an old man–about the fact that he was not an old man.

Their second argument was far more compelling to Ori. Nik explained that he and his brother had been well versed in Draoi essence and imbued items, not dissimilar from the war cuff, since before they were old enough to live on their own. They used the storefront of machinery and inventions to mask their true passions of experimenting with collected Draoi essence to create magical items of godly engineering. Ori pictured Percy's office above them that likely still had a multitude of utensils flying around the room with their own form of sentience.

She'd heard the term Xestoral before, but Ori had never met any herself. Of course, decades ago, any imbued items were to be turned over to the Grimm aristocracy for immediate abolition. She, along with everyone else in The Five Realms knew those items were likely held for "safekeeping". The Grimm family didn't and wouldn't let one ounce of power slip through their fingers. If anyone else claimed to be a Xestoral or have any Draoi items in their possession likely faced the same punishment as those born with the godly essence: banishment, imprisonment, or execution.

The Cromwell brothers shared that their family line had Draoi people as well. Though their father, Zander Cromwell, had no inkling of the essence passed on to him, his sister, Darcy Cromwell, had been blessed with the essence of Baasis.

Nik explained that their aunt had the gift of great strength and would often fight back against the raidsmen to protect her family. Nik and Percy's parents shunned their aunt from their family to "protect them", fearing that the outward use of her gift would endanger them all. During the last raid, Darcy was executed. Percy and Nik became overwhelmed in their young lives by the fact that these killings were senseless, leading them to pursue the very knowledge the Grimm family sought to destroy: Draoi people, their names, names of those who aided the Draoi in hiding, and the precious legends of the gods.

When they were of age to live on their own, the Cromwell brothers moved away from their parents in Grimmstone and to the village of Keld. Away from the mass of Nondraoi groupings and the furthest they could get from Grimmstone without leaving Baasaris.

The memory of the previous night's open conversations and the willingness of everyone to share intimate details of their past made Ori's heart lurch into her throat. She had found a family of sorts in the Celerity Channel, Draoi beings who had survived the raids bonding together in the name of their unknown histories. The network of thieves and dark dwellers knew they had to support each other because no one else would.

Ori had faced the hard reality of being *truly* lost throughout her young life alone. Meeting Callan, Ash, and the Cromwell brothers, and learning their stories, only made Ori harken back to her own past. When asked about her childhood, she would often tell people that her mother was executed in the last raid instead of the horrible truth she knew lingered in her veins. She would feel that cold dagger biting into her skin all over again.

Telling people that *small* lie began to feel wrong. Callan didn't know his mother and father, left to believe they were killed in the raids. Ash's mother was killed protecting her, something that Ori herself related to but in a very different way. Nik and Percy were stuck in the silent fight to learn about the forgotten histories of the realms all as a result of the death of their aunt. Ori felt as if she had done *nothing* and experienced *nothing* in comparison. She then recalled the familiar feeling of the void last night. That slippery slope that had become all-too-comfortable in her time alone. The disgust and hatred she often placed upon herself instead of the life she had been subjected to was the norm of her day-to-day. And the drink that followed blurred those lines enough that they were irrelevant for the rest of the evening.

Sitting up in her cot, Ori looked to her left to see that Ash was already gone, most likely in search of the first ounce of caffeine she could find. As Ori panned around the room, her gaze landed on Callan who was still in a deep slumber. He looked so peaceful when he slept. The past few days he seemed to have a permanent crease between his brows any time she spoke to him, or rather when anyone spoke to him.

She knew that *this* wasn't how he had imagined his little quest in the name of the captain to go. How could one brief trip to retrieve information turn into a potential search for a mythological weapon? She tried not to care. Ori was here to help her friend, not him. If it meant that she needed to deal with his attitude for a few more days, then she would do that for Lyra. The small part of herself that had begun to care about her traveling companions made it far more challenging to be indifferent about where they went next.

Callan shifted slightly before nestling back into his pillow, releasing a deep breath. Without the harsh lines of annoyance on his face, he was handsome. Ori openly stared at Callan, like a predator watching its prey from afar. She was merely observing him in the calm state she'd never before witnessed Then her thoughts moved to the loose curls of his hair, the subtle line of his jaw through his short beard, his long eyelashes that tickled the tops of his cheeks—

Ori shook her head, breaking from her useless thoughts. She knew it was not the time for thoughts of simple days. Days where friends could go out and enjoy their existence together and nights where a boy and a girl could get lost in each other's eyes. She didn't really know what that was like, but she knew that it was a futile desire. The books she read had sometimes talked about love, but Ori thought it to be only fantasy. She had only ever felt what she knew as love from her mother and from Lyra who was a little more rough around the edges compared to Cytheria's calm nature. But she loved Ori all the same.

Tossing her blankets away, Ori swung her legs over the edge of the cot, accidentally bumping into an empty drinking glass that had been left on the floor next to her. Callan shot up in a jolt of awareness, immediately finding Ori's eyes across the room. She would have atoned for startling him, but her devilish nature won out in the end.

Ori picked up the glass and playfully waved it at Callan. "It's just a glass, it doesn't bite or attack, not like I do."

A slow grin crept onto Ori's face, one with the trace amounts of joy she got from annoying Callan. He made no sudden movements, but he slowly sank, leaning his head against the wall and letting out a low huff from within. He watched her silently as she rose and walked across the room, his brow slowly unfurrowing the closer she got to the door and out of the room.

*****

Ori wasn't certain that there would be a continuing quest for the Cromwell brothers to join. Callan and Ash came to Keld simply to ask Nik and Percy what they knew and if they had any information that could help Captain Blackwell in determining the reality of this war cuff. Ori only wanted confirmation that Lyra wasn't tied up in some dangerous political scheme. They had accomplished their task of speaking with the brothers but found themselves with more unanswered questions and no solid confirmation that the gods-damned bracelet existed at all.

That afternoon, however, Callan wrote a letter to Captain Blackwell. The coded letter stated in some form that Callan had completed his assignment of finding information and that he planned to proceed ahead in the hopes of locating the item. The letter read as if it were in a foreign language, but Callan swore that it would make sense to Blackwell since he couldn't very well detail the specific findings and locations. There was logic to what he said, but there was no logic in the way he wrote that letter.

After paying a local messenger for its quick delivery, Callan returned to the Cromwell storefront. Nik and Percy had packed for a few days of travel, also supplying everyone with more food. Nik offered for Ori to borrow one of their four available horses so that she wouldn't have to ride with Ash. While Ori wasn't sure how to thank him for the gesture, she simply nodded and attempted a smile. She hadn't ever been offered anything, she always had to earn, *or steal*, everything that she owned. The warmth in her soul began to kindle for the first time in a very long time. With their sights set on possibly one of the most dangerous weapons to exist, the newly formed party of five set off to Qoohria.

*****

The night approached quicker than expected. Being on the western side of Baasaris meant that the blazing sun of Vytarrion made the days longer. As the sun found its resting place Callan suggested they set up camp off the roadway and while the others began unpacking bedrolls and supplies, Ash started the campfire. Ori was still bewildered by this endeavor that seemed to be nothing for Ash. It made Ori wonder what Ash was really capable of when it came to her power and how she controlled it so well.

Taking reprieve from the group, Ori ventured into the forest a little further to take a much-needed moment alone. She had been in a constant state of alert, not knowing who she could fully trust other than Ash whose trust was still only blooming. Something about her felt like home to Ori. Ash, of course, made Ori think of Lyra. She would catch a shimmering wing in her peripheral vision and begin to worry over Lyra all over again. Why did Lyra know about the cuff to begin with? And why was Captain Blackwell telling her of his plans to send Callan and Ash to get information about it?

Questions swam through Ori's mind day and night. Through all the voracious corners of her thoughts, Ash gave her a sense of security. The Cromwell brothers were benevolent men, truly too kind and Callan had even begun to accept Ori's presence with fewer eyerolls and sidelong glares.

She closed her eyes and took in a deep breath once she was far enough away from the other, attempting to clear the endless cycles from her mind. Ori focused on her feet, grounded to the Earth. Her breaths slowed to match the pace of the wind rustling the leaves in the trees.

The tiny issue she had come to face during this escapade was the hold she had on her shadows. Her shadows didn't fully manifest until she turned fourteen. She found that she was thankful for the sensation of darkness comforting her when she had nightmares or for hiding her a year later when she was in the nighttime streets of Grimmstone. She knew that this gift came from her father, and she had kept it hidden for that reason, she had only shown Lyra the gift by accident one time. Lyra never questioned her about it though, seeing that Ori wasn't forthcoming with the information. A great thief was never questioned if they did their job well.

Over time Ori had learned to beckon the shadows at will, but if she staunched the power for a few days, she could feel them push against her skin, forcing their way out. She remembered when she first joined the Celerity Channel, she had not summoned her shadows for five days straight to test herself. She wanted to test her ability, but she also feared that someone would see the dreaded gift that allowed her to sneak about and reveal her secret. On the fifth day of her homebrewed experiment Ori thought she would die. She had the worst sickness of her life; cold sweats, body aches, tremendous headaches that pounded so loudly she couldn't hear anything else. That last day ended with her room in the Celerity Channel partially demolished–the cracks in the ceiling standing as a permanent reminder of needing balance–and her head throbbing in pain for another five days.

Standing in the forest away from the others, Ori let a small stream of shadow run free from the tips of her fingers. The stream billowed and pulsed along with her heartbeat, flowing over the fallen leaves and patches of grass. Ori thought for a moment she could see the vibrant greens of the forest mingling with her dark mist. Feeling the automatic release from the strain that had built up over three days was instant—

Ori heard the crack of a branch. She snapped open her eyes and in the span of a blink the stream of shadows cut off and withered away but the mist of green remained hovering just above her ankles. How had she not noticed it before? Grabbing her dagger she searched the area. But she saw no one, nothing.

"Don't worry," a soft, lilting voice echoed around Ori. "I won't tell anyone."

Ori searched the surrounding trees again in a slow turn; the voice giggled. When she peered up into a darkened treetop, she could see glowing turquoise eyes. The figure leaned forward revealing a delicate green-hued face that blended in among the tree. Long hair strands the same dark shade of the tree bark slid over *her* shoulders.

"Who are you?" Ori's words were clipped short, partly in suspicion over the humanoid creature whose eyes were locked on hers, and partly out of fear for what the forest specter may have seen. The gift of shadows was one that only Ori possessed as far as she knew. Anyone who had any inkling of historical knowledge of the realms would know where the origins of her gift came from, she could not afford to be discovered, not now. She wanted more time.

"I am Sakura, the sentinel of the trees. What I would like to know is what *you* are doing in this particular forest?" The question felt specific, but Ori wasn't sure what this creature, Sakura, meant by *her* being there. Ori remained still, the grip on her dagger was the only comfort she had in that moment.

"Shy are we? And here I was thinking that *I* should be afraid of *you*." Sakura hopped down from her perch in the tree, landing mere feet from Ori, who was so petrified one may think her a statue. Sakura's pale green features continued down her arms and her legs, all the way to her bare feet. She wore a tattered white gown, and her waist was fitted with a brown corset that had ripped seams and patches from constant wear. She slowly walked around Ori. Two branch-like stems protruded through her hair like antlers and her arms were covered in what Ori thought were vines, but she realized they were tattooed swirling patterns that shifted on her skin. *Moving tattoos.*

Sakura put her hands in the air, evoking a position of surrender. "I am not going to harm you. I am not going to tell anyone about your gift," she let out a small giggle as she put her hands back down at her sides, "I do not see people often in this forest, so I find it interesting that not only you, but four others are here as well."

Ori was stunned. Stunned by Sakura's words, her appearance, and her reasoning. She watched the creature who stood waiting for Ori to respond. Sakura had the eyes of a young, curious child. Feeling as if Sakura truly had no intention to harm her, Ori sheathed her dagger before she finally spoke. "My name is Ori. My friends and I are traveling," she paused, trying to carefully place her words. Before she could continue, Nik pushed through the low-hanging branches behind Sakura.

He looked back and forth between them, mouth slightly agape. He cleared his throat awkwardly before speaking. "Well, I came looking for you, Ori, but I see someone else has found you first."

Ori winced, not knowing how to explain what this occurrence even was. But it wasn't long before Sakura skipped up to Nik and introduced herself.

*****

Back at the camp, Ori stood behind Nik as he introduced the strange woodland dweller to the rest of the group, "This is Sakura, she's the... what was it again?"

"I am the sentinel of the trees!" Sakura stated matter-of-factly, bowing at the waist flamboyantly towards Callan, Ash, and Percy.

Ash was the first to speak, "Okay then... would you like to join us for dinner? We don't have much—"

Sakura cut off Ash, Ori could tell that she didn't mean to but her excitement was like that of a young girl who'd just made new friends.

"Yes! I would love to!" Sakura jumped and clapped so excitedly that Ori truly thought she had shape-shifted from the creepy tree beast into a toddler in a matter of seconds without ever changing her outward appearance.

Callan's annoyance once more materialized but it faded ever so slightly as the conversations ebbed and flowed. Ash was the warm, welcoming presence Sakura was fixated on. Percy, on the other hand, was fixated on Sakura.

Ori saw what looked like longing in his eyes. She noticed that Percy would make useless attempts to avert his stares only to find him with his eyes closed instead. It was as if her voice was music to his ears and he was most content with listening to her orchestrations.

The party shared some food and water with Sakura, who was beyond grateful for the opportunity to share a meal with mortals. She told them that she would sometimes venture into the small villages that bordered the forests she inhabited to try mortal food, mortal books, and other mortal things that she found to be extraordinary.

Ori managed to sneak away from Sakura's excited chatter and walked over to Percy who was sitting a few feet away from the rest of the group. "Hey, do you know what she is?"

"She is a creation of the gods," Percy's eyes were again locked on Sakura as he spoke, "The Goddess of the Hunt in particular considering her likeness to the forests. Now, what she was created for is beyond my knowledge, but I can feel the godly essence when she is close. Hers has a stronger pulse."

"The godly essence? How can one even know what that feels like?" Ori's tone was coated in irritation. She found herself vexed by the constant state of learning new knowledge over the past few days,

"For the better part of six years, Nik and I have been collecting Draoi items. We have also used spells and cantrips to create our own items that have the essence of the gods imbued in them. I think I know what it feels like." Ori rolled her eyes at his explanation, but she knew it was in retort to her own tone. Percy continued, "Not unlike yourself and Ash, the essence is strong with Sakura. Instead of the essence being a part of her like a heartbeat, it is her very being. It is her heart. She is nothing more than a Draoi artifact herself. Just a living, breathing artifact."

Percy didn't deny himself the opportunity to look at Sakura this time. Ori realized that his awe wasn't just because she was beautiful despite her odd range of features but because he *sensed* her. Percy had spent so much time around items and artifacts imbued with Draoi essence that he could actually *feel* it when he was near anything that carried the essence.

"Excuse me?" Callan almost yelled in response to something Sakura had said. Ori and Percy moved quickly to return to the party who still sat by the fire, with the exception of Callan who was now standing and sliding towards his bow lying against a nearby tree.

"When you speak to the trees, you speak to me. I hear all things in the forests. I know what you seek, and I know where you intend to go."

The world went quiet. All that could be heard were the rustling of trees and the crackling of the fire. Everyone stared at Sakura, no one jumped to speak first or ask a follow-up question to that freely given confession. Sakura stated this in the most nonchalant way, showing how truly detached she was from mortal beings and the like who understood societal norms.

Percy was the first to speak. "I was just telling Ori that Sakura here was created by Baasis. Would I be correct in stating that?" Sakura gave Percy a small, thankful nod that accompanied a smile. "Sakura told us that she is a sentinel of the trees. She is, therefore, one with the trees and appears to have the ability to blend in with them and live among them. Would I be correct in that assessment as well, Sakura?"

Sakura nodded again and her smile grew wider. A slight tinge of pink stained her cheeks, but she did not hide her face.

"Baasis created me to collect information. Similar to yourselves, I seek information for the person who needs it. You all seek it for a captain, and I seek it for my Baasis. But, as I was going to say before someone got all defensive," she narrowed a glare at Callan who gave one right back, "the item you seek can only be used by Vytarr's celestial. *The Nameless*," she made air-quotations with her fingers, "is not Vytarr's celestial nor is he a man of any true power."

The group paused simultaneously to add up the miscalculations in Sakura's words. Only Vytarr's celestial–who died almost twenty years ago–could wield the war cuff, The Nameless had no *true* power, and Sakura just casually spoke with a *Goddess* on a regular basis?

"When you say no true power…" Ash was the first to break the silence.

"He has no Draoi essence in his veins. This was something that I overheard Baasis tell her coral sentinel one day." Sakura picked up a stray apple that was among the foods laid out and began eating it like this was truly normal dinner conversation.

While Ori was stuck on the title of *coral sentinel*, Ash asked another question, "So… you actually *know* the gods and goddesses?"

"Oh, I only know Baasis, I have never met the others. But Baasis doesn't like them very much."

Ash pressed further, "Why doesn't she like them?"

Sakura tapped her apple with a pointer finger as she thought of her answer. She took another bite and said, "Well, that's a long story. One I am sure she wouldn't appreciate me telling you all. After all, I would tell no one the secrets you all harbor, not even to Baasis. Unless she asked for that specific information of course." Sakura briefly glanced at Ori, subtly reminding her that she knew about her shadows but wouldn't tell anyone her secret. Not unless The Goddess of the Hunt herself asked for it. Ori wasn't sure if she felt comforted by that or horrified.

Callan, whose features had softened ever so slightly, probably in preparation to try and ask his questions level-headedly, asked Sakura, "If only Vytarr's celestial can use the war cuff, what would The Nameless want with it?"

"He may not know that he cannot wield it. Or he knows that there is a new celestial to Vytarr." Sakura's eyes scanned the wide-eyed looks she got from her answer. "I'll let you all in on a little secret, one that shouldn't cause *too* much of an uproar in the god realms. The Oracles of The Five Realms have foretold of a day when the celestials of each realm will come together again to claim their power." She paused to survey the now changed curious gazes that she held. "That foretold day is quickly approaching. In fact, it is only in a few days' time."

Chapter Eight

The Celestial Prophecy as foretold by the Oracles

The Fallen Star will slay a shadow to claim the Flame.

The Seadragon will tame the Red Phoenix.

The Fox will step out from the darkness and see the light.

The Flame will sacrifice the Sun to save the Knight, and

The Knight will find himself In the mirror.

The powers of The Five Realms will Unite as one and fulfill their Divine decree,

By joining life's essence into The Dyngheloi.

Ash

The Flame will sacrifice the Sun. Ash couldn't help but think of herself, her father, her *mother*. Pyre Faeries weren't the only beings who could maneuver or conjure flame. She had known some performers during her time at the Phenomicron who came through looking for work, but they could only do minor tricks and toils with fire. Throughout her short time on this plane, she had never met anyone outside of her own family who could wield fire as she could.

Her father and grandfather were both Pyre Faeries. When Ash was born, her father thought that she wouldn't possess all the traits of a Pyre Faerie since her mother was not of the same descent. Other than her eyes and hair which belonged to that of her mother, she was the spitting image of Kaster, and she liked to think her burning gift was passed down from him.

The Flame will sacrifice the Sun. What could it mean? Was her father the *Flame*? She thought it was outlandish, but *what if*? What if he could be involved in this prophecy? *How* could he be involved in this when she hadn't heard from him in almost two decades?

Kaster was integral in the forming of the peacekeeper's union during the height of the raids, but they had long been disbanded, decreed by the Grimm family to never reform. Kaster had told her not to contact him, that it would jeopardize Ash's safety. She couldn't even tell people her true family name for fear that she would be recognized as his only child. Even though Callan didn't know that piece of her, she had always let him believe she did not know her family name like many people of The Five Realms. Was her father involved in something bigger than she knew? Did he go against the Grimm law of rebellion against the Nondraoi ranks?

The Flame will sacrifice the Sun. The Sun. Ash looked down to her hand, which held the last piece of her family ties. The ring her grandfather *gifted* her the day her mother was executed. The delicate flower petals resembled the sun; the gold shimmered in the morning light as the party once more rode along through the thick maze of trees in complete silence. Everyone else seemed to also be lost in thought or desperately trying to ignore the rationalizations of the night prior.

Sakura had left in the night while the five of them slept. The prophecy she told them in the forests of Baasaris raised challenging questions that even Sakura didn't know the complete answers to. She told them that the Oracles of The Five Realms could see the past, present, and future. One of the oracles–whose name had been lost in time–that could see glimpses of the future saw the children of the previous celestials gathering to claim the godly power that was promised to them eons ago.

Sakura explained that Draoi essence had been spread thin throughout the last two hundred years, the raidsmen of the Grimms at the forefront of this quandary. The vast amount of executions of the Draoi people and the imbued artifacts destroyed plummeted the essence of the gods leaving The Five Realms with little to no essence left.

Sakura admitted that she had never met a celestial herself, but that Baasis explained to her once that when a celestial died, their essence returned to the *Dyngheloi*. This was a crystal of sorts formed by the gods to distribute their direct flow of essence to only the bloodline of their chosen celestials.

Ash recognized the ancient language that had also died along with the waning essence of the realms. The only terms from the vernacular of the god-made were used to describe the realms inhabitants; *Draoi, Nondraoi,* and *Corpoi.* Ash hadn't known *Xestoral* until meeting the Cromwell brothers, but knew it belonged to the long-oppressed language.

The children who gathered in the future oracle's prophecy were seen as weak until they united as one to gain the full extent of the gifted essence of the gods. Sakura wasn't able to advise on who the children were, how old they were, what they looked like, or where they might be. The oracle Enid, who could see the present and often spent time with The Goddess of the Hunt for one reason or another, deemed that the prophecy would be fulfilled before the end of the summer solstice. Callan remarked that it would *of course* be on his birthday that all the power of the gods returned to the realms. Callan's poorly timed joke was met with only blank stares from the rest of the party who were actively spiraling with the weight of this information. Ash smiled at the memory now; it was the kind of jest she wished they could share now. The silence was far too eerie for her comfort.

With the new knowledge they harbored, in addition to the small fact that Sakura could actually *hear* them through the trees, the five of them didn't speak much. Like herself, Ash was sure everyone else perused the prophecy and what it all could mean. Once night fell, they would have another day of travel to the seaport town of Greenside where they would find a ship that could take them to Qoohria. They were only a few hours away from the village of Midscar in which Nik, Percy, and Ash herself wished to seek a cot instead of the forest floors, but Callan was adamant that the village was too far out and would derail their arrival to Greenside.

Starting yet another campfire, Ash truly longed for the comforts of her bed back at the Phenomicron. She envisioned the feathered pillows and the downy mattress. Her dreams were snuffed out when she returned to the pressing matters of her aching back and the headache that came with this much travel. Ash thought back to the times when she had begged Callan to go on an adventure with her and explore The Five Realms.

Now it all seemed like much less fun than she had initially imagined.

She continued assessing herself, noticing the places her body had grown tired over the last six days as she sat on the ground in front of her fire. Her thighs were sore from riding, her wings were tender from being wrapped during the day, her hands had blisters from the reins, and she had a scar on her inner wrist. She examined the unknown scar, rotating her left hand in the firelight to better inspect the marking she had somehow not noticed until now.

"What are you doing?" Callan snickered from somewhere behind Ash.

She turned and looked up at him, deciding to actually tell him what she was looking at instead of following with the usual lighthearted insult. "I have a scar on my wrist, I just don't remember how it got there. It wasn't there yesterday."

Callan knelt down beside her and took her hand in his, he too tilted her wrist towards the light of the fire to try and get a better look. The sun had sunk quicker than usual, the forest already darkened by nightfall. Qoohr's moon was making its appearance through the thick foliage of the trees. Callan's brows pinched as he said, "It kinda looks like a constellation." Ash pushed him hard enough for Callan to fall over onto his side as he looked at her with mock confusion. "What? It does! It looks like a constellation I've seen!"

"I don't care what it looks like, Callie, I just want to know how it got there! I don't even see a drop of blood on me to indicate that I had been scathed at all."

Before Callan could reply, they were shushed by Ori who stood a few feet behind them. Ash and Callan snapped their heads towards her, both with mouths agape prepared to shush her back; then they saw *it*.

Ori had her back to them, facing a darkness that lingered around the trees like a heavy Grimmstone fog. Ash took note of Nik and Percy, who were off to the other side of the camp laying out bedrolls. They too had stopped their camp preparation to look into the thick, smokey murk that was beginning to spread across the ground around them all. When she looked back to Ori, Ash's eyes were pulled in by a pair of glowing yellow eyes that tracked Ori directly. It was then that the featureless figure spoke in a harrowing, disembodied voice that rattled Ash's bones. Even her fire light cowered in response.

"He's been searching for you. He's going to be so happy when he sees his Takar—"

The accent-heavy voice was cut short when a single arrow pierced the darkness. The yellow eyes snapped open wide before they too were swallowed in shadow and the hard *thunk* of its body hit the ground. Ash stood abruptly and looked to her left to see Callan standing, his bow already knocked with another arrow at the ready.

The unseen creature spoke no more, but the shadows remained around the campsite.

Was *it* dead?

Were there more?

Ash observed Callan's surveillance, his slow inspection of the void around them would've looked methodical and practiced to someone who didn't know him as a performer. Ori had brandished her dagger and took up a defensive stance, but her horror-stricken face told another story. Nik had loosed a hatchet from his belt taking up a similar stance while Percy stood only a few paces behind him.

It was in a matter of seconds that two large hounds the size of horses bounded through the darkness on either side of the camp.

Callan wasn't fast enough. The wolf-like beast leapt, jaws wide, aiming for Callan who had slain the first of them. Ash could only stand frozen, the world felt as if it had slowed. She couldn't move, couldn't think, she could only watch in horror as the razor-sharp teeth clamped down on Callan's arm.

He screamed in agony as his flesh was torn, but the beast was dragged back by an unseen force, its too large body clawing at the ground, a look of panic in its evil eyes.

Ash then saw the force that held the hound's leg back, pulling it away from Callan –who was kneeling and holding his arm, bow and arrows thrown to the side–was a tendril of shadow. The black tentacle was roped around the leg of the hound.

Before Ash could see who wielded the shadow, the sound of an agonizing growl made her jerk her head to Nik who had lodged his hatchet into the shoulder of the twin hound who had pursued him. But Nik was unscathed. A soft blue aura flowed along the entirety of his body, shielding him. How–

The roar of the roped-down beast rang through Ash's ears, when she followed the wretched sound, she found the beast free of its shackle and Ori lying far too still on the ground.

Ash felt the armored heat building under her skin—the anger that accompanied her flames ravaged her mind; her friends were going to die.

Her gift– her *weapon* overpowered the potent fear as she released a stream of flames at the hound. It shrieked as the angry orange flames licked at its body, eviscerating through its fur and down to the bone. It fell limp to the forest floor. As it fell, Ash turned to see that Nik had accomplished the same feat by embedding his second hatchet into the skull of the other hound, black ichor rolled down the lifeless face and seeped into the caked dirt.

Ash took one step towards Callan; his arm had already created a small pool of blood beneath him. She stopped in her tracks as a low growl hummed from somewhere behind her. As she turned to face it, a fourth hound zoomed in a straight path towards its biggest threat, Ash.

In that moment she saw her life flash before her, the mouth of the beast showing her every pointed fang that would end her very existence. Closing her eyes she braced for the impact.

Her flames hadn't had the time to replenish, she was exhausted and so too was her body. She knew Nik wouldn't get to her in time, she knew Callan and Ori lay behind her, the former wounded and the latter likely dead. She wasn't even sure if she tried to scream in her final moments as these revelations fell on her one by one.

Instead of gnashing teeth, she felt a warm tingling sensation on her skin. Surely she was dead. She was entering the afterrealm of Vytarr, she was being blessed by The God of Day for her sacrifice. The warmth of the eternal sun glowing on her skin, warming her soul.

When she dared to open her eyes, she saw no Vytarr. She saw no eternal sun.

She only saw wings.

Feathered wings.

Chapter Nine

Asvin

He heard the same scream. The very same scream that had plagued his dreams for the past week. Asvin flew with speed into the uncharted forest. He landed directly in front of a Shadow Hound, having fought a similar beast of its nature before, it was no struggle when he reached out into its coarse fur and snapped its neck with one twist. He heard nothing other than the crackling fire behind him. He smelled burning flesh and blood. He felt short breaths at his back. His senses were being attacked all at once as the mist shrouded forest had begun to show evidence of dusk once more.

When he turned, he saw… *her*.

Her hair looked like the brightest parts of the sun, the spattering of freckles adorning her face looked like the stars in Estana, and *her* eyes–wide with terror–were striking, as bright as lightning bolts in a storm. *Her* skin was glowing, a faint blue light shimmering along her face, neck, and hands.

The next breath he tried to take stalled in his throat when she spoke first. "Who are you?" She didn't flinch, she didn't even move, but her eyes still held fear, swirling flecks of gold floating in the pure silver irises.

He realized he was still staring. That *voice* was the voice in his dreams. Her pleading whisper that he'd flown through half of

Baasaris to find was just as he recalled. Clearing his throat, searching for any words he could manage, he finally responded, "I heard your scream and came straight here."

She nodded once, glancing around his arm to see the Shadow Hound lying still on the ground. He realized then that she too had been staring at *him*. The logical part of his mind knew that she had likely never seen someone like him. There were many who stared when he dared to put himself in a crowd, always perplexed by his wings and tall stature. But *her* stare felt different somehow.

She broke her fixation and ran to a man kneeling on the ground, his arm had large, gaping wounds. The sinew and familiar white of bone showing through his torn sleeve was enough to tell Asvin that the man would not be keeping his appendage.

"Callan, are you alright?" The panic in her voice was clear. He longed to hear *her* voice in some other form than sheer dread and anxiety. While having a face to put to the mystery voice made him realize he didn't mind her being in his dreams, he wanted to know what a peaceful tone sounded like from her. Asvin imagined it would be like Estus' *malachi*, the god's angelic crusaders whose songs were enough to soothe any emotion one could have.

Between gritted teeth, the young man spoke in only quick breaths, "Check. Ori." *Her* eyes filled with worry and disbelief. "I'm. Fine. Check. Ori."

She quickly stood and approached the woman lying on the ground. A large man with Shadow Hound blood splattered on his glasses was already leaning over the woman while another, older man cloaked in blue robes, had his hand over her heart, watching intently. Asvin didn't dare move, he didn't know these people, and they did not know him. Their perturbed state of being was familiar to Asvin; it was ill-advised to further disturb one who had experienced something traumatic. He only watched *her*.

The three of them—*she*, the burly, blood-splattered man, and the blue-robed elder—spoke in hushed tones. "Is. She. Alive?" The wounded man, Callan, grunted out from his fixed place in the middle of the small clearing.

She turned and nodded slowly to him; a small, sad half-smile turned the corner of her full lips. She was beautiful, she was graceful. She moved with complete confidence among the chaos that still lingered. Asvin leaned to the side and peered around the larger man to see the unstirring woman, red hair and pale features, lying on the ground and peacefully breathing.

The old man shuffled across the way to examine Callan's shredded arm. The wounds were deep; the muscles were likely torn and the unnatural angle in which the arm lolled was proof enough that Callan's arm was irreparable. Asvin watched as the elderly man knelt beside Callan and said, "I can heal small wounds. I have never healed anything like *this*, but I will try if you'd like."

"What. Other. Choice… Do I have?" Callan pushed the words out like it took every ounce of him not to pass out. His face was so pale from the extreme blood loss that Asvin questioned how the man still sat up.

"Well…" the larger man began, "If Percy doesn't try whatever loosely practiced healer spell he is thinking of, you will surely not be using that arm for the foreseeable future. In addition to not being able to use it, we have no way of cleaning it, and the amount of dirt, insects, and—"

"Please. Stop... Just. Do it," Callan interjected, his pallor had started turning green at the mention of insects crawling in the wounds he bore.

The old man, Percy, removed the bits of sleeve around the large abrasions and floated his hands over Callan's arm. A soft green light came out of the wounds as the skin stitched itself back together. Bone audibly snapped back into place. Callan didn't make a remark of pain, but the twisted look on his face revealed his distaste for the sound. Everyone watched in bewilderment; Asvin had seen healers work before but never with Draoi essence. When the viridescent light dimmed, four large scars remained on Callan's arm.

He rotated his wrist, flexed his fingers, and stared at his newly healed arm. "That was amazing. It still feels sore, but it's nowhere near the pain I was feeling. I can't believe that damn thing almost took my arm. Why didn't it take my arm?"

"I saw a shadow pulling it back... I... I don't know where it came from, who it came from." When *she* spoke, it was like silk gliding over Asvin's skin. He would be content hearing that voice and *only* that voice speak for an eternity. He felt the same pull that brought him to Baasaris, but... it was so much stronger. When she turned to him, they locked eyes again. This time, instead of the fear that consumed her stare before, her electric stare whirled with interest and curiosity. It took Asvin moments to realize that everyone else was also staring at him. "Was it you?"

"Was what me?" Asvin had been lost in those stormy eyes, her voice was a song.

"Are you the one who wielded the shadows to pull that dreaded *dog* away from Callan?"

Asvin, confused by this accusation, held up his hands, "No, I am no Shadow Wielder. The only Shadow Hound I touched was the one that came for you."

"Shadow Hound? You know what those things are?" Callan asked in shock and genuine keenness, standing up and crossing over his forgotten pool of blood towards Asvin. Asvin couldn't help but notice the defensive carry of Callan's form, he was assessing a threat.

"Yes, they are from Phyrus' realm. That's the only place Shadow Hounds and Shadow Wielders come from, if they leave at all." The four of them just looked blankly at Asvin. "Phyrus? The God of Oblivion and Souls?"

"We know who Phyrus is! We just didn't know these... *monsters* existed." Callan snapped this at him. Realizing that this odd grouping of individuals had just seen the likes of which none of them deemed to understand just yet, Asvin let Callan's tone slide.

Phyrus was the god who sought out the rancid souls of those who had wronged others in their lives. He also dealt in creating monstrous creatures to go out and do his bidding since he didn't have a celestial of his own. Tales of Shadow Wielders took many forms throughout The Five Realms, many of which served as warnings of morality. Shadow Wielders were the equivalent of a child's nightmare or the unnerving feeling you get that something is watching you from afar and waiting to pounce.

Asvin had heard similar tales of one called The Necromancer, a not-so-fitting name for someone who disposed of souls like an assassin rather than giving souls a semblance of life. This henchman of Phyrus was known to carry a shadow blade to claim the souls he was sent out for, wielding shadows in the name of The God of Oblivion and Souls. Shadow Wielders were very rare from what Asvin knew, never having met one himself.

"Who are you anyway? What brought you here and why would you stop to help?" Callan was about to lose the gift of kindness that Asvin was bestowing upon him; the gift of *choosing* not to render him unconscious. "My name is Asvin, I am from Estana. I have some investigations that have brought me to Baasaris on behalf of my people."

"And who might those *people* be?" Callan narrowed in on him, Asvin could clearly see that he wouldn't get by without giving details. He really didn't think they would believe in his truth, so he pretended to be who he often thought he could have been.

"I am a Cloud Giant of Titan's Terrain. My people have heard rumors of The Nameless and plans to start a war. My queen sent me to gather intel on what rumors are true before they reach unmanageable heights in Estana. I was flying ahead when I heard—" he paused to look at *her* again, "you... scream. I flew down to find two of you wounded, two of you finishing off another Shadow Hound, and *this* Shadow Hound launching its attack on her, completely unprotected."

"Ash was not unprotected!" Asvin barely comprehended the old man's words that cut him off, he was stuck on *her* name. *Ash.* "I had a shield spell cast on her before you even landed."

"Yes, but that spell wouldn't have stopped her from being decapitated," the large man retorted.

Percy turned to face the large and rather outspoken man. "Well, the next time you're in trouble I will be sure not to waste my abilities on *you*, *Nik*."

Nik threw his head back and let out a hearty laugh that echoed off the trees. His laugh had a contagion, soon everyone was laughing, even Percy–who had delivered the threat–let out a howl. It was likely the delirium that followed after four terrifying creatures threatened their livelihoods. Asvin stood awkwardly and waited until they quieted down and returned to their interrogation.

Ash spoke to him first with her silken voice. "I am not trying to sound offensive… but what is a Cloud Giant?"

Percy answered her before Asvin could even take a breath, "The Cloud Giants are Corpoi of Estana, gifted by Estus, The God of Stars and Sky. They live in Titan's Terrain, a floating city that only they can fly to. They are known to be eight feet tall or more, have stone-like skin, and of course, feathered wings. That description leads me to believe that you aren't *wholly* a Cloud Giant."

Asvin *did* look different. He was closer to seven feet tall, his complexion didn't have the granite look or feel, having more of a grayed human flesh. Of course, he had the same feathered wings that many other Cloud Giants possessed, but that was the extent of his likeness.

"Yes, I am the only *half*-Cloud Giant that I am aware of." Asvin made sure to emphasize the word "half", eyeing Percy so that he knew just because he wasn't a full-blooded Cloud Giant didn't mean he couldn't be the beast they were sometimes depicted as in nightmares. "My father was a human; my mother is a Cloud Giant. It's as simple as that." He stated that last part towards Ash as a true answer to her initial question. "I followed my instincts, and they led me here, to you."

Ash suddenly let out a hiss and jerked her left hand up to her face, directing a quizzical brow at her wrist. Callan moved closer to her, never taking his eyes off Asvin, and whispered to Ash, "Are you okay?"

"I… Yes, I'm fine." She dropped her hand and slid it behind her. Her demeanor shifted from confusion to diplomacy in an instant. "We are also looking to gather information on The Nameless. Given your skill in… fighting," she said the word like it was a question, "I suppose you would be an asset if you'd like to accompany us."

The men around her all whirled in her direction, each of them expressing their opinions on her invitation in rapid succession.

"Yes, I am aware that we do not know him. I am aware that he could be a danger. I am aware of what you are all concerned for, *I* too have been here and have seen it all just as *you* have!" Ash took her time staring at Callan, Nik, and Percy directly in their eyes as she spoke. Asvin could've sworn her eyes flashed white for a fraction of a second in her moment of rage, "But it was *he* who saved me. Who saved *us*! The beast surely would've come for one of you next once I was dead. If he hadn't been here, there would have been no point in our journey here.

"Can any of you confidently say you could snap the neck for a horse-sized dog if another came running up to us right now?" No one uttered a single word. "That's what I thought. Like it or not, if something came for us once, it could come for us again," Ash turned to address him once more, "Asvin, it is your decision alone if you would like to join us or continue your travels on your own. If you do join us, just be prepared for these *boneheads* to give you hell for the next few days."

Hearing Ash speak his name made the skin prick on the back of his neck. He had never heard his name sound so exquisite. This was his opportunity to figure out what this pull was, to see what the never-ending dream truly meant. He wanted to understand why the realms brought him to *her*. Though he would have to keep up his charade of looking for information for the queen of Titans Terrain that he hadn't even laid eyes on before. "I greatly appreciate your offer. I would like to accompany you. Truthfully, I do not know much about this realm and having people that know the area would be very helpful to me. I promise you'll hardly know I'm even here." The last part of his acceptance was pointed towards the men who stood defeated. Callan in particular had a grimace on his face that spoke volumes on his behalf.

Asvin offered to help move the sedated young woman, Ori, onto a few blankets, but Callan was adamant that Asvin would *not* be touching her. He stood by as Callan and Nik lifted her closer to the fire, both of them flanking her once seated. Percy had gone to rest on his own, lying not too far from Nik, who he learned was his brother. Asvin knew their ages didn't add up, but he set that slew of questions aside for now.

Asvin kept his distance, sitting and leaning against a tree on the other side of the camp. He kept his hands busy by sharpening one of his six knives with a whetstone.

Asvin hadn't realized that Ash wasn't among her friends until she sat down next to him and handed him something wrapped in a handkerchief. "It's bread and some cheese. I figured since you flew the whole way here from Estana that you may be hungry."

His fingers brushed against hers when he took the handkerchief from her. All he could manage to say was, "Thank you."

They sat in the stillness of the night for a few moments. He could feel the warmth that radiated from her, her arm almost touching his. He knew she was a faerie of some kind, though he had never met any faeries until now. She had unwrapped her wings, letting them rest on either side of her back, the ends of them were shredded. Asvin also knew that in Baasaris, wings were often clipped. He felt a rush of anger almost boil over at the thought of someone doing this to him, to *her*. He couldn't imagine being stripped of the gift of flight. To have the option of getting away from the terrible things life tended to present in The Five Realms, taken away from her. He had been told as a child that the ultimate punishment for Cloud Giants was not death, but to be stripped of their wings entirely.

"What is it?" Ash's voice was soft and comforting. His rage simmered down at the symphonic tone she carried. She had sensed something wrong; he realized right away that he was fixated on her delicate wings and the face he had been making.

"It's nothing." He looked away from her, carefully opening the neatly wrapped food she had brought him. He tore the bread and offered Ash half. "You're probably in need of this too after the night you've had." She smiled. Asvin had decided that *that* smile was his favorite thing in all the realms.

She nodded as she took the offered bread and mirrored his earlier response, "Thank you."

Asvin tried to come up with *any* way to hear her voice again, "So... you mentioned before that your party is also looking for information about The Nameless?"

Ash nodded again as she finished a bite of bread. "Callan and I were sent to locate intel on a Draoi artifact. It has led us on a path to Qoohria, the artifact's last known location. It's this piece of jewelry that's basically used to mind-control people. But we have recently learned that only the celestial to Vytarr, who has apparently been *dead* for almost two decades, can wield it. We also learned that The Nameless has no Draoi connection other than his hatred for the Nondraoi, his *own people*, and can't even utilize the artifact to begin with."

Asvin took in the knowledge of The Nameless' lack of power. He really wasn't there to decipher rumors, but this mysterious being always perplexed him. This terrifying being was a Nondraoi? One who didn't want the Draoi mass murdered? "The Nameless is Nondraoi? A *Nondraoi* man has stirred up the drama and even the hope of The Five Realms?" He didn't linger on her phrasing of the Draoi people's valid hatred towards the Nondraoi. He too held disdain for them upon initial interactions. How could he not? They had been the central cause of the realms' pain.

"Yeah. It was a shock to us too. I always figured that he would be Draoi given that he is pushing for them to rise to power. That hope seems far-fetched to me since the Draoi people are and have *always* been too afraid to be seen in large groups. Plus, not all Nondraoi are bad. My best friend is Nondraoi, and he has done nothing but accept me for who I am."

Asvin realized that Ash was talking about Callan as she nodded in his direction.

He was her best friend?

He shook his head, in an act of denial of her poor taste in friends. Maybe he had redeemable qualities; instead of changing into his other shirt from his shredded one, he had fashioned a pillow out of it for the sleeping Ori.

"I agree with you, a Nondraoi family raised me. I have never felt like all of them were out to get me. I am hesitant when meeting new people, but I'm sure that's a relatable feeling. That's not to say that there definitely haven't been Nondraoi who were actually out to get me. The last time I was in Baasaris, I almost had my wings clip—" Asvin stopped himself. But Ash didn't show one sign of sadness or longing for her wings.

"That is a hazard of being closer to Grimmstone." She changed the topic so effortlessly. "You were raised by Nondraoi? I thought your mother was a royal Cloud Giant?"

Asvin felt his eyes grow wide at his mistake. It really was too soon to let his disguise falter. "She is royal. She just didn't have the time to raise me. All I have of her is my name and my wings." He was surprised by how quickly he came up with the response. It wasn't a complete lie, his mother didn't have the time for him, or so he always told himself. He couldn't tell Ash that he'd been ousted from Titan's Terrain without raising questions of his true reason for being in Baasaris.

Ash looked at him with surprise "You know your family name?"

"Falak. It means, 'One Who Decorates the Sky'." Ash smiled again, Asvin wasn't sure what he had done to deserve that smile, but he never wanted it to leave her face. "Do you know your family name?" His question quickly brought his dream-like state crashing back to reality. Her smile slowly slipped away, and he could feel himself reaching for that smile as it contorted into a frown.

"I don't. I lost it a long time ago."

Before Asvin could ask her what she meant by *lost*, a guttural scream erupted from the other side of the camp.

Chapter Ten
Callan

She was alive.

Ori's scream was so loud it rattled Callan's eardrums, but she was alive. He watched Ori sit up in a panicked sweat, reaching for her dagger. Callan sent a quick prayer of thanks to the gods that he'd had the sense to put her dagger with her bag instead of back in her sheath.

Callan–bravely–took Ori by the shoulders and shook her until their eyes met. "Ori! You're okay, I'm here. You're okay." His words grew softer as he spoke, calming her down enough to realize she was safe, and the hounds were still dead. Of course, Callan couldn't blame her for waking up in defense mode. When she had been knocked unconscious two hounds were still on the prowl, and she hadn't even been aware of the third.

Her eyes were locked on his, it was like she couldn't trust his words and endlessly searched for truth behind his stare. Her irises looked like the setting sun and had a tinge of orange next to the glow of fire. Callan felt the warmth in those heated pools of gold. "You're okay." He said again, whispering this time.

Callan waved everyone else away, not tearing his eyes from hers, in an attempt to create space for Ori. He had done this many times before for Ash when they were younger, when she would get overwhelmed or upset and needed the room to cool off. Ash was quick to understand his intent, he could hear her cooing at Nick, Percy, and Asvin as she ushered them to the other side of the camp.

"What happened?" Ori practically demanded this, but he could hear the fear that shook her normally steady voice. Callan let his hands slide to the crooks of her arms, loosening his grip from her shoulders now that she had stilled.

"You were knocked out somehow, no one saw exactly what happened. Nik took down one of the beasts with nothing but hatchets and Percy put up a magic shield around him, it was incredible! Ash literally set one of the Shadow Hounds on fire! And then that giant *bird* over there showed up out of nowhere and killed the third one."

"Wait. Shadow Hounds?" Ori's brow was creased with worry as her terrified stare moved from Callan's eyes to his scarred arm as if she remembered that horrific moment. He ducked his head down to meet her eyes once more, hoping that it reassured her in some way that he was fine.

"Yeah, Asvin, the aforementioned *bird*-guy other there, said that they were called Shadow Hounds, so that explains all the dark fog that covered them. But that doesn't explain why they were here in the first place."

Ori broke her stare and looked down at her hands. She balled her fingers into fists. It wasn't until he heard her sniffle that he noticed the tears falling onto her wrists. Callan pulled her to him, letting her weep in the place between his neck and shoulder. He brushed her hair with his hand and rocked her gently until she pushed him away and sat up across from him, distancing herself.

He didn't understand her sudden change of accepting comfort to rejecting it. Then again, he knew she had to have been terribly confused and maybe even still in shock. He felt the same way though the lingering emotions were more residual now.

He was just doing what he had always done to comfort Ash, but he should've known that Ori wouldn't be the same. She was nothing like Ash. She was otherworldly to him. The skin around her eyes was swollen and her face was stained pink. "I need to be alone." She bit out the words.

"Let me come with you." Callan tried to make it sound less like a plea, but it came out that way. Ori was quick with her response, "No, I just need a minute alone. I won't go far."

"Ori, less than two hours ago, four Shadow Hounds were attacking us. We almost died. We almost lost you. Please, just let me go with you. To watch your back at least." Callan almost couldn't believe his own words, he hoped the last few took away the awkwardness he felt at asking to stay by her side.

He wasn't sure when exactly he had decided that she wasn't a threat, but his mind had been muddled with the overwhelming travel and learned information that still gave them no clear answers. Ori was simply a bystander to his iron whim. She was strong-willed, smart, and crafty with a dagger. In truth, he thought she was brilliant. Seeing her before, lying on the ground unmoving, solidified Callan's view of her. She was just as vulnerable as he was, though neither of them would ever admit that aloud. When he couldn't see if her chest rose with life, he immediately imagined the worst and blamed himself.

Ori stood up so fast that Callan almost didn't react in time to catch her as she stumbled. She slowly pushed him away but held onto one forearm to steady herself. "Just let me go with you, I understand that you need to get away and clear your head. But you *clearly* can't even walk on your own, much less protect yourself if another one of those demonic dogs shows up." The crease between her brows appeared again, anger or annoyance, *or both* swirling in her eyes. She gave him a curt nod and turned, walking slowly into the woods just beyond the camp.

When they were far enough away from the earshot of the others Ori turned to face him and held up a hand signaling for Callan to stop. Ori closed her eyes and took a deep breath, letting her trembling shoulders relax and lowering her hand that flexed, opening and closing at her side. Callan had no idea what to do, so he just waited. He felt at that moment that waiting for her was the best thing he could do.

When she opened her honeyed eyes and they met his, Callan could sense somehow that she was afraid. This was different from the look of terror she had upon awakening. This was anxiety, *panic* that painted her face. He did his best to appear as open as possible even though he too began to fear what could make her look at him that way. She was brave, any fool could see that, even him. In their night of chaos she stayed, she fought, she sacrificed herself to help people she hardly knew. What could *she* possibly fear if not what they had just experienced?

"I have to tell you something. Well... show you something." Ori lifted her hand once more and Callan braced himself for whatever was about to come next.

Callan found himself anchored to his spot on the forest floor as wispy tendrils of shadows wrapped around Ori's delicate hand and snake their way down her arm. He scanned his surroundings in search of another hound. Didn't Ash say it was a *shadow* that pulled that hound from him? A *shadow* that kept him from being devoured?

As the realization hit Callan like an angry ocean wave. Is this what the bird-giant was talking about? *Shadow Wielders*? That meant... Ori was from the realm of Oblivion and Souls. Callan wasn't even sure what that meant. Was she inherently evil because she could wield shadow? Asvin made it sound like it was extremely rare, but not necessarily *bad*.

He forced himself to school his riotous thoughts when he saw tears streaming down Ori's cheeks. He could hardly make sense of his own thoughts, much less hers. Her tear-slick face was a mixture of the same bundled anxiety with something like relief. She'd probably been carrying this weight on her own for so long. Callan had absolutely no idea what that immense pressure felt like, but he found himself sympathizing for her anyway.

Callan felt something warm and soft touch his hand, looking down he saw the same tendrils of shadow wrapping around his fingers, spiraling up his wrist and arm. The sight of this brought panic into his already tight chest, but the warmth of the soft shadows gave him an odd sense of peace. He focused on his composure; the last thing he wanted was to upset her more by being *afraid* of her.

"I have always been afraid of this. I never asked for this gift." Ori's words were short and whispered, through her soft weeping. "It didn't develop until I was a little older and there is only one person in all the realms who knows about this. And it is for her that I have followed you all this way. I am trusting you to keep this secret."

Callan gave her a gentle nod of agreement and stayed quiet, giving Ori the space to speak or to remain silent if that was what she needed. The smoky tendrils clung to his arm like *they* were drowning. His mind turned over the past few days as he tried to configure how she'd kept her shadows a secret for so long. She'd said she was from Coulteron in Phyruh and was an arctic fox Corpoi. *Fox.* It was then that the gravity of Ori's situation dawned on him. She had said she was the only one that she knew with her features. The singular line from Sakura's prophecy fell from his lips in a whisper, *"The Fox will step out from The darkness and see the light."*

As he recited the prophecy of the celestials, Ori's shadows snapped back, causing him to shudder at the speed in which they moved and the chill they left behind. He could see the devastation that plagued her. She fell to her knees and sobbed. Callan calmly walked over to her and knelt down next to her.

"When I heard the prophecy, I knew it had to be me. I am the only Corpoi of my kind, I have never met another like me other than my mother. I am also a Shadow Wielder, and I have never known another. I don't want to be *his* celestial. I don't want to be a celestial *at all.* I don't want *this.* To be *this.* I wish that I could be anyone else other than myself." She held her face in her hands as she cried. Callan once again pulled her into his arms and comforted her. As Ori calmed, she didn't push Callan away this time, he felt the warm shadows wrap around his back like a pair of arms, like a hug. Her words hit home for Callan. He had always wondered himself what had been so wrong with *him* that his parents left him at the Phenomicron. In some, very small, way he understood how she felt to loathe being in her own skin.

When she finally pulled away, it was gentle. She had cocooned them in a blanket of shadow. Ori wiped her remaining tears on the back of her hand before she looked at Callan for the first time since her confession and softly whispered, "Thank you."

Callan looked to the hand that he left resting on Ori's arm, his ring was glowing. It was brighter than the times he had seen it before. Something told him that he was in the right place, that this little purple beacon was telling him to stay. "I can't quite understand what this is like for you. I also can't understand the weight of knowing what you are and what you may become. But I do know that you are stronger than what you know yourself to be. I've seen your determination, and I've seen the way you care for others; you saved me back there, I realize that now. You risked revealing your gift to drag that Shadow Hound away. I would be dead if not for your willingness to sacrifice your secret. I vow that I will do what I can to protect you, and I will do what I can to *help* you. You just have to let me help, and this is a good start."

Callan gave Ori a smile, one that she surprisingly returned. He didn't want to push her any further, understanding that she had likely already been pushed to her limit for the night. The eyes that were once dull with an unknown despair were now lighter, vibrant even. What was once a tarnished bronze shone as the brightest gold. Callan found himself lost in those eyes and Ori didn't break her stare either. He'd never felt so intimate with another person. She bared her soul to him, and he had nothing to give in return other than comfort and a promise to keep her soul safe from those who would wish her harm. This wasn't like his brotherly promise of protection to Ash. This was *different. Wholly different.*

They heard branches snapping and leaves shifting from the direction of camp. Ori cleared her shadows in the blink of an eye as Callan quickly turned and faced the direction of the sound. It was Ash that slid through the brush, "Hey, are you okay?" Ash looked to Ori with concerned eyes.

"Yeah. I am now." Ori said as she began walking toward the camp. Ash turned to Callan with a raised brow. Callan rolled his eyes in response to her insinuation of why they were away from the camp *alone* and signaled to her that everything was truly fine, even if that wasn't the whole truth. It hurt him to lie to Ash, even if it meant Ori's safety and now, her trust. Something he found himself not wanting to give up so easily.

*****

As the three of them returned to the clearing, Ash and Ori made their way to their neighboring bedrolls by the fire and Callan found a spot near the edge of camp to sit for a while. Ori had shared something with him that he never anticipated. A Shadow Wielder. And the likelihood that she was possibly the celestial of Phyrus, given her gift of shadows likely came from his realm, that was a lot to take in. But he meant what he'd told her. She saved him. Sure, it could have just been an arm he lost, but he very well could have lost his life if it weren't for Ori and her…gift.

She didn't see it as a gift, but it was to him. He ruminated on the way her shadows felt warm and safe. They didn't feel like a curse in the way that the shadows from the hounds did. Those shadows made the air around feel colder than death itself. When he looked at Ori, he felt the opposite. She wanted everyone to think she was cold and harsh, but she, like her shadows, was warm and…beautiful. Her shadows were even beautiful in their own way. The way they exuded their own personality separate from Ori's made Callan curious. Her shadows were a part of her, yet they had their own emotions. How did that work? He ascertained that he wanted to know about more than her shadows and the way they functioned. He wanted to know *her*.

As Callan sat, lost in thought, Percy had awoken from his rest and trudged over to where he sat. "Ori looks better now than when she woke. Is she alright?" Callan nodded in response, not willing to risk any more details. Percy must have noticed this and quickly changed the subject from Ori, "So, how do you feel about our new winged friend?"

"*Friend* is the last word I would use for him. I don't know. Ash trusts him so I am willing to give him a fighting chance. But I am *certainly* not going to make it easy. Especially if he keeps staring at her *that* way." Callan wrinkled his face and Percy chuckled quietly. Callan then changed the subject once more, not really wanting to talk about Ash's *savior*, "What do you think of what he said about The Nameless starting a war?"

"Well, I suppose that rumor makes sense. Even his moniker rallies those whose names have been taken from them as a result of the raids. The Nameless is like a sign of hope for the Draoi people. Hope that maybe one day the nameless generations won't have to hide or fight any more for their survival.

Callan saw a purple light cast on Percy's cheek. When he looked to his right hand, his ring's glow was as bright as it had *ever* been, even more than it had been when he was alone with Ori. "Has it always done that?" Percy's eyes were wide with curiosity.

Callan thought of his answer to Percy's question. He had only recently noticed that it was a glow and not just the stone catching the light from time to time. He sat transfixed on the ring, trying to put his very few puzzle pieces together before he finally spoke, "When I was young, if the light caught the stone just right, I could see hints of purple. It had always been just that, just a shimmer and nothing more. Within the past few days of travel, anytime The Nameless is mentioned in some way or another, it *glows*. It has done it a few other times as well, but I haven't made any other connections. I honestly thought I was maybe losing my mind." Callan reflected on the times he had seen the glow. He remembered the stunts he did at The Phenomicron; the ring would shimmer when he was nervous about acts with heights. Any time The Nameless had been mentioned, the ring would faintly glow as if it knew he was getting closer to the truth. Then, it had made its appearance when he was alone with Ori. He wasn't sure what the instances meant or if they were even connected to each other.

"No, I see it too, you're not imagining it. Do you know where this ring came from?"

"This was the only possession my mother left with me when she brought me to The Phenomicron. I have gone to dozens of jewelers and metalworkers over the years, and no one has ever seen one like it."

Percy nodded introspectively and there was a beat of silence before he spoke. "The ring seems to be charmed to react to certain situations. The questions to be asked are why those specific situations and why was it charmed in the first place. With it being gifted to you by your mother, I would imagine it serves as a protection charm."

Was the ring warning him? Was he getting too close to The Nameless? Too close to danger? Too close to Ori? Was she truly a threat to him? He blurted out his worry before he could stop himself, "Should I worry? It's just all confusing. I don't know what it's trying to tell me."

"It's what your mother is trying to tell you." Percy's words cracked Callan's heart in a way he had never felt. He had never thought of his mother caring for him, trying to protect him. He had marked his mother and father off as two people who never wanted a child since the day, he was dropped off at The Phenomicron.

Percy interrupted his spiraling thoughts, "We should go to Midscar."

"What does Midscar have to do with anything? I told you it would be too far out of the way to get to Qoohria." Callan heard the frustration in his own voice and winced at his own temper.

"We should go to Midscar to rest, yes. But, in my research I have come across the possibility that one of the three oracles resides there. Enoch Ferraille, he is the oracle of the past. The thought crossed my mind when Sakura mentioned the oracles and their prophecy. He may be able to give you some answers if he truly resides there. But..." Percy paused as if he were debating on whether to finish his sentence, "... if we go to see Enoch, we will have to bring those Shadow Hound corpses with us."

Part Two: Adrift in Dark Shadows

The Way of the Nameless

Chapter Eleven

Ori

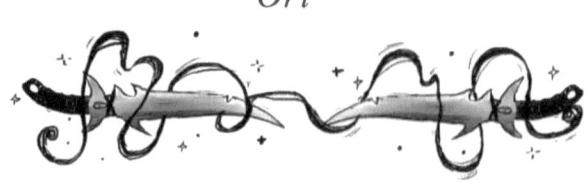

Arriving in Midscar was a relief. Finally having the opportunity to not attempt sleep in a dark forest was something Ori didn't realize she would long for. Nor did she ever think of the forest as a bedchamber in any capacity. She found herself missing the caves of her found home in the Celerity Channel, surrounded by the protection of the ancient stone walls instead of the vast open spaces in the night. The night didn't scare her, but the creatures in the night now did.

Callan shared with the party upon waking that they should change course to Midscar for much-needed rest. Given that Callan had previously told them Midscar was too far out of the way of Greenside and their trek to Qoohria, his change of heart was a surprise to everyone with the exception of Percy. Ori ascertained that he *must* have convinced Callan to change his mind somehow. She soon learned that she was correct in her assessment.

Callan confided in Ash that he would be seeking an oracle in Midscar. Of course, Ash immediately told Ori about this shocking revelation. The urge to talk it out with someone else had been too strong it seemed. Ash had told her that Callan didn't believe in fortunes or prophecies; Ash believed that he perhaps needed guidance, that he seemed more clouded and distant than usual with her. Ori couldn't help but think that she played a part in that distance since she had divulged her secret to Callan and not

Ash. It wasn't that she couldn't trust Ash, but she truly thought that if she knew, *Ash* would no longer trust *her*.

Ori was used to distancing herself from others, she was comforted by it at times, feeling as if her shadows were nothing but a danger to them if they knew. Deep down Ori knew that it was not her shadows that were a danger, but the source of those shadows. That was the truth she harbored on her own and truly feared.

Callan told Ash that the Oracle of the Past, Enoch Ferraille, was rumored to be hiding in Midscar. It was easy to see by the detached manner that possessed Callan that he was concerned about something. He rode alone lost in thought instead of speaking with the others. Through talking out loud, Ash deduced that he wanted to know about his own past. What had been hidden from him, why no one would tell him of his mother and father, and why there was no trace of them at all. Ash, in her true fashion, convinced Callan to let her see Enoch as well, though Ori was sure it was for hope rather than fear of her own past.

Thus, the party all agreed to change their course for Midscar, with two of the Shadow Hounds in tow. Callan told Ash that Enoch would request an animal, or being, that had been slain by the person who would receive the reading. Coincidentally, they had the perfect specimen. They gathered branches and ties, fashioning stretchers to pull the beasts behind them. The horses pulling the hounds heartily proved their tenacity for the last leg of their journey into the town of Midscar, not stopping once to rest.

Ori wouldn't let her gaze linger on the hounds for too long. Memories of the attack kept resurfacing. She had *felt* their presence. Before the trees darkened and the light of the setting sun was suffocated, she felt something prick the skin along her spine.

When she locked eyes with the first hound, she knew it was for her. She knew that she had run from her truth for far too long and they had come to collect. She was more than grateful that Callan cut off the sure-to-be revealing speech of the first hound before she'd had much more to explain. More than that, she hated herself for bringing them straight to Callan, Ash, Nik, and Percy. She couldn't have known they were coming for her, but she felt an immense amount of guilt for putting the people *near* her in danger.

She knew she had to do something to protect them, and she had the notion that getting too close to one of the hounds would've resulted in her capture. Restraining the hound with her own shadows had been risky enough, but the strength it took to hold the beast back was insurmountable. It was like its shadows negated hers, the pressure it took to hold the grip of her essence was shut off and knocked back into her. That was the last thing she remembered before she was thrown back, and the shadows *she* once controlled, controlled *her*.

She had been trapped in another nightmare that she couldn't escape. The walls of her childhood home would come into focus, but her sight was blurred by her shadows. The gloved hand would clasp over her mouth, cutting off the screams that would reach no one. She would feel the scrape of that damned dagger on her cheek, cutting open the scar that had been a permanent and constant reminder of who she was. Then, the agonizing pain of her tail being slowly ripped from her back—

And then she would wake. It would always be the pain that woke her from the restless sleep, still searing through her body, jerking her forward and in search of the man cloaked in black who had done this to her, again.

Ori squeezed her eyes shut in an attempt to rid herself of the terrifying memory. She replaced it with the calmer one that occurred after waking this time. While it was initially filled with fear and anger, Ori reflected on the fact that even without Lyra, she had been taken care of. Ash stayed up with her until she was able to fall asleep and even moved her bedroll closer so that she wouldn't feel alone.

Then there was Callan. The way he'd held her, it was nurturing. In his arms she had the innate feeling that she was safe. He was so understanding of something she knew was beyond foreign to him and he was even willing to risk his own friendship to keep her secret. Ori still wasn't completely sure how to feel about his... kindness. Callan wasn't kind to her; he had only ever expressed annoyance in most situations. But when she saw the Shadow Hound bounding for him, she knew she couldn't just let him die, she knew somewhere in her soul that he was too important. To the realms? To his friends? To her? She didn't know. But waking up to his eyes, the swirling green pools were filled with misery and fear. She wasn't sure what to make of that either, not then and not now.

*****

Midscar was nowhere near as coated in dust as Keld, but some of the same dryness lingered without the dreaded heat. The storefronts and homes were modest ones that weren't closely built on top of each other and decaying like the homes in Atreyu. Ori also noted that these weren't like the homes in Grimmstone either with no luxury spared. Midscar was simple and its people didn't seem to have a single care in the world.

As the party dismounted and stretched their tired bodies, a young woman approached them. She carried with her a basket of yellow flowers that bordered on looking gold. "Welcome travelers, would you like a Grian rose?"

The woman's body fiercely started when Asvin landed from the cloudy skies above, causing her to drop the flower she held in her fragile hands. Asvin strode towards her, bending at the waist to retrieve the flower and place it back in her basket. "I apologize if I startled you, lady. Would you happen to know where our party can eat, stall our horses, and rest for the evening?"

The stunned woman only started up at Asvin, mouth still agape. She broke her gaze, seeming to realize that everyone was now staring at her, with the exception of Callan who had narrowed his *glare* towards Asvin. The woman stuttered over her words once she had collected her bearings, "Uh—Y-yes, there is a tavern just this way. I can take you to it."

Asvin bowed his head in thanks, and they followed the woman, making sure to give her a wide berth so there wasn't the possibility of scaring her again. Ori was somewhat perplexed by the shock that followed Asvin when he was noticed by others. Sure, he was really tall and had massive wings. Ori had seen the likes of many Corpoi in the Celerity Channel, Asvin's features paled in comparison to those she had come across. She had to admit; he was handsome, charming even. Ash definitely thought so though she hadn't said it aloud, Ori could see the way Ash would steal side long glances at the avian.

The woman who led them quickly departed as soon as she located the tavern owner, casting weary eyes towards Asvin. Ori couldn't *completely* blame her, Asvin was a Corpoi that people rarely saw in Baasaris. Thinking through all the hybrid Draoi beings she'd met, Asvin was the first Cloud Giant. Ash practically swooned over him when she told Ori about how he had killed the fourth Shadow Hound with his bare hands. A fighter then. She told Ori that she was bracing for her death at that moment and likely would have been dead if not for Asvin. The half-Cloud Giant was a mystery to them all, but Ash was convinced that he was good.

The tavern they were led to doubled as an inn. It was a three-story structure with wrap-around porches on each level. However, the first thing Ori noticed were the flickering candles set in each window. This was a safe place for the Draoi people. It reminded her of the painting she'd purchased in Atreyu, and of her childhood home in Phyruh where the candles were lit to remember those lost by the raids.

"Welcome! Varis tells me that you all seek shelter for the evening. My name is Rohan. I am more than happy to show you where you may leave your horses and then to vacant rooms that are already made up and ready for rest. The Obsidian is open to you all." Rohan, the tavern owner, was a tall man with deep brown hair, almost appearing black when the sun wasn't able to peek through the cloud-covered sky. Through tufts of his chocolate hair were bone-white antlers.

Ori had never known of a Corpoi to *own* their own establishment, much less a Corpoi who wasn't scarred or maimed in one way or another. His caramel skin had a golden sheen to it when he moved under the lights of the tavern. Ori noticed that he didn't take any lingering looks at anyone in their party, he simply acknowledged them all and *truly* welcomed their presence. Something that most of them probably weren't used to. The friendly nature of the village stunned Ori. It had likely stunned them all; the further one was from Grimmstone the more one felt as if they could breathe for the first time. At least she noticed the slight change of the usual pressure on her chest.

Nik, Asvin, and Callan led the horses to the stalls that were located on the eastern side of the tavern while Ori, Ash, and Percy were led inside.

The main room was open with a bar and tables spread over oak floors that were well-worn from visitors' past. To the right of the entrance stood a podium where Rohan marked off available rooms for the group. When Callan, Asvin, and Nik joined them once more with packs and travel ware in hand, they spread out to claim rooms. With only three available in close proximity to each other, they split off in pairs. After a minor argument over who Asvin would share a room with, prompted by Callan, Nik offered for Asvin to share with him and for Percy to share with Callan, leaving Ori and Ash to claim the third, largest room. Once they had time to settle in and clean off days of travel, the party met back up again downstairs to eat their first warm meal in days.

"I think it would be wise for us to take a watch over the horses and the hounds throughout the evening." Asvin, having not spoken during dinner, had opted to change the subject from lighthearted stories to the serious topic of not being familiar with Midscar and its people.

Callan reluctantly nodded in agreement. "We can take shifts, Percy, you can take the first and come wake me for the second." Callan went through and listed out who would relieve who throughout the night. They already knew bringing the Shadow

Hounds with them was a risk, someone standing by with them throughout the night should help to keep wanderers from becoming interested in what was hidden among the horses between the stalls.

Chapter Twelve

Ash

She knew she could never fill the gaping hole in the earth with the sparse dirt she was shoveling. It felt as if she had been there for hours, not having stopped once in her endeavor.

She was in the meadows near her childhood home in Vytarrion, but she was alone. Or rather, her family was not with her. Being truly alone would've meant that the beast lying in the proximate tree line wouldn't have been there either. She couldn't make out its features, but she could see that it was large, larger than her house—which she realized could no longer be seen from a distance. The beast's striking white eyes, swirling with iridescence, bore into hers. She knew even then that if she stopped shoveling, if she turned to make a run for home, she would not make it.

Digging her shovel into the endless pile, she turned once more to the pit. It was dark and cavernous. She couldn't see the bottom and each time the dirt trickled in, there was no reassurance that it ever hit the bottom floor.

This time, however, when she returned to the pit, she saw a light. A pulsing light of the brightest blue. As blue as the sky above her. The light didn't show any sign of an end to the pit, but it drew her in anyway. She placed the tip of her slippered foot at the edge *of the hole to peer in closer. Before she could focus in on the speck of light, a low-bellied growl rippled through the blades of grass. She felt heat carried in the breath of the beast as it slowly rose, its spiked head climbing above the trees. The creature was still covered in darkness though the sky held not one cloud.*

The sound of a voice forced her attention back to the pit, to the light that drummed faster than before. She tried. She tried to hear what it was desperately struggling to tell her.

The beast huffed hot air again but before she could turn away from the light and discover how close the obscure monstrosity had come, she was surrounded by burning white flames.

*****

Ash woke, eyes wide, scanning the bedroom. Ori was still next to her, sleeping peacefully. It would seem that her self-medication of mead kept her from experiencing the nightmares Ori said she often had. After the one Ash just experienced, she began to understand her wayward friend and her choice of bad habit a bit more.

The moonlight beamed into the room, lighting up the end of the bed and the dresser against the wall. She was still at The Obsidian in Midscar, *not* home. Glancing at the old clock in the corner, she knew it was almost time for her watch to begin. She quietly rose and dressed in a loose white shirt and brown breeches. After sliding on her boots and wrapping herself in a spare blanket that decorated the foot of the bed, she left her nightmare and chances of sleep behind.

When Ash rounded the corner of the inn and into the horse stable she could see Asvin. He was sitting on the hay-covered floor, leaning against one of the stalls. She watched him for a moment as he sharpened another of his knives. She wondered just how many he carried. His peaceful demeanor was stunted when Ash noticed him taking in a few deep breaths, only to let out a whooshing sigh.

Maybe he was deep in thought? Maybe he was just tired. Ash couldn't help but acknowledge that maybe Callan's behavior toward Asvin may have annoyed the congenial giant. Ash made an attempt at a lighthearted joke to sway his attention, "Is that all you do? Sharpen weapons?" she asked with a grin plastered on her face.

Asvin didn't even jump at her presence, it was like he already knew she was there, watching him. "Do you often watch people without announcing yourself?"

Well, she now knew the answer to that assumption. He was quick to match her sarcasm, but he didn't share the same grin or meet her eyes, only his brows furrowed as he continued his work.

Ash took a seat on the ground across from him, crossing her legs and gathering her blanket closer to her. While the heat from Vytarrion was still close by, the nights in Midscar were rather chilly. "You still have some time before your watch if you'd rather wait inside," Asvin said but still didn't look up. How he even knew she was cold was beyond her comprehension since he had yet to look at her. She began to wonder if she'd done something to annoy him herself.

"I'm fine, I couldn't sleep much anyway. You can go early though if you'd like, I'm sure you're tired. You should get some more sleep." Ash made a note to herself to talk with Callan about his deliberate choice to place Asvin at the center of the watch rotation. The man had *saved* them all, this was far from the appreciation he deserved.

It was then that Asvin grinned, but it carried a wicked gleam to it. "Yes, your *best friend* put me at the worst of the watch times." Only silence lingered between them and Asvin had paused completely. Ash wasn't sure if he was making a joke or being serious, so she waited. Asvin took in a deep breath, resuming his blade sharpening as his features softened. "I can finish my watch. I also couldn't sleep, so I might as well be useful."

Ash wasn't sure what to say. Was he truly that upset with Callan? She knew he could be an ass at times but… "Did Callan say something to you?"

Asvin froze again, but this time she didn't see the same precarious look as before. "No, no. He just doesn't seem to like me very much."

"Callie is like that when he meets new people. It takes him a while to open up. I'm sorry if he has given you the cold shoulder."

"*Callie*? I'll have to remember that the next time he pisses me off." His laugh was genuine; his shoulders shook a bit as the low tone danced and twirled around Ash's bones.

"So, why couldn't you sleep?" Ash wasn't sure why she asked but she just wanted him to keep talking. She liked being around him, being near him even though she wasn't sure exactly the reason. She really didn't have a *good* reason.

Asvin placed his knife in an empty sheath over the right side of his chest and reached to place the whetstone in a pouch secured to his belt. Then he finally dared to behold her, the slow trailing of his eyes made her feel more seen than ever before.

She wasn't positive on how it made her feel: *scrutinized* or *revered*. He started at her boots, then moved to the blanket she securely wrapped around herself, before he finally *looked* at her. When their eyes met Ash felt the same sting on her wrist she had before. She hissed through her clenched jaw before tossing the blanket open to inspect the wound.

"What happened? Are you okay?" Asvin was already crossing to her side of the stalls, kneeling down. When she finally felt the sting subside, she opened her eyes and saw not a scar... but a tattoo? "What the—?"

"It's the constellation of Vytarr and Qoohr," Asvin said with such certainty that Ash didn't doubt him, but all she saw was a small collection of dots and stars. Callan had said it looked like a constellation.

Her look of pure confusion must have been enough for Asvin to speak again. "Estus created all the constellations in the sky. He placed every star with detailed precision; it was like a master painting for him. He wanted to tell the story of The Five Realms and part of that long epic is the tale of Vytarr and Qoohr." Ash remained quiet, brushing her thumb back and forth over the quickly healing markings on her wrist. "The God of Day and The Goddess of Night have been lovers since the beginning of time.

Legends say that there was only one day each year that they could see each other—"

"Eclipse Day?" Ash guessed, remembering the holiday of lovers that many throughout the realms celebrated.

"Yes, Eclipse Day. The one day where the sun and the moon unite as one. A *day* where lovers can meet in the *night*. May I?" He hovered his finger over her wrist. She wasn't sure what he was asking permission to do but she nodded anyway. He emanated security, safety. She'd known him for only twenty-four hours, but the trust was there for him.

He began to trace invisible lines between the markings, explaining the shapes and what they meant. "Here, this symbolizes the eternal flame, Vytarr." He drew slow lines over her wrist with the lightest touch, Ash wasn't sure she was breathing as his calloused finger moved in small patterns, connecting the stars that stood out from her freckled skin.

"And here, this represents the changing tides of the seas, Qoohr. One will always chase after the other until they meet. They collide on this day, spending every moment together until they are inevitably torn apart again." Asvin drew his fingers up the center of her palm, to the tips of her fingers before he retracted his hand and sat beside her. His stone arm pressed into her shoulder.

Shaking from her momentary stupor, Ash finally let out the breath she had been clinging to. "I still don't understand why it's here. How does a tattoo just magically show up on your skin?" At that point she no longer cared about the meaning of the markings; she hardly cared about the marking at all. Her mind was tangled with mixed emotions ranging from bewilderment to curiosity to misplaced desire.

"Honestly, I have no idea. Maybe Percy or even the oracle could tell you?" Ash snapped her gaze from her wrist and found Asvin already staring at her, his sky-blue eyes held a sense of serenity in them. Like the blue skies of her home above the meadows. The grin spread across his striking face said she was too naive. "How do you know about the oracle?"

"If *Callie* acted a little less inconspicuous then maybe I wouldn't have eavesdropped on his conversation." His grin widened into a smile and Ash couldn't help but let the giggle she had suppressed rear itself. His rugged laugh made another appearance. She decided that she really liked that laugh. *His* laugh.

Before Asvin realized she was blatantly staring at him, Ash turned her head and focused again on her wrist. A constellation about... love? A truly tragic love. She started to slip into silent thought when Asvin spoke again. "You have a beautiful smile."

Ash felt the heat creep up her cheeks. Any thought that once occupied her mind was wiped blank at his words. Ash managed to say, "Thank you." It was merely a whisper past her lips, but she didn't know what else she could say in response to his unexpected compliment. She had never been told that any part of her was beautiful, at least not in a genuine sense.

Asvin stood and dusted off his leathers. "Well, I am going to try to get some sleep. Be safe, okay?"

Ash met his eyes again; she didn't want him to leave. She gave him a parting reply anyway, "Sleep well." She smiled again; she couldn't stop herself. The smile she received in return was equally beautiful. No one had ever looked at her the way Asvin did. It was like he saw through her, all the way to her very soul.

Ash was beaming throughout the rest of her watch. She fell asleep after, though the butterflies fluttering through her core made it difficult to do so. She woke up the next morning with sore cheeks and a glow that no one would be able to extinguish.

Chapter Thirteen

Callan

It was early when Callan and Ash left The Obsidian. Callan spoke with Rohan and asked him where he could find a man by the name of Enoch Ferraille. The innkeeper was quick to tell him that Enoch owned the butcher shop towards the end of town. Rohan gave them confused looks at their excitement over a local butcher, but Callan quickly sedated his puzzlement. Callan explained their party had brought animals with them from their hunt that they hoped to sell the meat and hides before their trip to Greenside. Callan wasn't sure if Rohan actually believed his white lie, but it was enough to get the information he needed.

Callan and Ash took two horses, each pulling one of the hounds behind them, covered in sheets to conceal their bodies in the daylight. Callan hoped that his explanation to Rohan would aid in dismissing curiosity about what lay beneath the stained white cloth. He and Ash quickly rode to the edge of Midscar where they saw the sign for Ferraille's Butcher Shop.

Walking into the establishment, Callan first noticed that the small front room had a granite-topped counter with a chalkboard on the wall behind it listing different cuts of meat. The next thing he noticed were the lack of people in the front room. No one waited on their previously made orders, and no one waited to place them. No one was there to take any orders to begin with. Callan heard nothing and no one, but the smell of roasted meat and seasoned cooking wafted through the air. While the scent was a pleasant one, it was not what Callan had expected in a place that should smell of meat and blood.

"Do you think this is the right place?" Ash whispered to Callan from his side. She too was inspecting the layout of the room and making an attempt to peer behind the curtained door in the back. Before Callan could respond to Ash, they heard heavy footsteps sounding from the curtained doorway.

When large hands pushed the tattered curtains aside, they revealed a boisterous man with a tall, muscular build and a full round belly that shook when he spoke. "Hello! I do apologize for not hearing you enter. What can I do for this lovely couple today?"

Callan wrinkled his face in disgust at the thought of being... *romantically* involved with Ash of all people. Ash had apparently mirrored his expression because the large man was quick to correct himself. "Oh, I am sorry, I see I've assumed before asking."

The man's ebony skin darkened, the apples of his cheeks blushing from embarrassment. "It's okay, I'm Callan and this is Ash. She's... more of a sister than anything else." Callan gave the man a smile in hopes that it would ease the awkward tension.

"It truly is okay," Ash repeated, "we are attached at the hip, so it was bound to happen one day or another." Ash's smile must have been far better than Callan's attempt. The man let out a laugh that rolled throughout his belly and shoulders. Callan wasn't entirely certain that the windows didn't rattle from the quake of his rich laughter. Callan and Ash laughed along with him; his joy was a much-needed contagion. When the man's cackle came to an end and the room was once more quiet, Ash asked, "Would you happen to be Enoch Ferraille?"

"No one has asked for me by name in a very long time." The silence in the room was palpable, Callan felt his heartbeat through his entire body, waiting for Enoch to say something, anything. "I take it you two aren't here to procure various meats for a lavish dinner party, eh?."

With an awkward clearing of his throat, Enoch led Callan and Ash through the back of the shop which held a plethora of doors. Some doors led to workshops for conducting business while others led to storage rooms for keeping meats and various other foods chilled in iceboxes or hung to dry.

The door Enoch opened and led them into was a sitting room with old high-backed chairs, the fabric ragged from years of use. A bare wooden table sat in the middle, dark stains and scratches coating its top. Callan should've felt uneasy about the room that was otherwise barren, but he was more uneasy about what he could learn from an oracle. Percy's urgings had brought Callan this far, if it weren't the scholars' request that he take this detour, Callan would happily be trotting to Greenside already.

Enoch offered them something to drink and a bowl of the roast he had been working on through the night. Callan and Ash shared one quick look before agreeing that it smelled too good not to taste. Enoch smiled wide and hastily collected three bowls of his homemade roast and three ales, successfully carrying them all in one trip, using his large hands and arms as serving trays.

"I have always held a fondness for cooking. It's the one thing I do that helps me to feel normal in this world." Enoch shared this as they took their last bites. Callan had finished his roast and ale long ago, Enoch topping Callan's glass off with another pour. Ash took a few sips of hers but wasn't the biggest fan of the drink, so Callan was apt to finish hers as well but thought better of it. He somehow knew that experiencing an oracle reading while intoxicated would sway him to keep believing it was all hogwash. He did his best to keep his skepticality from his face.

"You are a fine cook, Enoch. Honestly, I would travel all the way here just to simply enjoy this meal again," Callan admitted. "But we do come asking for a favor. We have heard stories about your gift to see the past. Would you be willing to read ours?" Callan tried not to recoil at his own words. Of all the gifts of essence he had seen in his young life, gifts of telling fortunes and fates were not among them. The fortune tellers at the Phenomicron were all scam-artists looking to earn the money of the gullible. Poor fools, he thought. Now *he* would be a fool. He hoped Percy was right about this man.

Enoch's ever-present smile slowly faded, his eyes tracking to a dark corner of the room. Callan and Ash both turned to follow his lost gaze, but they saw nothing, just a cobwebbed corner.

"You know, I haven't read someone's past in a very long time. Almost been a hundred years if I remember correctly."

Callan tried to make sense of what Enoch had just confessed. He was at least *one hundred years old*?

Enoch moved on, not noticing the shocked look Callan and Ash both held, "When I first came to Midscar, I wanted a simple life, one where I could live among those who didn't truly know who I was. I remember holding large parties and serving every dish I could conjure up to anyone who would walk through the doors. Drummers and string players would always join in on the merriment, bringing joyous music and dancing. I miss those nights. The townsfolk of Midscar have never treated me poorly, but they became weary over the years when they saw that I did not age along with them. I only have a few gray hairs and not many have joined them in quite some time. Not enough to give them proof of my aging." Callan looked up to Enoch's shiny, hairless head and raised a brow before he looked at Enoch's long beard, spotting all of two silver hairs among the thick black locks. "No one has come asking for me–the *real* me–until today."

Callan wasn't sure what to say, and it was in that moment he was glad that Ash convinced him, or rather forced him, to let her join. She broke the silence in a far more gentle way, "Have you heard of The Celestial Prophecy?"

Enoch didn't meet her gaze, but he nodded his head sheepishly. "I had a small feeling your visit may be about that."

"How do you mean?" Callan couldn't hold his tongue— how could he have any idea what they were here about without even knowing *who* they were?

"Let's just say, my siblings and I have known about that prophecy for a long time, and I was recently made aware that it should come to pass in a few days time." Well, Callan couldn't exactly argue with that, not that he knew how he would argue with the insanity that was the unknown. Sakura had told them the same when she first told them of the prophecy. "What do you seek to learn from your pasts?"

Ash answered first. "I believe my father may be in danger or somehow tied to The Nameless. We have been looking for information about The Nameless and I am worried that the prophecy may involve him. I want to know if there is anything I may have missed or didn't understand as a child, something that would tell me my suspicions are wrong."

"And what if your suspicions are correct?" Enoch's question was not answered. Ash shook her head, and Callan saw a small tear escape from her wide eyes, falling from her cheek to her lap. He took her hand and gave a light squeeze—if giving her that small comfort was all he could do, then he would do it. "And you, Callan, what is it you seek to know?"

"Everything. I know little of my past. I know my mother dropped me off into the hands of the woman who raised both me and Ash. I know she left me this ring and nothing else. And I know there are no records of my family name, leading to the conclusion that I know absolutely nothing." And neither will you, Callan wanted to add. He didn't mean for his words to carry the heat that they did, he was angry, not at Enoch of course. He wasn't angry with himself. He didn't even know he was angry until that very moment when he felt Ash squeeze his hand back in solidarity. Who wouldn't be frustrated by the unknown?

Enoch stood from the table, pulling in a deep breath as he rose. He looked between the two of them for a few moments before he spoke once more. "Do you know how I read the past?" Callan and Ash shared a look before they both shook their heads. "The other oracles, my siblings, have different methods. The one I use is rather... bloody. I require a creature whose life was taken by the person I am to read."

"We actually brought those in the event you said yes," Ash interjected with a saccharine grin.

Enoch caved in at her smile again. "Well then, my question remains, do you know exactly how it is done?" The two said nothing. Callan began to question how strange this method would be given Enoch's persistence. He didn't have the time to dwell on it before Enoch declared, "Well, let's get started."

*****

Ash would go first. Mostly because she told Callan she wanted to get it over with. He understood and accepted her request, though he was still dreading his eventual turn.

Enoch didn't question the Shadow Hound corpses, only raising one impressed brow when he removed the bloodied sheet from the first. Callan assisted him in bringing the beast back into the room where... where they had just eaten food off the table that Callan now realized was used to carve into dead animals. He swallowed the bile that threatened to escape from his upturned stomach, his face he realized was scrunched in disgust. The half-burned body of the hound rid the room of the godly seasoned roast and replaced it with the scent of charred fur and flesh.

"When I read the past, it does not always answer the questions you seek. It tells me what the past believes you should know to prepare you for your present and future."

Callan and Ash nodded as he explained the process. It took Callan great measures to school his features into neutrality. Enoch told them that each organ in the body held different portions of the past; the liver would tell him of the important figures in their past, a lung would tell them of dire situations they may have faced, the heart would tell them about the love that was bestowed upon them, and so forth.

Enoch focused in on Ash as he handed her a serrated blade that was longer than her forearm. He instructed her to make a slice from neck to navel on the beast, explaining that only the person being read could open the creature. Ash took a deep breath before she plunged the blade into the throat of the hound. Dark, coagulated blood oozed from the wound and continued to pour out as she dragged the blade down. The stench of the dead overwhelmed Callan's senses and the bile threatened him once more.

When Enoch reached his hand into the beast, sleeves rolled to his elbows and his stained white apron traded for a dark leather one, his eyes closed. He searched for a moment for the organ he sought while Ash held her breath and clutched the base of her throat.

Enoch's eyes opened slowly, the warm brown irises and the pupils were gone. His eyes were bone white when he settled his gaze again on Ash. "I see white flames. A woman with pale hair and silver eyes. She was worried for you. A man with strawberry hair, freckles on his face, wings like yours only whole. He takes you away. He speaks to a man, a captain. The winged man does everything for you, he cares deeply for you, in part because he knows who you will become." Callan tore his wandering eyes from Enoch's blood-soaked hands. Ash was as still as a statue, she didn't move an inch, but tears were streaming down her face.

Enoch continued as his hands moved around in the dismembered belly of the hound, "Blue eyes, they look upon you, the first star in the sky. Parastella. You are loved by more than just the man and the woman, your parents. Grian Roses. I see them spread across a field of green. A strong tree with a swing, you could fly then. A place where you were safe."

Enoch pulled his hands from the beast; he blinked a few times as his eyes returned to their natural warm state. Ash sobbed. Callan had never seen her in so much pain.

Enoch's face was pooled with sympathy for her, "I know you must have questions. I am sorry to tell you both that I cannot interpret what the past tells me, only you can." Callan nodded in muddled understanding. Ash continued to cry as she lowered herself into one of the chairs that had been pushed back. When her tears ran dry, her body still trembled with what remained of her devastation. She stilled and stared at the hound with its innards laid open to the world.

Callan reached for her, but she held up her hand, her voice shaking as she said, "I'm okay, I jus—I just need a minute." She took a few paces back, her unblinking eyes would not meet his, "Go ahead, learn what you need."

Callan hesitated, not only because he knew Ash was *not* okay, but also because he didn't think he was ready for what Enoch would see. Was Ash able to make sense of anything he'd said? Callan only picked up on the description of Ash's father, everything else translated into nothing for him. What part of Enoch's words caused her so much anguish?

Enoch handed Callan the newly cleaned blade and he repeated the same movements that Ash had before him. When Enoch placed his hands into the beast that still held the arrow in its brow, the oracles' russet eyes once again were wiped clear of the darkness, replaced by the eerie white. "A woman with lavender hair and bright eyes," Enoch took in a short breath, "Your mother. Violet smoke, she controls it. She struggles, and shadows take her down." At the mention of shadows, Callan's thoughts painted a familiar pale face with a deep scar running along her cheek.

Shadows come from Phyrus' realm. The realm of eternal darkness. The realm of terrible creatures.

Enoch continued, unaware of Callan's mind piecing together what little it knew, "A man, dark hair and green eyes like yours, he is devastated, he disappears. You are not alone, but you are not known."

As Enoch removed his hands from the beast, Callan couldn't stop himself. "That's it? That's all you see?"

"That is all that is decipherable. I can only see the past and your past... it's as if it's covered in fog. It was strange, it was like it wasn't your own. And as I said before, I cannot tell you what it means for I did not live it."

Callan's chest rose and fell rapidly as he took breath after breath, shaking when he exhaled. His fists clenched, and he felt the same anger as before, only then it was just simmering, now it was boiling over. He felt a small vibration at his hand, but he ignored it. "What the hell am I supposed to do with that? What the hell is Ash supposed to do with that? This only made things more confusing than before."

"I see you're protected." Enoch spoke with such a calm nature that it snapped Callan from his rage.

What was he talking about?

"Your ring, it has a protection charm on it. It looks the same shade of purple as the smoke I saw in your reading. Your mother is protecting you from the grave, even now."

Callan felt that crack in his heart open again; his mother was dead. There was no reunion, there was no knowing her, there were no answers. The rage-fueled panic settled in over his bones. He didn't know what to do or say. He stared at the arrow-slain beast before him, hands clenching and unclenching at his sides.

"Do you dream of her?" Enoch's question stunned Callan even further, the anger seeping into his blurred vision.

"Why?" The one-word question was all he could muster through a clenched jaw.

"Your ring protects you from what your mother chose to place in the charm. Chances are she was trying to protect you from the truth, many harsh truths."

"What truth would that be?"

"Your mother was a celestial. I recognize her, she was the celestial to Baasis." Enoch turned to Ash. "I knew your mother too, and your father. Your mother was the celestial to Vytarr. This is why The Celestial Prophecy was revealed to you; you are two of the children it speaks of."

Callan shook his head; denial took over every thought. His panic transitioned from anger to disbelief. He was nothing, he had no gifts, he had no essence. He was no one.

He was nameless.

"I ask about your dreams because celestials have prophetic dreams. Dreams that can carry hints of the future." Enoch's gaze slowly returned to the dark corner of the room, and again, it was empty when Callan followed his stare.

"What do you keep looking at? There's nothing ther—"

"Do you dream?" Enoch interrupted, asking his question again, but his voice remained at the same volume it had for their entire visit.

"No, I don't dream, and I have never dreamed of my mother." Callan was short with the oracle; his patience was too thin. His skin was coated in a layer of sweat. The room he thought once cold from the neighboring icebox room, felt degrees hotter.

Callan's disoriented mind showed him the drawn image of a woman that he had believed to be his mother. He was a small child when she left him with Madame Loch, but he knew in his heart the image of the woman that flowed from his mind to his pen was his mother. But he didn't want to share this with Enoch, he hadn't even shared this small part of him with Ash. He had stashed the picture in his desk drawer and that is where it remained, not wishing to hurt himself by longing to know the woman who'd *left* him, *abandoned* him. His anger was replaced with a deep sorrow.

Callan shook his head in an attempt to clear the woman's sorrowful eyes from his mind. He pressed his palm into his chest to calm his racing heart to no avail.

"I've had a weird dream. It was seldom and blurry at first but now I have the same one every time I sleep." Ash's voice was barely a whisper, she stepped forward, her eyes were now red, but her face was dry, no longer streaked with tears.

Ash looped a supporting arm through Callan's; he felt his panic subside ever-so-slightly at the presence of his friend. She spoke softly as she described her dream, "I am shoveling dirt into a bottomless pit while a faceless beast watches over me, forcing me to keep going. I can't see my home, but I know I'm in the meadows I used to run through as a child. The meadows you saw with the Grian roses, those were my favorite flowers. When I look into the pit, I see a blue light shining and then I am surrounded... by white flames."

"Your mother harnessed white flames when she was Vytarr's celestial, it could be that she is trying to protect you from something." Enoch turned to address Callan. "Have you ever taken that ring off?"

Callan shook his head. With a deep inhale, Enoch began wiping his hands clean of the hounds' blood on a nearby towel.

He walked over to Callan and clasped his shoulder. The jolt shook Callan from the stupor that had overtaken his body. "There is a good chance that the ring has stopped you from dreaming, an even better chance it has suppressed your gifts." *Gifts*? He had no *gifts*. This man was another scam-artist, just like the rest. But... Ash. Ash believes.

Enoch continued, "You are not Nondraoi, but you are also not a celestial yet, merely the child of a former celestial. If I remember the prophecy correctly, you are the Knight." He turned his head again to Ash. "And you, you are the Flame. We didn't always know what the prophecies meant when they came to us but based on your past readings and recognizing your parents, I know who you could become. But I understand the weight this has placed on both of you." Enoch addressed Callan directly once more, "Your dreams could help you to understand this reading, you just have to take off the ring and see if anything comes to you."

Callan looked down at his ring, the only piece of his mother he had, the only tangible piece of his past. He felt his mind running in circles, trying to understand and put together the puzzle that still had many missing pieces. But he had no choice other than to try. He couldn't focus on the prophecy, he couldn't focus on Ash, he couldn't even begin to think about the fact that he was Draoi; he could only think of his mother and her sacrifice. What had she done to keep him safe? And from what?

He tapped the stone on his ring with a finger, and the purple light shuttered, almost as if *it* were afraid. He saw his own fingers tremble as he slid the ring off his finger.

Then there was nothing. Darkness was all he could see.

*****

The purple smoke appeared slowly at first, coming in and casting the darkness aglow. When the smoke began to clear, he was surrounded by life. Green plants, trees, vibrant vines, and flowers. As he swept his gaze across the clearing teaming with jungle-like greenery the likes of which he had never seen, he spotted his reflection. An oval-shaped mirror sat angled against the tree directly in front of him.

Approaching the mirror, he saw the ornate patterns on the frame, swirling leaves of gold glittering. He knelt down and picked the mirror up. When he studied his reflection closer, the forest behind him was not the same as he had seen it, everything was dead. The trees were barren of leaves, the flowers were withered in shades of brown and gray, and the once-long vines were shriveled. Yet, when he turned and observed the scenery around him, it still teemed with life.

His face appeared paler than usual, his hair was shorter, and his beard was clean-shaven, his skin smooth. A crown of golden leaves, matching the mirror, sat upon his head.

Before Callan could reach up and touch the spires of the weightless crown, purple smoke gathered again behind him. He set the mirror down and slowly turned to face the amethyst cloud.

He could hear what sounded like a struggle, a fight. He took one step towards the mist but found that he couldn't penetrate the cloud, an invisible wall held him back. He heard the striking sounds of weapon on weapon, of punches being swung through the air and landing their target along with grunts and cries of the surely wounded. Then he heard a voice. The voice was feminine. If Enoch was truthful, Callan's mother *wielded purple mists.*

"You know not what you do. The only thing you accomplish by killing us is borrowed time. You remember the last time, you remember when we came back with even more power than before. They have no idea what they have created."

A dark voice shouted over hers, "You are the one who does not see the truth! You will see that it is those who return that will suffer the wrath of the gods. Of him. *They will learn from your mistakes, or they will fail just like you have."*

Tendrils of shadows replaced the vines around him, the shadows wrapped around the smoke until it was smothered completely like a python to its prey, and the darkness returned.

Chapter Fourteen

Ori

The night before felt like one of Ori's nightmares. When Ash returned to The Obsidian, Asvin following closely with Callan thrown over his shoulder, Ori imagined the absolute worst.

Ash explained to Ori, Nik, and Percy what had happened with the oracle, Enoch. When Ash got to the part about she and Callan learning they were the children of former celestials, Ori felt her heart drop into the pit of her stomach. They were part of the prophecy too.

Ori knew she should've told Ash then that she too was one of the children mentioned but she didn't know where to begin. They wouldn't be subjected to the same imminent wrath as she. Ori couldn't just come out and say that she was a Shadow Wielder or who her parents were. She couldn't, *wouldn't* jeopardize the budding relationship that she found herself clinging to without Lyra around. But she also knew that Ash would have to know the truth, soon. Especially now.

Ori did what she could do at that moment, she took Ash to their room and she comforted her, the way Lyra used to comfort Ori. She held her as she cried and rambled through every thought and emotion that plagued her. Ash told Ori about her mother and father, about her nightmares, about her home in the meadows. Ori stayed there with Ash until she fell asleep.

She left their room once more that night to check on Callan. Upon entering the room, she found Callan sitting up in his bed, awake after hours of unconsciousness. Percy was nowhere to be found, likely occupying Nik and Asvin's room. Ori hated that she hadn't been here when he woke. She'd sat by Callan's bedside for what felt like hours, just like he had for her, only for him to wake up alone.

Callan didn't raise his head when she entered, his focus stayed locked in on the ring he always wore. He had it between his finger and thumb rotating it, inspecting it.

"How are you feeling?" She choked on the words as Callan broke his concentration and shot a dagger-filled stare in Ori's direction.

"I don't know why that's any concern of yours."

She was stunned; these words didn't carry annoyance like before. They had no hints of the sweet and kind notes he'd used to make her feel safe with him. These words, *his* words, carried hatred.

Ori stared at him blankly, she didn't know how to respond other than to utter, "I don't understand."

"Oh, I'm sure that you do, actually. I knew you were keeping secrets. I told Ash that there was no way you could be trustworthy. I don't know why you're here, but I know it's not any of the bullshit excuses you're concocting right now. I should've known better when I saw your *gift*."

His words cut deep. Deeper than the pain that she felt when the man in black ran the blade down her cheek.

Deeper than the pain she felt when her tail was sawed from her back.

Deeper than the pain she felt when she realized her mother was gone.

The pain of fear, the pain of the unknown.

The pain of being outcast.

"Either you tell me now who exactly you are, or you can leave." Callan's chest rose and fell rapidly. His anger radiated throughout the room, but his words were just above a whisper sending a chill down Ori's spine. She tried to speak but she couldn't. Her throat closed up and she began to choke on the stagnant air she desperately tried to take in.

Her heart started to race; her vision grew clouded at the edges before they became blurry with tears. Ori ran from Callan's room, slamming the door behind her. It wasn't until she flung herself downstairs and out the front doors of the inn that she could breathe again, gagging on the bile that had risen from the depths of her stomach.

What made him say those things? What had she done? Would he still keep her secret? Would he tell the others of her burden? Of the one thing that she could not control?

She took in deep breaths, counting between each inhale and exhale until she felt herself grounded once more to the wooden deck of the porch she stood on. She looked down to her hands, small wisps of shadows danced along her fingers. She knew they were trying to comfort her but in that moment, it felt like they taunted her.

When Ori returned to her room, Ash was still curled in the same spot she had left her, she crawled into the bed and silently cried until she too drifted into the sober sleep she often avoided.

*****

She was surrounded by dark, cave-like walls. These were not the walls of the Celerity Channel. These walls rose higher than the white towers of Knife's Edge and looked more like obsidian slate than stone. Ori cloaked herself in her shadows, blending in with the darkness that surrounded her.

She moved along the wall until she saw the glowing light at the end of a hall. Following it, gliding along the floors in silence, she heard a voice.

"Takara. It has been far too long." It was the name she had run from her entire life. The name that she did not claim. The name was given to her by her father. Takara. Treasure. "I told your mother that I would stop at nothing to find you. You, my Takara, the one who will bring death to the realms."

She couldn't move. She couldn't breathe. She stood flat against the wall, not willing to move even though he *knew she was there. She could feel his eyes burning through her. The eyes he gave her.*

"Treasure, Infinite Death. You know your purpose already. It is only time that stands between you and your true destiny. Takara Orelia Keres."

The Way of the Nameless

Chapter Fifteen

Ash

Ash had the same dream again, filling the pit with dirt while the beast watched over her. Enoch's reading relieved and terrified her all at once but she supposed she could understand her dream better than the nights before the reading.

Her mother was a celestial. She was the Flame in the prophecy. Callan was the Knight. Enoch answered some of the questions Ash had but he created so many more unanswered ones that now plagued her waking hours.

Ash thought about her dream again. Enoch told her and Callan that celestials would have prophetic dreams. Her mother Reya wielded white flames, was her mother the beast in her dream? Was she trying to protect her from the light at the bottom of the pit?

Then there was the word she had never heard of. *Parastella*. The first star in the sky. Her mind ran wild with all the possibilities. Someone loved her, other than her parents. She knew her parents loved her, the reading only confirmed that her father had hidden her with Madame Loch to protect her. The reading mentioned her father speaking to a captain. The only captain she knew was Blackwell, but he would've only been a child at the time

Kaster brought her to The Phenomicron. Ash still worried that her father was in trouble somehow.

The Flame will sacrifice the Sun to save the Knight. She was the Flame, Callan was the Knight, but who was the Sun? Who would she sacrifice to save Callan? She knew that she would sacrifice many things to protect him. The only family she had now was Callan, her brother not by blood or bone but by soul.

As Ash continued to examine her racing thoughts, she watched Asvin and Nik sparring behind The Obsidian. A welcome distraction to her incoherent inner ramblings. After she woke from her restless sleep she found herself walking down the stairs and to the back set of porches before she even knew she had gotten up from bed, leaving a slumbering Ori. It was like Ash's body was ten steps ahead of her mind. Or maybe she was so transfixed on yesterday's events that her body was simply moving for her.

The sun was just beginning to rise, turning the morning skies various shades of pinks and purples. Asvin had his sword brandished in a defensive position, taking Nik through the series of movements needed to knock the sword from his hand. Nik had a hatchet in each hand, flipping the one in his right over and over as Asvin spoke. Sweat poured from Nik's brow and made an appearance through his shirt. Meanwhile, Asvin showed no signs of tiring at all. It made her wonder just how often he had to use these techniques and on what or whom they were used.

Asvin had chosen to go without a shirt this morning, giving Ash a view that made her coursing thoughts come to a very bemused crawl.

She reflected back to what Percy had said about how cloud giants typically appeared, eight feet tall with stone skin. Asvin was

179

admittedly tall, she thought Nik was a pretty big guy, but Asvin takes the position of tallest in the party. He had paler features, but Ash didn't think he looked like stone. With her latest view of his body, she did note that he was chiseled like stone. He looked just like any other man, with the exception of his feathered wings. From his wide shoulders down to his legs, the muscle was packed onto every limb like he used his entire body to train and fight.

Okay, maybe he wasn't like any other man she'd known.

Ash's thoughts had ventured quickly from Enoch's reading to the confidence in which Asvin moved. Nik steadily circled him, but Asvin was clearly in complete control of the situation. Ash came to this conclusion when the practiced battle angel met her stare and gave her wink, his eyes off of his opponent.

Nik charged Asvin, raising the hatchet he had been flipping high above Asvin's head and coming down with brute force. But Asvin was faster.

In the span of mere seconds, Asvin evaded Nik's swing, ducking to the left while he grabbed Nik's arm and flipped him over and onto his back. Asvin stood above him, the tip of his sword poised right above Nik's throat. The dominance in his stance radiated over his face, his chest, and his back. The corded muscles seemed to ripple as he lifted his sword and placed it in the sheath down his back.

"I see watching people without announcing your presence is a common occurrence." Ash had no idea Asvin was referring to her until Nik, still lying on the grass in an attempt to catch his breath, jerked his head to her place on the porch. Nik slowly sat up and took the arm that Asvin offered to pull him up. Clasping Nik's shoulder he said, "Never give your opponent an opening like that.

Your body has to be on guard at all times. If you're up for it, I do this every morning, you are free to join me."

With a curt nod and a tired smile, Nik clipped his hatchets back to his belt before removing his sweat-coated shirt to wipe his face as he walked around the inn. She didn't watch as Nik rounded the corner in favor of resuming her mildly inappropriate staring without an audience.

Okay, it is highly *inappropriate.*

Ash cleared her throat and broke her gaze. "Sorry, I couldn't sleep, and I just found myself here watching the spectacle."

"Spectacle? I hardly thought it was that intriguing." Asvin said this as he climbed the steps, practically prowling towards her. No, she was making this up in her head. Her very tired, mixed-up head.

He sat in the chair next to her and ran his fingers through his silver hair, the subtle breeze blowing the smell of a summer storm in her direction. "How are you feeling? Aside from being beguiled by our *spectacle*."

Damn, she was still staring. It was difficult to draw her eyes from his. His aquamarine irises pierced hers, coated with unmistakable amusement and a hint of concern.

He had rescued her again yesterday. After Enoch told Callan about his mother's ring blocking out his prophetic dreams, Callan removed the ring, and he collapsed. Ash was overwhelmed by such a surreal panic as she held Callan, begging him to wake. It was only a few moments later that Asvin came bursting into the room, eyes scanning for an unseen threat. When he saw her there, he said nothing. He didn't touch her, he didn't try to move her, he just stayed. He knelt down next to her and waited until she could confirm that Callan was still breathing, merely unconscious. She wasn't sure how Asvin knew where exactly to find her or why he sought her out in the first place, but she found herself comforted by his presence.

Ash hadn't said much to him after the fact. She did, however, tell Ori about what had occurred when they were alone in their room. Ori just listened, her eyes held what Ash thought might be fear but she held Ash as she cried. Tears of confusion, frustration, and absolute terror took over Ash's body. And while it was usually Callan who would distract her from these overwhelming feelings, Ori was there, and she held her until she was able to fall asleep. She was becoming a true friend.

"I'm feeling okay. I'm still not sure how to process yesterday, but I'm just going to take it one day at a time." Ash didn't truly believe her own words, and she knew by the look on Asvin's face that he didn't believe them either.

He leaned his head back and closed his eyes, taking in a full breath. "I know what it's like to have emotions and thoughts that you can't express or discern. But, if you need to talk about it, I'm here."

Ash felt tears gather in her lashes as he spoke. He didn't have to offer that. He didn't have to come and find her yesterday. And he didn't have to be... she didn't even know what to call it.

"Thank you." She could barely manage to whisper past the knot lodged in her throat.

She closed her eyes, willing the tears to dissipate. She took in a few shallow breaths before she, too, leaned her head back to rest against the chair. She could feel the warmth of the morning sun on her skin, the greatest comfort of all.

It wasn't until she once again caught the scent of a summer storm that she noticed Asvin was standing in front of her, his open hand extended. "Come with me. I want to show you something."

Ash's mind searched for a response, but her body once again took over when her mind wasn't fully capable of making the choice for her. She took his warm, calloused hand and he led her down the stairs and to the soft grass of the yard. Ash hoped he didn't plan on taking her anywhere else—she realized then that she didn't have shoes on.

Then something else popped in through her clouded mind, "Wait, I'm definitely not sparring with you if that's what you're planning."

Asvin all but cackled as he threw his head back, laughing with that symphonic sound that forced a simper onto Ash's face. "No, I am not going to spar with you. But I need you to trust me." Her smile slowly faded as she pursed her lips and scrunched her brows in confusion. It was his turn to grin this time, albeit mischievously. "I need you to stand on my feet."

"What?" Now she was thoroughly confused.

Asvin's smile became toothy as he said again, "Just stand on my feet."

Her body once again moved for her. She really started to question her sanity. But then again, her mind wasn't in the clearest state, so she cut herself some slack as she stepped onto the tops of Asvin's feet. Ash used his stable forearms to steady herself. He didn't seem to mind the pressure on his feet at all. Ash knew she was small, but she wasn't the lightest being in the realms having always been on the curvier side.

Asvin ran his hands down the length of her arms, this sent a shiver through her entire body, as he placed her hands around his midsection. She felt the soft feathers of his wings graze the tops of her knuckles. "Hold on."

"Wait, wha—" Ash's words were cut short as Asvin beat his wings twice before they began to rise into the air. She nuzzled her face into his warm chest squeezing her eyes closed tightly.

"Open your eyes," he whispered onto the top of her head.

"No, thank you, I think I'm good."

"Just look, please?"

Ash hesitantly opened one eye and turned her head enough to see the horizon. From a distance she could see the southern shores of Baasaris. The sun was bobbing just above the waters, casting a soft orange glow on its surface.

"When I can't clear my head, this is what I do, I change my perspective. I know you haven't been able to do this..." Asvin's words trailed off. He paused before changing his unspoken apology. "I can't imagine what it's like to have this taken away from you."

Ash, still clinging tightly to Asvin's waist, tilted her head up to him. He was looking in the direction of the rising sun, his pale features cast in a shade of gold that made him look godlike.

"Thank you." Those two words were all she could govern over the lump in her throat.

This was something that *had* been taken from her. She had never learned to fly before her wings were clipped and shredded to the point of no use. She felt the ever-present tears return to her eyes. She was tired of crying, but these were not tears of frustration or sadness. They were tears of appreciation. He did this for her, he took her to the place where he felt the most himself, the skies.

Asvin turned his head down to meet her gaze. She could've stayed in this very place, suspended above the realms forever, with him.

Chapter Sixteen

Asvin

The morning sun had fully peaked when the party had packed and readied their horses. Asvin found himself solely focused on Ash. Merely hours ago, he held her in his arms. He watched as she fussed over Callan, who was clearly alive and able to function on his own. Granted, Callan was more rude than usual.

Asvin's eyes followed her as Ash kept circling back to Ori who wouldn't speak more than a few words herself at a time. She didn't seem to speak much anyway but he had noticed how she and Ash would huddle together and whisper secrets throughout the past few days he had been with them. Ori kept her distance from the party, barely acknowledging anyone and constantly surveying her surroundings.

Asvin had a hard time tearing his persistent eyes as he spoke to the Cromwell brothers. Both of which had taken a liking to him in comparison to Callan. Ori seemed rather indifferent to his presence, and he had an inkling about how Ash viewed his being there.

"I think you've caught a certain faerie's eye." Percy leaned over and said this from his perch on the white horse he rode.

"What do you mean?" Asvin desperately tried to conceal that he knew *exactly* what Percy meant.

The brothers laughed in unison. To his left, Nik too leaned down from his steed and said jestingly, "She can't keep her eyes off of you. And you can't seem to keep your eyes off her long enough to talk to anyone."

Asvin snapped his head to the larger brother and shot him a glare to remind him exactly what position he had been in earlier—the dangerous end of his sword. Nik still had a wide smile plastered across his face, his mustache following in shape.

Asvin gathered the courage he felt he needed before turning back to Percy and asking, "Do you know anything else about Cloud Giants? Any lore or legends about them?"

Percy seemed confused by his question. "Do you not know anything else about your own race?"

Asvin sent Percy the same menacing glare that he had given Nik, figuring that was answer enough. Percy, too, only smirked in response as Asvin tried to reign in his frustration. "My mother didn't have the time to tell me the history of our people. I was primarily raised by humans. So, no, I don't know everything about my own race."

Percy and Nik didn't laugh that time. "I know a little about cloud giants. Mostly legend given I haven't met a Cloud Giant until you. Are you looking for specific information?"

"Do the legends say anything about being tied to another? Like having a bond or tethering to another being?"

Percy sat in thought for a moment, he looked to be scanning through the catalog in his brain. Asvin could only imagine the vast amount of knowledge stored in that mental library.

"There is a story about Cloud Giants having what they call a *Parastella*. It loosely translates to *a pair of stars*. I thought of it as being a glorified version of 'soulmates, but *Parastella's* could feel each other's emotions, feel each other's pain, and even help them to locate each other if they were apart. But that's the only thing I can think of when it comes to a bond between two Cloud Giants."

Parastella. It had to be what he felt pull him to Ash. How else could he have sensed her fear when the Shadow Hound was bounding for her or when Callan collapsed in the butcher shop? He could even sense her confusion and fear when he sat with her on the porch of the inn. His mind couldn't move past this revelation, this crystal-clear understanding of what brought him *here*, to Baasaris.

To *this* party.

To *this* woman.

It was Ash, his *Parastella*.

The party rode mostly in silence to the end of Midscar's streets. Asvin kept stealing glances of Ash, who he noticed doing the same from time to time. Catching a glimpse of her exquisite smile every time their eyes met.

When they came to the edge of the town, Asvin saw the butcher—or rather, the oracle–Enoch standing in the doorway of his shop as they approached.

Enoch stepped out into their path and the group came to a halt. "Callan, I was hoping to stop you before you left. I need to impart one more piece of knowledge upon you." Callan shook his head but before he could keep moving and ignore the oracle, who harbored a solemn expression, Enoch tried again.

"I have seen Einar. The Oracle of the Future. My sibling only appears in times of great change. Their appearance, you saw it during your reading the other day. They were who I saw standing in the corner of my reading room. I tell you this because the future that I saw was not one of reward but one of loss. Know that you and your fellow celestials will have the power to change the future, they are a malleable being when you challenge them. Approach *your* future with caution."

Asvin wished he hadn't heard the man.

The oracle's foreboding words lingered over them as they rode to Greenside. The seaport town would have glittered if not for the decaying homes and buildings taking away from the beauty of the sea. The decay felt symbolic of Enoch's warning. Great loss, devastation instead of triumph. All Asvin knew was that he would not submit Ash to this future. He knew in his soul that she deserved more and she would have it.

She would have everything he could give to her and more. Whatever she wanted, he would make sure she had it. This *Parastella* was a tangible thing, something he wanted to nurture and take care of. He would do just that.

They didn't stop for shelter this time—Qoohr's moon replacing the golden hues of Vytarr's sun with her silver rays that glistened along the waters. Percy had stated there would be no use in trying to find a ship this late in the night, but Callan rode along, not acknowledging Percy in the slightest.

Right when Asvin had decided he had had enough of Callan's ignorant attitude, he saw the massive ship bobbing a short distance from the docks along the beaches. A familiar ship. One with white sails boasting the image of a red phoenix.

Chapter Seventeen

Callan

Callan never thought he would be more relieved than when he saw the sails that belonged to *the* Captain Blackwell. When the party dismounted at the nearest dock Blackwell and his small crew were there with tenders to take them to the ornate ship in the harbor.

Blackwell donned more simple attire in comparison to the last time Callan and Ash had seen him. Clothed mostly in black, with the exception of the red feather adorning his hat, the captain lacked the dramatic flair that Callan had grown so used to seeing. He looked tired, worn down.

When Callan thought to ask the man if he was well, Blackwell's charismatic baritone voice greeted them. "Well, if it isn't Mister Callan Bram. I'd say you have outdone yourself on my little task. Not only did you find the information I asked of you, but you have gone out and assembled your own brigade I see." Blackwell clasped Callan's forearm in greeting as he assessed the mixed company behind him. The captain's voice didn't match his fatigued eyes. Callan was discombobulated by his conflicting speech.

Nik approached Blackwell and gave the same warm greeting in return. "Blackwell, it is good to see you again!"

"Ahh yes, it has been quite a while since I've been in the company of the Cromwells. Percy, I see your brother didn't mention how well you have aged. Still a handsome one." Blackwell's snide comment towards the younger brother was accompanied with a cheeky wink.

Percy rolled his eyes as he shuffled towards Blackwell, giving the captain a vulgar hand gesture before bracing forearms with him as his brother had done.

Blackwell practically floated over to Ash and bowed deeply. "Lady Ashlun, it is a pleasure to make your acquaintance again."

Ash inclined her head to him with a bright smile as she introduced Ori. The captain was just as polite to her, but he seemingly noticed Ori would not be one for flattery. He sufficed with a simple incline of his head.

Callan still wondered why Ori hadn't left after he confronted her. What did she know? She was likely the only shadow wielder in The Five Realms; she *had* to know something about the nightmare he'd seen after taking off his mother's protection charm. He thought about the vibrant glow of his ring when he'd been alone with her. A warning. *Of what though?*

He couldn't trust Ori, could he? She had hardly said anything about her shadows and where they'd come from after she'd divulged her secret onto him. How could he know that she wasn't a part of something bigger? Something far more dangerous than he could comprehend in that moment.

Callan shook the thoughts from his mind. The constant intramural battle had been waging since he'd awoken. He didn't want to trust her. But he did. He didn't want her to stay with them. But he did. He didn't want to see her shadows near him again.

But he did.

As Callan's head began to thump from the persistent backpedaling in his reasonings, he desperately clung to his surroundings as a means to not drown in the tempest that was his mind.

Captain Blackwell had moved on from Ori when Callan focused once more on the world around him. Asvin was the last of the group that Blackwell was to greet. He did so with a similar clasp of his forearm as he'd done with the others, but it was what he said to the flying-giant that halted *all* of Callan's thoughts.

"Asvin Falak! It has been far too long since I saw you last. The greatest hunter in all the realms!" The party openly gaped at the two men reminiscing on their *apparent* past encounter.

"Did you ever find your beast of the seas, captain?" Asvin was the very essence of cool, calm, and collected. Callan found himself to be envious of his eminence.

"Ahh yes. Shortly after your departure, I did indeed find her. My greatest conquest, or perhaps it was she that found me. Anyhow, I would've never come close without your guidance." With a pat on Asvin's shoulder, the captain turned to address everyone who still stared at the two men.

"Now that you are all here, I believe I have some guests I've brought along with me that you all should meet. Let us be off to the ship!"

Was Blackwell not going to mention how he and Asvin knew each other? Perhaps he felt that he didn't need to? Callan's weary psyche was already pushing near its limits, and he didn't think he could handle much more confusion.

Callan couldn't find an adequate reason for why, but he had an infinitesimal inkling that the guests Blackwell ominously mentioned weren't simply *just* guests at all.

*****

The ship was massive. The helm was that of the red phoenix that Blackwell himself chose as the sigil of the White Knights. Callan couldn't quite place why the symbolic bird had meant something more to *him,* but he dismissed it then, too enraptured by the infamous vessel.

The detailing of the ship was carved out in various woods, and each board on the main deck was clean and polished to the highest degree which felt fitting for the captain with his need for the flamboyant.

When Blackwell and his triage of shipmates had retrieved the party from Greenside's docks in its entirety, he led them to a lower deck of the ship which held a large room and two hallways with doors Callan assumed led to various cabins. The main room was a lounge with red velvet couches and chairs, far more pristine than the ones in Blackwell's quarters at Knife's Edge. This ship was the captain's true home, the one he cared for greatly and likely spent the majority of his days sailing to distant shores.

It wasn't until Callan heard Ash suck in an exaggerated gasp that he became aware of the two people sitting in a far corner. They were in adjacent chairs, turned slightly away from the entrance the party had begun to fill.

One figure was hooded and dressed in dark leathers. He could tell the figure had a feminine frame by the shoulders, but they remained concealed, still unaware of their audience. Perched in their lap was a white cat with orange-striped spots looking perfectly content to be loved by the mysterious figure.

The other subject was a man with well-maintained strawberry blonde hair sprinkled with grey. The clean cut put the man's pointed ears on full display. His shoulders were broad, but his form was slender. As Callan's focus moved lower he could see wings. They were wrapped neatly behind the man, but he knew those wings.

Those were the wings that he had seen nearly every day of his young life. They were just like Ash's but they... they were whole.

"Dad?" Ash whispered her plea across the silent room. The man rose suddenly and that's when Callan had the full picture.

He had Ash's nose and her smile. He even had the same splatter of freckles along his face. "Ashlun."

Both the man and Ash crossed the room in a matter of seconds, embracing each other so tightly Callan wasn't sure they could still breathe.

The hooded figure had risen from their seat as well. As she turned to face them, Callan saw her once hidden wings wrapped behind her. They looked like Ash's too, but they were darker. The iridescence didn't shimmer with yellows and golds from the sconces on the walls but with shades of blue and silver. When she turned she lifted her hood revealing short midnight black hair that framed her face. Her silver eyes were soft in contrast to her sharp angled face as they landed on Ori.

"Ori!" The woman practically leapt over the arm of her chair and ran for Ori. She embraced her the same way Ash's father had his daughter. Like *family*.

Ori stood in a state of shock before she slowly wrapped her arms around the woman who held her so tightly as if waiting for Ori to float away. Ori closed her eyes and buried her face in the crook of the woman's neck and shoulder.

Blackwell's smooth voice carried notes of joy when he interjected the strange reunion. "Everyone, meet Lyra Nocte and Kaster Tanwen." The white and orange cat trotted up to Blackwell as if it had its own reunion in mind. Blackwell leaned down to allow the cat to jump into his arms.

Even Callan knew that this should be a joyous occasion for Ash… and Ori he supposed. But he still felt the fresh wound in his heart fill with sorrow.

He would never reunite with his mother.

The Cromwell brothers would never see their aunt again.

And, though he really didn't care much for Asvin, he knew he probably had someone he would never see again too judging by the look of longing on his strong face.

Ash finally pulled away from her father's embrace, wiping the happy tears from her face with the back of her hand. When Lyra stepped back from Ori, she stopped and looked Ori over, as if she were looking for any damage or wounds. "I can't believe you just left like that! Knowing now where you have ended up, something tells me you were *eavesdropping.*" Lyra forced a tight smile as she continued her inspection. Ori sheepishly nodded as her only response.

Callan couldn't remember the last time Ori had spoken aloud. At least, not since he'd challenged her at The Obsidian. He thought he may have rendered her speechless. Didn't she come all this way *for* Lyra? The friend she was so worried for? Wouldn't she have anything to say upon being reunited?

The frustration he felt building up only made his insistent headache worse. He didn't understand her. He wanted to. He wanted to ask her all of the questions that were adding to the pressure behind his skull, but he didn't know where to start or if he could ask any of them without fear.

Fear that he would learn something he wished he hadn't.

Fear that he would lash out again.

Fear that he would come to *hate* her.

Fear that she would actually leave this time and disappear from his life. He *didn't* want that.

Callan forced himself back to the unfolding scene as he pushed his endless questions down deep in hopes they would remain there forever.

Kaster kept Ash within arm's reach as he surveyed the rest of the party. He looked over Asvin, Ori, and then the Cromwell brothers. When he landed on Callan he said with a somber tone, "We should all sit. We have many things to discuss. Things that you all need to hear."

Chapter Eighteen

Ash

His eyes hadn't changed. They were still the same mossy green that she remembered. The very same green that reminded her of the rolling hills back in Pyrecliff. *Home*. His hair had begun to sprout greys amongst the tufts of red and blonde, and he had slight wrinkles around his eyes that contorted his freckles. But he was still her father. It was actually her dad standing in front of her. Ash felt as if she had to pinch herself to make sure this wasn't some surreal dream.

Captain Blackwell offered seating to the new arrivals. As they settled he practically floated around them all with trays of tea and sweets. His traveling companion, Lucy–the sweet white cat that had spots of orange fur–was also doing her walkthrough, greeting everyone as they found a place to sit or stand.

As Blackwell rambled on about the various flavors of tea he had on the ship, Ash found it difficult to think of anything other than Kaster. Ash's thoughts moved about from one question to the next just as Blackwell and Lucy moved from guest to guest.

Where had Kaster been? Was he okay? Was he in danger?

How did he get here? How did he know Blackwell?

Why hadn't he contacted her all this time?

She didn't get the chance to start her rigid questioning before her father cleared his throat and addressed the room. "There are some things that we should shed some light on now that *all* of you are here."

Ash wondered what he meant by *'all* of you'. By looking around the room at the tense faces she had neglected upon reuniting with her father, she could see that they too were bracing for whatever Kaster prepared to tell them.

"Captain Blackwell, Lyra, and I are part of an organization known by only its members as Prism Shield. Some of you may be familiar with stories of the disbanded peacekeepers union, this is the newer version of that failed mission. Except now, we have more pressing matters to oversee than the raids of the past." Kaster's words lingered in the ship's lounge. Everyone was locked in on him, eagerly waiting for the next piece to the puzzle.

The emotion that clouded over Ash's own eagerness was shame. Her father hadn't contacted her because he truly couldn't. He was out trying to unify The Five Realms as he had once done before. She remembered her mother's soft voice when she would try to explain her father's absences. Ash realized then that she had not changed much in adulthood. She was still selfish.

Ash had begun to resent him over the years, maybe even hate him for leaving her. But all of her emotions were now overshadowed by the fact that her father was dealing with something bigger than just his child. He was fighting for the *future* that his only child wouldn't have without his intervention. She understood then that Enoch's reading had shown Kaster taking care of her, keeping her safe all this time.

Kaster continued. "Have any of you heard of The Celestial Prophecy?"

Ash was sure the question would earn Kaster eye rolls from her troupe of traveling companions after how often the prophecy had been discussed over the last two days, but the only changes in demeanor she saw were a curt nod and a paling face. The former from Callan and the latter from Ori.

"Well, I hadn't planned for that." Kaster gave an uneasy look towards Blackwell–who shrugged–and Lyra, who gave him a half-smile of reassurance before he shifted his eyes back to Ash. His face emanated nothing but a neutral calm, yet his eyes brimmed with worry and fear. "And do you all know who the prophecy speaks of?"

Callan didn't hesitate to answer, as if answering the quickest would make Kaster answer faster in return. "Yes, well…" Callan hesitated for a breath, "we have some *theories*. Are you insinuating that you *know* who they are?"

"Yes, I believe that we *do* know who the prophecy details. It has taken years of *research*, *secrets*, and *blood* to obtain the information that we have now." Kaster didn't quite spit this at Callan, but Ash felt the vexation in her father's words. She could sense that his heated tone was not directed at Callan or anyone else in the room, it was something that rested far deeper than the surface.

"Prism Shield was formed after some of its original members from the peacekeepers union left or… met their untimely demise. All that remains now are myself, Blackwell, Lyra, and Madame Loch, each leading their respective troops."

Loch is in on this? Ash thought that it honestly *did* make sense given her constant fight to protect the Draoi performers in Phenom. The woman was a brute, but she cared. She fought for the protection she offered her performers.

"I know this will likely come as a shock to you all. I'm sure *much* of what I have to say may surprise and terrify you, but you all must know your true destinies and the history that has been hidden from you. I am just sorry you have to hear it at all."

Ash's entire body locked up in anticipation of her father's next words. Everyone in the room was solely focused on Kaster. Callan didn't blink, Asvin more closely resembled his statuesque heritage, Nik and Percy sat on the edge of their seats in unison, and Ori looked as if she might pass out soon. It was only Blackwell and Lyra who had looks of concern plastered on their faces.

"You are all here by more than just coincidence; you are all here because it is what *fate* demanded." Kaster paused for a few heartbeats and took in a breath before he began again. "I will start at the beginning of what we know.

"Myrsky Dorrin was the Celestial of Estus, The God of Stars and Sky. During his time in the union, he gathered information on the heretic human clans in Estana. During his time there Myrsky learned that the clans had largely denied working under Grimmstone control. They led their raids of their own accord, mercilessly killing the Draoi people in revolt.

"Myrsky also met and fell in love with a Draoi princess during his travels. He was so smitten by her that he convinced her to run away with him. The last communications we had with him detailed his findings and his desire to leave the union and start a new life. One where he could protect the woman he loved. It was only a matter of time before who we believed to be the princess' family tracked them down. Myrsky was *thought* to have been executed under Titan law for kidnapping." Ash felt the lamp-light blaze in her mind with a sudden understanding. *Titan* law. *Titan's Terrain.*

"Was this princess a Cloud Giant?" Ash couldn't help herself. She stared into her father's eyes, and waited, not willing to let him continue on before she knew for sure.

Kaster's answer was soft, almost kind. "Yes."

Ash slowly turned her gaze to Asvin whose eyes were already locked onto her. The blue pools stirred with an emotion she couldn't quite place. Her heart lurched into her throat. She began to rise from her seat on the settee next to her father, but he placed a hand on hers, silently pleading with her to be patient.

"The princess's name was Bronte Falak. She is now the queen of Titan's Terrain. If my calculations are correct, I believe this young man here," Kaster gestured toward Asvin, "is her son. And Myrsky was your father. What is your name?"

Asvin had already torn his gaze away, now looking towards one of the portholes that showed the moon reflecting across the waters. Ash knew then that he was waiting for the first opportunity to fly away, to leave and never return. His escape from reality. She wished she could fly away with him.

His reply was short and to the point. "Asvin."

"The first star in the sky." Kaster's words were like a dagger to Ash's heart.

Enoch had said that someone else loved her during her reading. *The first star in the sky. Parastella.*

Asvin told her the meaning of his name in the forests of Baasaris when they first met. How had she not recalled it before?

He loved her? How could he love someone he just met? Why did her heart hurt thinking that his love was misplaced?

Kaster continued as she went over Enoch's words in her mind, "You are the Fallen Star in the prophecy. It was the forlorn death of your father that began the downward spiral we find ourselves in.

"Before we *truly* knew what was happening, the celestials were being killed one after the next. After Myrsky, Lyra's parents– Cordelia and Jaxe Nocte–were both cruelly murdered. They were Lumi Faeries. They are similar to Pyre Faeries like myself and Ashlun, but they follow the ways of Qoohr, The Goddess of Night. Jaxe was the Celestial of Qoohr, and he was found slain next to his wife by their only daughter. Lyra is the Seadragon in the prophecy."

Kaster's words faded in and out. Ash tried to listen, but her mind was racing, her list of queries growing. But the first question at the top of her list was no longer one that her father could answer. The man who might be able to answer it was still lost in the night beyond the window he'd glued his eyes to.

"Reya Tanwen." Her mother's name broke through the dense fog of Ash's mind. "My wife, Ash's mother. She too was killed a few years later."

Ash's heart dropped from her throat and into the lowest part of her stomach. She pictured her mother lying dead in her arms, she felt her cold body stiffen as the minutes turned to hours, she heard the door of her once warm home opening and her father's panicked footsteps.

"Reya was the Celestial of Vytarr, The God of Day. She was fierce, beautiful, and by far the most powerful celestial to have ever existed. We initially thought that the raidsmen took her from us, Ash was too young to recall the one who took her wings and her mother. It was then that I began to piece together the details of the killings. Unwilling to lose anyone else, I took Ashlun to Madame Loch. She always held a safe haven for the Draoi people, and I knew she would care for you while I figured out what was happening."

It wasn't until Kaster spoke to her directly that she realized he had turned his body to face hers.

He took her sweating palms into his worn, tired hands. "You are every bit of your mother. You too are beautiful, and determined, and I know you will be just as strong as she was. And you have the only gift that a father like myself could bestow. You *will* fly again."

Ash's vision blurred. She couldn't focus on his face anymore. The face that she had longed to see one more time for most of her life. She turned her gaze to her lap; her legs spotted with the traitorous teardrops that began to fall in earnest. "Ashlun is the Flame in the prophecy. She will be the celestial to Vytarr, just as her mother was."

She squeezed her eyes shut, white stars dancing in her blackened vision. Every sound around her dulled to nothing but static noise, her breath turning to short gasps.

Then she felt Callan's arms around her. She knew it was Callan who'd come to comfort her, just as he'd done so many times before. He pulled her into his chest and cradled the back of her head as Ash was transported back in time to the nights he'd held her while she cried over her mother and father.

The panic slowly began to dissipate in his embrace. Callan would always be a hero to her. Her best friend, her brother.

When she felt calm enough, Callan steadied her in her seat before he stood and took a step back. Ash looked again to her father to implore him to continue. She expected to see sympathy in his eyes but found admiration in its place. Ash didn't fail to notice a streak of what she believed to be sadness across his face. Or maybe longing? Grief?

With a heavy sigh, Kaster turned to Callan and said just above a whisper, "You are just like your mother, Callan."

Chapter Nineteen

Ori

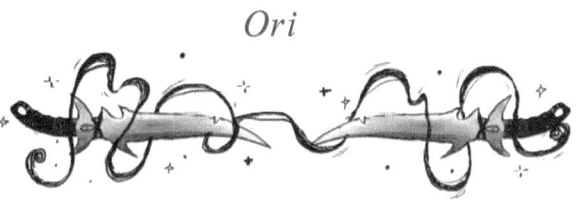

The only thing that suppressed Ori's panic was the fact that Lyra was there. Lyra was sitting next to her on one of the several pieces of velvet furniture. Lyra was there with Ori on Blackwell's ship. Lyra was there.

Every time Kaster spoke Ori felt her shadows press against her skin, as if they were trying to protect her from his words. Of what he would reveal to the waiting ears on this ship. The beginning of her end.

But her spiraling stopped in its tracks when she saw Ash go quiet. Ori only knew what was happening when Callan crossed the room to pull Ash into his arms, just like he had done for Ori after the Shadow Hound attack. Ash had explained to Ori that night by her fire that Callan had always done this for her when she felt overwhelmed.

Ori began to feel more at ease once she realized that Ash was okay. That wave of calm quickly receded when Kaster began speaking of Callan's mother. Ori knew it was what Callan had always longed to know. She didn't have to hear him speak it to know that he wanted to know about his parents. She knew what it was like to be alone in the world.

It was for Callan that she was able to tuck away the looming anxiety over her own fragile secrets.

"Your mother, Callan, was Hyacinth Baas the Celestial of Baasis, The Goddess of The Hunt. She was unbelievably kind and intelligent beyond her years. Outside of Reya, I like to think Hyacinth was my best friend. I miss her dearly.

"You have her confidence and her demeanor. I see that in the way you speak and the way you care for Ashlun. But, you have your father's eyes."

Ori watched Callan intently as Kaster spoke. She felt the sudden urge to move as close to him as possible, to comfort him, to be there for him. But she knew he no longer wanted that. Ori still questioned why she had chosen to stay with the group after Midscar. A question with an answer she didn't have.

"Your mother and father met when they were very young. Your mother had already claimed her place as a celestial and had begun working with the union when she met your father, Ezra.

"Ezra Ellis was the son of a well-known politician who worked very closely with the Grimm family. Ezra was primed to follow in his father's footsteps, but Hyacinth was the one and only thing that came to matter to him. Hyacinth convinced Ezra to join the peacekeepers union while still working with his father and learning of raids that were to take place." Kaster took too long of a pause between his words.

The silence lingered so heavily in the room that Ori finally broke her stare from Callan. Kaster had averted his gaze to the floor, his brow furrowed in maybe anger, or confusion.

"One day, your mother disappeared. We had no idea why she would just leave. Hyacinth was the closest thing we had to a leader in the union and she just… left. Ezra drove himself mad looking for her and stopped at next to nothing to find her. It was like she didn't exist anymore. She was gone for months. Ezra left to go find her, insistent that she wouldn't have simply left him, and none of us ever saw him again." Kaster paused again. Callan had a matching furrowed brow and Ori could see the concern flowing through his bright eyes.

"Hyacinth, however, *did* come back. She had seemingly disappeared off the face of the realms for almost a full year. When she returned she was different. She no longer had the optimistic outlook she once did. She was full of fear at every hour of every day. A few short weeks after she'd finally come home, we found her dead."

The room was silent once more. No one dared to look at Callan, Ori sensed the tension clinging to the very air they all struggled to breathe. She couldn't stop herself from peering up at Callan, hoping to steal a glance at him, hoping to see him relieved instead of the spiral of despair and anger he had been in for days.

When she instead found his eyes on hers she couldn't look away. She didn't know exactly what she saw on his face or in his eyes, but she held his stare anyway.

If that was all she could do to simply be there for him, she would do it. She would face the urge to run. To run away like she had done all those years ago.

This time, she would stay.

"You, Callan, are the Knight in the prophecy." Kaster broke the moment of silence. "All I can assume is that your mother learned that she was pregnant with you, remained hidden from the realms until you were born, and then searched out a place to keep you safe. I should've thought to question Madame Loch about it, but I was suffocating in my own grief. It wasn't until I saw you with Ashlun today that I realized who you are. Your mother would be proud of the man you have become."

Callan didn't respond to Kaster's kindly meant words. Ori could see that Ash was waiting for him to say something; he'd finally learned the truth of his mother's life and death, something he always wished to know, but he said nothing.

Even Ori knew it was unlike him not to have a retort, a question, or some other statement in return.

"The last part of the prophecy is one that even I don't quite understand. But I am left to believe that *the Fox* is here with us as well." Ori snapped her head back to Kaster and he nodded in confirmation as he observed her golden eyes and her pointed ear that had been on full display when she tucked her hair back out of habit.

"I believe you are the daughter of Cytheria Keres, the Celestial of Phyrus, The God of Oblivion and Souls. I only met your mother once. She wanted to help in our efforts, and she would never have admitted it, but she was too afraid. I can only imagine that Phyrus wasn't the easiest of the gods to work with."

Ori didn't move; she wasn't even sure she was still breathing as her shadows once more pressed against her skin demanding that they be let free to protect her.

"I am sorry that I do not have any further information for you. I never heard from your mother again after our initial meeting and I can only surmise that she too is no longer with us."

Ori could only manage to shake her head as validation for Kaster's assumption. She felt a tremor in her hands. She opened her mouth to speak but there was no sound.

Lyra spoke for her. "Ori's mother was murdered by a man in black. Just like the others."

Ori could practically feel Callan's stare burning through her, but she couldn't convince herself to meet his eyes this time. She would run after all.

"I am sorry for your loss, Ori. I am sorry for the loss that *all* of you have witnessed or experienced in your young lives. Your parents–your celestial parents–were supposed to be the ones to guide you in the ways of this life. Instead, life has left you to be trained in the way of the nameless. You have all led a life of secrecy and hiding yourselves from the world, afraid to be who you truly are." Kaster met Ori's eyes again when he spoke next. "You do not have to hide anymore. You are with the people you were meant to find."

It was Percy who chose to speak for the ones who were still processing their unknown histories, the forgotten legends they were destined to be a part of. "You say that you now know who committed these atrocities against the former celestials?"

"Yes, based on the reports we were able to collect, a man dressed in black was either seen entering before the murders or leaving after. Aside from the children who may have witnessed the murders of their own parents, only one being was there when one of the celestials was killed, and she refuses to speak on the subject, to anyone." Kaster lifted his head to Asvin. "Bronte Falak."

Asvin's jaw was clenched, his arms crossed over his chest. Even Ori could see that this was a topic he didn't particularly care for. Maybe he was used to running like she was.

Percy interjected again, "You said that we were with the people we were meant to find. What do you mean by that?"

"The oracles are usually the beings who believe in ideas such as fate, but how else would the five of you have ended up in this very place at the same time? We are only two days from the summer solstice and that's the exact day that The Oracle of the Present says you will come to your power. We know of only one person that could possibly have an artifact like the Dyngheloi in the prophecy. I know very little of the ancient language, but I believe the word roughly translates to 'The Crystal of Essence'."

Ori took note of the faces in the room. Some had looks of confusion or anticipation to know who Kaster was referencing. Others shared a look of knowing, of a clear understanding. Ori gathered up enough courage to look at Callan once more, but he was no longer looking at her, he was looking at his ring.

It was glowing a soft shade of lilac in his hand.

"The Nameless."

Chapter Twenty

Callan

Hyacinth Baas and Ezra Ellis. They finally had names, his parents. It all made sense now, why he couldn't find records of his last name Bram, it did not exist. He wasn't sure what name he was supposed to take but he was content to know that he had ones to choose. He had a name, a history, a family.

Kaster had taken the time to explain to the party that once he'd figured out the recurrence of the man in black at each murder of the former celestials, he knew there was something far greater going on in The Five Realms than the Agenda of the Grimm's and the Nondraoi. He knew that to assassinate not one, but all of the celestials, was an act of the gods. Knowing his daughter was to be one of the next celestials he had done everything he could to protect her and find out who the remaining four children were.

Madame Loch served as a lookout among the Draoi who took refuge in the Phenomicron as well as a guardian to Ash and–unknowingly–Callan.

Captain Blackwell's parents were members of the peacekeeper's union before their retirement and objectively peaceful passing. Blackwell was raised under their tutelage, to ultimately believe that everyone in The Five Realms should have the equal opportunity to live unharmed and happy lives.

The young captain rose through the ranks of the Grimm military by way of his parents. Former Captain Robert Blackwell being a prestigious military leader and Mary Blackwell having a seat amongst the high ladies in Grimmstone's political hearings. When Blackwell became just as well-known as his predecessors, he gained the permissions to establish the White Knight's guild on the island of Knife's Edge. Unbeknownst to Art Grimm, the White Knights were under the instruction of the captain alone and working alongside Prism Shield. Their front of being a mercenaries guild helped to keep them in the good graces of Grimmstone's leaders.

Working closely with Kaster when he stepped into the role his parents left behind, Blackwell began his hunt for the fallen star and the seadragon in the Celestial prophecy. Callan recalled the way in which the captain told this story to them all, as if he were reciting a monologue in a drama play.

Captain Blackwell, through connections of the guild, heard of a famed hunter in Estana who had become known for his tracking skills. Blackwell told the story of the day he'd met Asvin Falak and how he aided him in locating a beast of the seas.

Asvin, being the only Draoi with half of his traits belonging to Cloud Giants, was recognizable to the captain. After he'd met Asvin that fateful day, he knew he'd succeeded in finding the fallen star.

It was only a few days later that he would meet Lyra. The captain didn't share his story of meeting Lyra in the colorful way he did for his meeting Asvin. He took on what Callan saw as a defensive nature in comparison to the demeanor that Callan had come to expect from him. Callan quickly assumed that Lyra meant a great deal to the captain.

Lyra told the party that her friendship with Ori was one that became far more important than she had realized initially. When Ori opened up to her about her childhood and heritage, Lyra knew she had to have found her in the alleys of Grimmstone by fate. Lyra took Ori into the Celerity Channel which–under Lyra's lead–also worked in tandem with Prism Shield. Though Lyra admitted to them all that she often left two of her most intimidating thieves in charge of the channel in her absence, as she didn't enjoy the role of being at the helm. Callan noted Ori's pinched brows. Did she not know Lyra was the leader of the organization she was a part of? Callan had assumed they were close.

Callan couldn't help but wonder what it meant for Ori to truly open up to someone, to be *close* to her. Lyra didn't divulge any information about Ori's shadows to the rest of the room, nor did she say anything about how she knew Ori was a child from the prophecy. Callan felt a surge of irritation. He knew that they were getting so close to the full picture, but there was still so much left to uncover. And there was so much being left unsaid.

Kaster moved on to explain that they had planned to seek out The Nameless who had a base of operations in Qoohria for at least the last decade. Callan could see all of his questions from the past weeks forming answers in his newly cleared mind–without the help of their rather guarded company.

The war cuff was a rare Draoi item. Rumors circulated around the realms that pointed Prism Shield in the direction of The Nameless who proclaimed through his disguise that he was looking for Draoi people and Xestorals, like Percy and Nik, to join his cause. Or... for Draoi *artifacts*.

Callan thought back to the Dyngheloi, the crystal, in the prophecy. He hadn't given it much thought after learning that he–

215

along with Ash and the people he just *happened* upon while traveling–were supposedly the children portrayed in the prophecy. He realized then that his quest to collect information about the war cuff–the war cuff that could only be wielded by Vytarr's celestial, *Ash*–was initiated because he was Ash's best-friend. And if The Nameless had the cuff, he may have the crystal in his possession too.

Blackwell used Callan's interest in becoming a White Knight to his advantage. Callan supposed he couldn't blame him, after all the fate of the realms rested in the hands of Prism Shield.

He had to admit, if only to himself, he felt a little used. Perhaps even taken for granted or overlooked? If this wasn't the twisted scenario he ended up in, would the captain have even looked his way when he inquired about being a White Knight?

Callan tried not to dwell on the thought. There was no use in dreaming of being a hero to the realms. He was to be a celestial. Whatever *that* meant. Did that mean he could still be a hero? He had a purpose to his life now. It was the one thing he wanted but it wasn't the one he'd thought of since the first day he laid eyes on that uniform.

What did it mean to be a celestial? Of all the stories and explanations they'd received over the last few hours, he still had no idea what his *alleged* destiny entailed.

Why him? This whole series of events felt orchestrated.

But it was apparently *fate* that brought the children of the celestials together.

The Fallen Star will slay a Shadow to claim the Flame. Asvin had killed the Shadow Hound that was about to attack Ash... who was the Flame.

The Flame will sacrifice the Sun to save the Knight. Ash would sacrifice someone to save him? Callan was the Knight... he didn't think that part of the prophecy had come to pass yet. And what did his part of the prophecy mean?

The Knight will find himself In the mirror. He remembered his celestial dream after taking off his mother's ring. He had seen his reflection in a mirror perched in the middle of a forest.

He didn't think that the dream counted as part of the prophecy, but what did it mean?

Callan lay staring up at the ceiling of the lower level of Captain Blackwell's ship. Everyone was still processing the information Kaster *bestowed* upon them within the first hour of being on the ship. Blackwell offered to reconvene in the morning over breakfast, leading people to sleeping arrangements for the night.

Captain Blackwell gave up his sleeping quarters in favor of–in his own words–sleeping among the Qoohrian stars, and offered them to Ori, Ash, and Lyra. Thus, he led the rest of the party to the lowest level of the ship with storage and numerous sleeping cots stacked upon one another. Likely where the small crew and handful of White Knights slept.

Callan felt the ship slowly sway, which he believed would've taken him quickly off to the land of dreams any other night. If it had only been any other night. But his mind raced on, not wishing to rest for one moment.

He looked around the room; many sailors and White Knights slept peacefully occupying most of the cots available. Nik and Percy seemed to have found sleep easily as well. Nik was snoring like a bear and Percy lay in a position one would find a body in on a burial pyre, his legs straight and arms crossed over his chest. Callan noticed that Asvin was no longer leaning against the staircase as he had been moments ago. Perhaps he too found sleep to be nothing but a hindrance.

As Callan's eyes lazily panned the cabin, his eyes snagged on a piece of faded-red cloth. He realized it was Captain Blackwell's red phoenix signet on a torn, battle-worn banner hanging from a banister. The red phoenix.

The Seadragon will tame the Red Phoenix. The *Red Phoenix* had to be Blackwell. Kaster told Lyra's story during the meeting, he said that she was the Seadragon in the prophecy.

Had that premonition come to pass already? What had she done to *tame* him?

She didn't seem to be of the trustworthy sort given her status as queen of thieves–Callan grinned at his own joke–but he didn't truly know her. Of course, she had been instrumental in Prism Shield, working alongside Captain Blackwell and Kaster who he knew had likely sacrificed many things for the safety and peace of others. Maybe Lyra was like Ori, misunderstood.

Ori. She hadn't been lying about her friend. Lyra was the one she had left Grimmstone for, the person for whom she felt she had no other choice but to follow two complete strangers into unknown territory just to get answers.

He recalled Kaster's story about Ori then. She had nothing to do with his mother's demise. His dream showed him shadows snuffing out his mother's purple haze. The only Shadow Wielder he knew of was Ori. But she wouldn't have been old enough to partake in his mother's death. He had been wrong. The deaths of the celestials, their parents, had taken place two decades ago.

Overwhelming guilt plagued his mind and body. He jolted upright, holding his cool palm to his burning face in hope to quench the dread that spread through him. He was up and moving to the stairs before he realized it. Placing his booted toe on the first step to the cabins above, he stopped.

What would he say to Ori?

What *could* he say? He *hurt* her.

He hurt her after he promised he would protect her the way she had protected him. She had been afraid and alone her entire life, just as he had. They both had a friend to get them through the hard times, but they had no one truly, no one to call *home*.

The Fox will step out from the darkness and see the light. Ori had shown Callan her true self. She trusted him enough to share her darkest secret, the one thing that she felt she could not reveal. The same *gift* Ori's mother had hidden from, perished from. And he had pushed her away over some stupid dream that he couldn't halfway begin to translate. Because *he* was afraid.

Callan shuffled his way back to his chosen cot, laid down, and resumed his staring at the wood grain of the boards above his head. He had been wrong. The same mysterious figure in black had killed all of the previous celestials.

Callan remembered Ori's Corpoi fox tail. She said it had been removed. Did the man in black do that to her? The image of the scar on her delicate face burned into his mind. Not only had he taken her mother, he marked her, *scarred* her so that she would never be able to forget that night.

Callan couldn't even begin to imagine the death of his own mother, much less the traumatic events that Ori had been subjected to.

He tried to clear his mind; he took in a too-shallow breath and closed his eyes. He could still see Ori there, her golden-pooled eyes, her auburn hair loose of the braid she usually wore. He had only seen it down once when they had stayed on the top floor of the Cromwell brother's home in Keld. He liked the way the waves fell on her face.

Her face–that damned scar brought him right back to the guilt-ridden emotion that almost made him seek her out in the middle of the night. Who was this man in black? Whoever he was, Callan promised himself, his mother, Ori, Ash, and even Asvin and Lyra that he would find this man, this coward who took the lives of those who mattered to someone. To him.

He calmed himself once more, this time he tried to imagine the picture he had drawn all that time ago of the woman he believed to be his mother. Hyacinth. It was a beautiful name, the name of the purple flowers that grew in the forests outside of Atreyu.

He could remember the days that he and Ash would venture out–without Madame Loch's permission–into the outside world. Ash would always pick those same purple flowers and bring them back with her where they would sit in an old glass bottle until they withered and she would make him accompany her to gather more. He felt now as if his mother had always been with him.

He felt a soft vibration on his chest. Callan reached into his breast pocket and retrieved his mother's ring. The small stone was glowing softly, as if it, as if *she* had heard his thoughts. He didn't feel the usual looming dread or confusion that normally accompanied the glow, this time he felt comfort.

He held the ring, the one piece of his mother that he had left, tightly in his closed fist as he drifted into sleep.

*****

He was again in the forest. The forest with the fullest trees, with the longest flowing vines, and lush greenery with the most colorful flowers and blossoms.

The mirror with gilded leaves of gold was still perched, leaning against the same tree right before him. When he approached it this time he did not see his reflection. He saw a man standing with his back to Callan. The man was standing in complete total darkness, but Callan could still make out the long, faded cloak the shade of dark violet. The man had dark brown hair with loose waves, thin streaks of gray marked his temples, and a body with a broad frame. The man cupped his hands on either side of his mouth and called out, "Hyacinth!"

Callan audibly gasped. The man turned in one swift movement as if he had heard him through the mirror. The man's eyes bore into Callan's. His eyes were a sea-green color, like his own. The man's face too reminded him of his own, but older. He had a full beard like the one that Callan was growing after not having had the opportunity to shave nor the will to.

The man stepped closer to the other side of the mirror. He looked at Callan with a face of true bewilderment. "Hyacinth... she..." the man's words trailed off.

Callan wanted to know why the man was looking for his mother, was this a reflection of himself in the future? "Are you, me? Is your name Callan?" Callan felt foolish as the words left his mouth.

But the man answered, "Callan? No... I..." The man's face softened but he took on a look of turmoil and disorientation throughout his features.

Callan realized that he too probably had a similar look on his own face. This had to be himself that he saw, this had to be a vision of himself.

But why would he be calling to his mother, who was... dead?

The man took in a sharp breath. His features paled and his face revealed his emotions once more. The fervor of realization, of conclusion, of recognition. "I have no name. Do you?"

Chapter Twenty-One

Asvin

The open air of the seas aided him in finding the peace he had long forgotten once he set foot on the captain's ship.

He was grateful, wasn't he? To know of his father, to know his name and his importance? He was grateful for that. But, he did not feel grateful to the woman who he knew as his mother by blood.

After the night's conversation, he wanted nothing to do with her. He had always wanted to meet his mother, to *know* her, but not now. How could she remain silent about a murderer who had killed arguably the most important people in The Five Realms? The man who had killed her lover? His father?

Now that Asvin understood that Bronte was not forced to give up her child, but that she likely gave him up of her own free will–her own choice–that hurt. It was a pain that stuck him like a blade in his side. If she truly loved his father–Myrsky–why would she give up the one thing, the *child* that had become of this so-called cherished union?

It was the anger and frustration that called him to the night skies, stepping off the edge of the ornate railing and gliding over the sparkling oceans of Qoohria. It was the knowledge of his past and now his destiny that kept him from any hope of sleep. His father, who he had known nothing of, was the former celestial to

Estus. *He* would be the celestial to Estus in less than two days' time. Did he have a choice? Would The God of Stars and Skies force his hand?

He supposed none of that mattered. He didn't find himself here because he was some prophesied being. He was here on this ship because of *her*, Ash. His Parastella. It resurfaced in his mind that Kaster, Ash's father, had mentioned Parastella. Did Ash know about it? Did she know what it meant?

He thought of her beautiful face, full of shock when he'd said it, when Kaster spoke the true meaning of his name–Asvin–the first star in the sky. She had panicked shortly after that, undoubtedly overwhelmed by the new knowledge and the traumatic memory of her mother. Asvin hadn't known much about her past other than a few stories about growing up with Callan. She had never spoken of her family, of her name. She did have a family name. Ashlun Tanwen.

She had a name to be proud of, a name to live up to. Unlike himself.

Asvin wasn't sure what to do or how to approach her about the Parastella. He didn't want to scare her away or make her think that he was insane for talking nonsense about some legend that she wouldn't have heard of. He hadn't known of it himself until Percy told him the story of the Cloud Giants who had a bonded mate, a partner tethered to them for life. Would she want that?

To be cemented to him forever?

Asvin didn't think anyone would want that for themselves given no one had wanted him before, and no one wanted him now. He didn't think that she deserved to be leashed to someone like him. She deserved far better; she deserved the world. Asvin could see her father believed the same.

He couldn't help but feel shame. The weight of it pressed down on his back. His wings were more akin to lead than the feathers he knew were stretched out behind him.

He had the opportunity to comfort Ash when she panicked in the lounge room, he had the chance to show her that he cared for her, and that he *wanted* to be there. But he stalled, he stood frozen in fear for her. He didn't want to burden her with the Parastella. He didn't want to trap her like she had been trapped all these years. She had gone through too much already.

Asvin landed back on the ship. The night sky had started to brighten ever so slightly with hints of teals and greens, it wouldn't be long before the day had finally arrived.

He could smell the ocean in the light mist that had begun to gather through the night. Then he caught the scent of citrus and smoky embers.

Leaning on the ship's railing, he turned his head to see the most bewitching creature he had ever laid eyes upon.

Ash's hair cascaded down over her shoulders, almost to her waist, in curls of silver under the light of the moon. She wore the white cotton gown she had worn once before but she didn't have her belt cinched at her waist. Her feet were bare as she padded her way across the deck towards him.

"Couldn't sleep?" Her melodic voice danced along his skin. She leaned against the railing next to him, her elbow touching his.

"No. I'm assuming you could not find rest yourself?"

Her voice was soft. "No. Lyra and Ori drifted off pretty quickly. I think that all things considered, they are happy to be reunited. I tried, but I couldn't calm my mind."

He felt the same urge to comfort her, but then his thoughts of her entrapment to him returned. He couldn't, *wouldn't* trap her.

"Are you alright?" Ash sounded worried and that pained him, he didn't want to hurt her either, he didn't want her to worry. He almost felt as if her worry was causing his heart to beat rapidly. He didn't want her to feel panicked again.

"I think so. After the meeting I... I just had to get away to process it all."

"I can understand that. To be honest, I already knew or had at least pieced together what my father had said about me, about my mother. When Callan and I visited Enoch he told me that my mother was the celestial to Vytarr. And of course, I know what happened to my mother." Asvin heard her speak confidently, but he could sense the pain and fear in her voice. His heart beat against his chest faster. It had to be her emotions he could feel through–

"Enoch mentioned something else in my reading. Something that my father spoke of during the meeting."

Asvin tensed, locked in place he waited for her to speak again. Her emotions fell away as his own returned to the forefront. He wouldn't put this on her, he wouldn't force her into this.

Ash stayed silent. He could feel her gaze on him, unmoving. He summoned the courage to meet her eyes and when he did, the pearlescent irises instantly broke down the wall he had begun to build. "What did the oracle mention?" he finally asked.

"Parastella." When she said it, his heart skipped a beat, Asvin was unsure his breathing could slow down the pace his heart had set. Then she asked, "Do you know what it means?"

He couldn't lie to her; he couldn't bring himself to even dismiss her questioning.

He took in a shaky breath, "Parastella is from an old legend of the Cloud Giants. It means a *pair of stars*. I was told that it was a bond between two people, a tethering between souls. When the two accepted the Parastella they could feel or sense each other's emotions or locate one another if apart. It is like an invisible string linking two people together."

Ash didn't look away, she was completely focused on him, her eyes burning into his. Asvin found himself unable to turn away from her, he could feel the same pull that he felt to get to her. The other end of the string, tying his soul to hers.

"You are the first star in the sky, it's what your name translates to?" Asvin only nodded in response. "Are we Parastella?"

Asvin's heart began to pound at his chest, begging to be let free, begging to be cared for, held, loved.

He tore his gaze from hers, his control unraveling each moment he looked into her eyes, longing to remain there. "I... I don't know. I don't know if it can happen outside of Cloud Giants. I don't even know if it's *real*. Besides, I don't want you to feel like you are chained to me if it *were* true."

Saying the insecurity out loud hurt him more than when his mind was turning it over moments before. He'd never felt so dimwitted. He *knew* no one could ever want him, and he had to be okay with that. He had forced himself to settle with that piece of him—the piece that no one wanted.

Asvin felt the lightest touch on his face. Ash palmed his cheek and forced him to face her, to look her in the eyes once more. He felt as if he may have broken right there, the half-torn wall had been completely obliterated.

She placed her other hand on his arm where it still rested on the railing. His body strained at the tension in which he held himself.

Afraid. He was afraid of what she would say. He had never feared anything in his life, not like this.

"All I have wanted my entire life is to be reunited with my family. With my father and my grandfather. I have wanted nothing more." She spoke with certainty, though her voice had the smallest tremor.

"I wanted nothing more, until now. Until you. I can't explain why I feel drawn to you. I can't explain why you are the only thing that occupies my mind when it feels like the realms may fall apart at any second. I don't know if the Parastella is real, but Enoch saw it. He saw your eyes, your eyes when *I* first saw them. When you came to me during the attack, you weren't following a lead or information. You were following the *pull*, the same connection that I feel to you now. Parastella or not, I could never feel chained to you. I would never feel trapped by you."

Her words felt like being drenched in a Phyrian river. His heart may have come to a complete stop. The shock of her admission holding the fragile organ in a vise-grip. But he didn't spare his heart any thought.

He took her face between his hands and placed his forehead to hers, breathing in her smoky-citrus scent, feeling her short, rapid breaths on his lips, mere inches from hers.

He tried to stop; he tried to push her away though his body wouldn't let him. He tried to convince himself that she would never want him. She had all but proclaimed how she felt yet he didn't know how to do the same. He didn't know how to tell her that it was *she* who brought him here, it was Ash who made him want to wake up and never fall asleep again if it meant he was with her. It was Ash who he needed. Who he selfishly wanted.

She didn't wait any longer for him to gather his thoughts. Her movements were impatient as she lifted herself high on her toes and brought her mouth to his.

Her kiss was soft, but he could feel the heat that radiated from her. He met her heat with a passion that he could not express in words. He leaned down to meet her halfway, wrapping his arms around her waist. He never wanted to let go, never wanted their lips to part again.

A sudden, sharp pain broke his hypnosis. He felt a searing sting on his right wrist. Ash saw his flinch in pain, her eyes filling with immediate worry. Asvin looked down to his wrist and Ash's gaze followed. On his wrist was the same pattern of stars that Ash had on hers, the constellation of Vytarr and Qoohr. It was glowing, bolts of light connecting the stars and forming the shapes of the eternal flame and the changing tide. The light dimmed until it left identical markings to Ash's wrist.

Ash's hushed tone could barely be heard over the waves lapping against the ship, "Parastella."

Part Three: A Knight in Heavy Armor

M.M. Bartlett

Chapter Twenty-Two

Ori

When Ori woke, she was in the bed alone. Lyra and Ash were no longer in the large cabin that Captain Blackwell had generously allowed them to occupy for the night.

The sun poured in through the large windows with colored glass. Blackwell's quarters were placed at the stern of the ship and was a sea of reds, blacks, and golds from furniture to paintings and sculptures. The whole space seemed far more grand than any living quarters she had seen on land. She could see that Blackwell took pride in his ship, his true home.

Collecting herself, Ori scooted to the side of the bed and took her time sliding on and lacing up her boots. She really had no desire to leave the room, she wasn't ready to see everyone again.

She may have been making it up in her own mind, but things were a little different now that everyone was aware of her link to The God of Oblivion and Souls. Her own paranoia was likely the culprit of this change.

They still didn't all know about her shadows, they still didn't know what she was–or rather *who* she was. Out of everyone, Callan and Lyra knew the most about Ori, but even they had the absolute bare minimum.

Callan.

She should be angry with him, furious even. He had no right to say what he did or to take his frustrations out on her. Ori wasn't even sure why he had gotten upset with her in the first place, but she was sure it had something to do with Enoch's reading of Callan's past. Ash couldn't even shed light on his outburst, Callan had remained distant from the whole party until he stepped foot onto the ship, and his world was turned upside down; along with everyone else.

Ori truly felt sorry for Callan. His mother, whom he never met was likely dead before he could walk and his father had simply disappeared from the realms. The former being something Ori could try to understand seeing that she too lost her mother at a young age. But she had the chance to know Cytheria, she was kind and warm; she still had her memory with her always. Callan didn't even have that.

Ori took in a deep breath, grounding herself and clearing her thoughts before she finally rose and crossed the room to the door. She caught a glimpse of her reflection in the floor-length mirror between a set of gilded drawers and a matching armoire.

She hadn't kept a mirror in her room at the Celerity Channel and the person looking back at her now reminded her of that purposeful choice.

Her hair and her pale skin were both traits of her father. Her mother told her about him only once and she never mentioned him again. She told her that Ori's given name—the one her father bestowed upon her, the one that sealed her fate—was never to be uttered aloud or she would be discovered; she had been "Ori" ever since.

Then there was the glistening white scar on her face that stared her down in her reflection. The marking that reminded her of the one day she prayed often to forget. The same man, the same *beast* who gave her this scar had murdered the loved ones of the people she had come to care for in the passing days. They may not know every facet of her, but they had accepted Ori anyway, so she accepted them too. Callan might be the beginning of that acceptance faltering in the group, but Ori felt prepared for that.

The walls she had built around her were sturdy and she had always been alone to begin with. But she found herself almost happy with Ash, with Nik and Percy. With Callan, still. She didn't want to lose that, she wanted to be where she belonged, and this felt like the place. Ori couldn't place why it felt right, but it did.

She looked at her mirror-image once more and smiled. She wasn't sure if she had ever seen her own smile, but she liked it. She liked the feeling of being content.

A flat line replaced the faltering grin quickly. She knew she could never be happy, at least not for too long. She knew that when she walked out that cabin door, that faint happiness would begin to chip away.

She looked down to her hands, letting small tendrils of shadows dance along her fingers. They almost seemed happy too. Ori took in another deep breath and hesitantly walked out the door, leaving the hope for a happy future with the smiling twin on the other side of the mirror.

*****

Breakfast was quiet. Not many words were spoken outside of a "Good morning!" by the boisterous captain. He was greeted with small nods and smiles.

Ori found Callan staring at her numerous times over the course of the morning meal. He didn't have the same hatred in his eyes the last time they had spoken. This time, his bright green eyes were swirling with what looked like concern? She wasn't sure what to make of that and tried to avoid him as much as possible. She wouldn't let that sliver of hope grow.

She did everything she could to avert her wandering eyes back to his. The Cromwell brothers ate on either side of Callan, neither of them deeming anyone at the table more important than their meal.

The first distraction Ori was interested in at the table came from Ash and Asvin. The fair-haired pair couldn't keep their eyes off each other. Ash would giggle and blush without being spoken to, and Asvin's greyed cheeks would be stained pink when she did so. The Cloud Giant almost looked like he wasn't made partly of stone.

Ori saw that Kaster noticed this interaction too. She wasn't sure what type of father Kaster was to Ash, but Ori was very glad she wouldn't be involved with *that* conversation. There were– believe it or not–pros to having no parents. No one to butt into your choices in life.

Her next distraction came from the direction of Lyra. She wasn't as obvious as Ash, but Ori saw Lyra stealing glances of Captain Blackwell. Of course, the captain likely saw no need to be sneaky, openly winking at Lyra a handful of times across the table. Kaster seemed to take notice of this exchange too, but instead of a concerned father he would morph into an embarrassed partner, rolling his eyes each time Blackwell winked one of his. This only made Blackwell grin with satisfaction, and he would send a wink in Kaster's direction as well.

The ship arrived in Qoohria only an hour after breakfast. Ori managed to avoid Callan and his awkward body language and found a place on the top deck to just sit and talk with Lyra.

It was nice to hear her voice again—Ori thought that she may never have gotten the chance after leaving the channel and encountering the monsters she had, both beast and mortal. Ori also didn't think that she would find a whole host of people who were destined to the same fate as she, or that she would meet another faerie–a Pyre Faerie no less–or that she would ever find trust in another to reveal her shadows. Ori felt the pang of regret in her chest at that.

Ori told Lyra about the Shadow Hound attack and how she had used her shadows to save Callan from certain death. As Ori recounted the travels and people she had met, Lyra's brow furrowed further and further.

"You said when you used your shadows on the hound that the force made you blackout?" Ori nodded in response, wondering how that was the one detail Lyra latched on to. "You said that the first hound *spoke* to you? *Directly?*"

Ori nodded again in confirmation. This time *her* brows pinched in confusion and the dread in the pit of her stomach began to grow, threatening to push aside her breakfast.

"Ori, they were coming for *you*. You are the celestial to Phyrus. You may not have known it then, but they were coming to collect. The gods have to know that their celestials will claim their power on solstice tomorrow and Phyrus is looking for you."

Ori let that settle in her mind. Tomorrow. Tomorrow she would be a celestial, *the* celestial to The God of Oblivion and Souls. Would she have to report to him? Would she have to do his bidding? After all that Kaster had told them, she still didn't know what this power meant, what it meant to be a celestial, and what it would be like once they assumed their predestined roles. *Does anyone else feel this way?* Ori immediately wanted to ask the others how they felt; if this was what they wanted.

Was there a choice?

Lyra broke Ori from her steady stream of thoughts and questions. "You have to be vigilant. I know you are and have been your entire life, but I won't let him take you. God or not, you have a choice, you always have a choice."

Lyra's words should have made Ori feel better. It was like she knew what Ori had been thinking, but they instead felt like weights pressing down on her shoulders. If she truly had a choice, what was she doing there? If only Lyra knew who she really was. If only she knew that Ori's choice in the matter was null and void.

*****

The party left the ship at the docks of Tregaron, a small port town. When they set foot on the saturated land the first thing Ori noticed was the lack of greeting. The entire town appeared to be empty. Aside from feeling weary over her decisions made and yet to be made, the eerie town was at the forefront of her mind.

Where were the inhabitants? Had they all fled? Did they just relocate? Why?

Blackwell made the decision to leave his group of White Knights with the ship in the event they would need to have it ready to leave. Before departing, he made sure to scratch his feline companion Lucy under her chin and whisper to her like one would to a child.

With hesitation looming over them all, Ori, Lyra, Ash, Callan, Asvin, Nik, Percy, Blackwell, and Kaster set off to find The Nameless.

After making their way through Tregaron, most of them on horseback while Asvin and Kaster flew overhead, the old buildings were slowly replaced by frail, thin trees.

Qoohria–so far–reminded Ori of swampland, the air around them was moist and the realm was practically void of color with the exception of the deep green moss that coated everything. She was almost positive that there was no way Asvin or Kaster could see them from above. The low-hanging clouds blended into the mist, blocking out much of the sun and the winged scouts above her.

Nik and Percy rode on either side of the captain, chatting aimlessly about his adventures and the places he had seen. Even Ash was nearby to listen to the vehement stories he shared. Lyra wasn't far behind Ori, likely not willing to let her out of her sight for one more moment. Ori could understand the sentiment of wanting to keep her safe, but she really wished she would travel next to her.

Even with all the people around her, Ori felt alone.

Callan was merely feet ahead of Ori and before she realized it, he was slowing his black mare's pace to match hers. She could feel the tension between them, the lingering emotions of that night at The Obsidian sat heavy between them among the clopping of hooves and the squish of the path below them. Callan didn't look at her. She could tell that he was trying to find his words but failing each time he opened his mouth.

"How are you?" She had to break the silence. It was the only question she could think to ask. The only question she really wanted an answer to when it came to Callan, he had learned so much about his past in the last few days, she knew that had to weigh heavy on him.

"I'm okay. I just—"

"You don't have to explain if you don't want to. I just wanted to know if you were alright. I'm sure it's a lot of information to digest all at once between your parents and this whole celestial thing." She was still angry with him. She didn't want to be, but she didn't know how to forgive and forget his actions–his words.

Callan looked at her then, his face harbored a look of grief and regret. "I'm sorry."

Ori tensed at the words. She had wanted them when he yelled at her, hurt her, but now she just felt the sorrow that coated his voice. The weight of his apology only hurt her more.

"I shouldn't have said what I did. I jumped to a conclusion that wasn't even possible and I... I hurt you in the process. I meant it when I said I was going to protect you and that you could trust me, I still do. I know I have probably ruined all possibilities of you trusting me again, but I needed you to hear it. I need you to know that you are not a monster, you are not the darkness of your gift. I've seen your soul and I know how beautiful it is beneath that darkness."

Before Ori could respond, Callan sped back up ahead of her. Ori just watched him as they continued on and played his words over and over in her mind. She wasn't a monster. She was not the darkness that consumed her. She didn't know until then that those were the words she needed to hear. Ori thought back to her hopeful reflection in the captain's mirror. She smiled to herself as she let that fragment of desire for a bright future away from the darkness take root in her heart.

She used the light pressure of her legs to urge her horse into a trot, moving to match pace with Callan. She had to tell him how she felt about his words, about his admission. She had gotten to his side and met his bemused gaze when Asvin called out above them in a panic.

"HOUNDS!"

Asvin and Kaster dropped from the skies as the party came to a halt and dismounted. Ori felt Lyra at her back and Callan remained at her side, enacting his renewed promise to her. Having someone beside her felt... nice.

She was safe, equal, empowered.

Ash quickly approached Asvin and Kaster and asked, "How many?"

"We saw at least five of them up ahead. Looks like there is another abandoned village with only a few old houses." Asvin reached for Ash's hand as he spoke; Ash's delicate hand was encased by Asvin's and the look on his face was one that Ori had never seen from him before. One of apprehension.

"They are here for Ori." Lyra was firm in her statement, but Ori heard the tremor in her voice. "These hounds are from Phyrus' realm, and she is to be his celestial. They are coming for her just as they did before." Lyra turned to face her. "You cannot use your shadows, they possess the same energy and while you can incapacitate them, they can do the same to you very easily. You cannot try to fight these things—"

"I won't just stand by helplessly—"

"I will NOT lose you again!"

Ori snapped her mouth closed; tears welled in her eyes as Lyra confessed what she already knew. She cared for Ori; she would protect her at all costs just like Ori had wanted to do for her.

Callan's hand brushed against hers in solidarity. All she had to do was lace her fingers through his, but she was afraid she would never let go. The last time Ori clung to someone they were savagely ripped away from her. If she didn't let them in, she didn't have to lose them.

Kaster stepped forward to the center of their partially formed circle. "We will approach cautiously, Lyra, myself, and Blackwell will lead in—"

Kaster's words were cut short when the snap of a branch was heard from too close a distance. Kaster and Asvin turned and slowly began to approach the sound.

They no longer had time for a plan.

The dispersed trees opened up from the worn pathway into the soulless village. Not one hound was visible, but Ori felt their presence, it was like they were a part of her, connected to her. Her shadows danced anxiously between her fingers.

Blackwell, Nik, and Callan spread out to Ori's left. Percy stayed close behind her and Lyra as they began veering to the right. Kaster, Asvin, and Ash continued down the path between the houses.

The breath Ori took in died in her throat when she felt her shadows rush through her body, sensing the Shadow Hound that was now bounding towards Ash from the left.

Asvin was faster.

He swung out his body catching the hound by its throat and snapping its thick neck in one twist. His movements reminded Ori of a violent dance.

When the body fell limply to the ground, Ori felt the revolting presence only grow stronger. She could see another hound prowling slowly straight ahead of her, another matching the set tempo to its right.

"Get her out of here." Kaster's hushed words weren't directed at anyone in particular but Asvin clearly understood. He wrapped an arm around Ash and with two beats of his gray-feathered wings they were in the skies, Ash fighting him to get back to the ground. The hounds didn't break their strides, their focus only on one target.

On Ori's left she saw another Shadow Hound rushing towards Blackwell and Nik. Nik withdrew a hatchet and threw it with a precision that Ori had never seen, the hatchet embedding itself in the beast's shoulder. The hound slowed but it continued its path barreling towards the captain as he drew a sword from the sheath under his blood-red cloak.

Callan disrupted her vision—he'd run up next to Ori, knocking and releasing arrows in rapid succession towards yet another hound bounding straight for her from the left side of the path. His fourth arrow pierced the sport right between the dog's putrid yellow eyes.

When the second beast had fallen, she heard a muffled growl coming from her right. Her head snapped in its direction. She feared the worst, but she didn't quite understand what she saw.

Lyra stood untouched and unscathed, a Shadow Hound writhing at her feet, gurgling on something in its throat. Drowning.

Bewildered by the sheer chaos, the sounds of flesh being torn, swords clanging, and arrows flying, Ori had forgotten the hound that was positioned straight ahead. It was still locked in on her, moving with the grace of a cat on its too-large, clawed feet.

Callan was focused on the hound that Blackwell and Nik were battling, Lyra was finishing off the hound convulsing at her feet; Ori was alone.

She reached for her dagger. If she couldn't wield her shadows, she could wield a weapon.

It was then that she felt her skin tingle, a warm sensation wrapping around her. She didn't take her eyes off the hound to look; she wouldn't give it the chance to attack. But that didn't matter. The hound charged into a full run, its claws digging up the soggy ground.

"ORI!" Lyra shrieked, too far away to make it to her in time, in time for this beast to either meet its end by Ori's dagger or for her to meet her end. She prepared for either cessation.

The beast was only feet from her as it burst into flames. Angry orange flames seared its fur in an instant, and its flesh bubbled and melted off bone until its body was unrecognizable.

It had happened so fast, she couldn't comprehend what she had seen. Her stomach threatened to falter from the gore that littered the ground. Small flames still lapped at what remained of the corpse.

She tore her eyes away in an attempt to free them from the horror that she had just witnessed. Casting her gaze downward she watched her trembling hands. That's when she saw the soft light blue aura that traveled up her arms.

Her awe was cut short when Lyra–who had finally made it to her side–came to an abrupt stop. Her face relaxed and a tight smile kicked up one side of her mouth when she looked past Ori.

When she followed Lyra's gaze it was Percy who stood with arms stretched before him, casting the shield that shimmered over her body. Percy's shield was fixed to Ori, but his stare was aimed at the skies, his mouth ajar.

Ori looked up to see Kaster floating down and landing in front of the incinerated carcass that was once a hound.

Flames. Kaster had been the one to scorch Ori's four-legged assailant. He met Ori's gaze and gave her a short nod before he took off again, assessing the remaining threats from above.

Ori did not feel fear any longer, she felt cared for, accepted, *loved.* These mere strangers chose to protect her with the knowledge of what she was. They may not have known the details of her past, but they knew the hounds were there for her. They could have just as easily handed her over. Yet, she still remained out of the hands of her worst nightmare. They fought *for her.*

The emotion was overwhelming. She felt Percy's magic fall away as she took in the bloody scene before her. Her stomach was confused by the butterflies that flitted around the twisted sickness that remained. She didn't know whether to cry, scream, or laugh at that moment.

She counted the dead creatures around her. The hound Lyra had drowned above land lay on its side, eyes rolled into the back of its head. Then there was the hound that had several arrows buried into its hide and the first hound not far from it whose neck sat at the wrong angle.

When she looked back to Blackwell and Nik, she could see the faint outline of a hound's body and its head lying a few feet away. Blackwell's once-shining blade was coated in a thick layer of blood, and Nik was retrieving the hatchets lodged into the hound's shoulder and on the ground by its limp legs.

Ori couldn't shake the feeling that this was far from over. All five of the Shadow Hounds lay dead around them but she could still feel the dark presence that they brought with them. "There has to be more. I can't explain it but I can *feel* them."

Kaster met Ori's concern with understanding. "I believe you. I do, but I didn't see anything els—"

The ground quaked beneath them.

On the other side of the village, past the small, dilapidated houses, shadows spread over the ground.

Callan stepped closer to Ori, placing her behind his protective arm. Lyra had already armed herself with the matching dagger to Ori's and another curved Qoorhian blade she had never seen before.

The shadows climbed up from the sheet of black mist that had gathered on the ground. The amorphous cloud stretched over the houses as it started to take its true form.

It stood a little over three stories, black fur covered its muscled body. It stood tall on two hind legs that bore black claws the size of her arm. Its head was that of a Shadow Hound but far larger and there were bright red bulging eyes placed above its snout. When it opened its mouth Ori saw three rows of glistening teeth that were easily the length of her hand.

The screeching roar that left its body shook her bones, forcing her and the others to cover their ears with their hands. Her palms did nothing to stifle the ringing in her ears.

"Penumbra!" Blackwell yelled from where he stood across the clearing.

Kaster looked to the skies to see Ash still in Asvin's arms. Ori didn't miss the fear that took over the man's handsome face. That fear shifted into determination as he bounded towards the beast.

Ori heard Ash's scream, a scream that she would never forget. One of the same frustration and terror that radiated from her father seconds before.

Lyra, Callan, and Percy flanked Ori as they all watched in horror after the man who had given his life for the protection of the realms time and time again. Why did no one run with him?

The beast, the Penumbra, screeched the same horrid sound from deep within as its beady stare honed in on Kaster.

Kaster left the ground, flying to the height of the Penumbra. He hovered in the air for a heartbeat until he surrounded himself in flames. The same irate orange flames.

The inferno grew larger as it lashed red tails of fire from within. The beast stared in awe at the sight. Everyone had stopped in their tracks to take in the sight of the isolated firestorm as its gargantuan form towered over the Penumbra. He was the sun itself.

The flames began to dissipate and in their place stood a dragon.

The Way of the Nameless

Chapter Twenty-Three

Ash

Her father was a dragon.

She could remember stories about dragons from her childhood, whispered by her grandfather to lull her to sleep, but she couldn't comprehend the image before her.

Ash's dream forced itself into the forefront of her mind and the white dragon who watched over her. But this dragon was not the same.

Her father's dragon was like a living flame—orange scales covered the majority of his colossal body, blending into gold scales on his belly and darker red scales along his spine. The crown of his head had gold spikes that sparkled when he shook his head and let out a defensive growl.

The Penumbra took a rumbling step back. The closest emotion Ash could place on its monstrous face was shock. That shock quickly spilled out and was replaced with fury.

Ash struggled again in Asvin's grip. "Take me to him!"

"I can't. I can't." She could sense the dread in his words, she could feel it coursing through her own body as he spoke. "He told me to take you away from this, to protect you. I will not disobey him."

A strange mix of anger and love wrapped around her heart. The anger was something she couldn't help but... love. Love for the father that she thought she had lost once and may lose again. And love for the man who respected that father. Love for the man who held her and understood on the deepest level how she felt in that moment. The pain in his crystal blue eyes told her that much.

Kaster let out a guttural roar that rattled Ash's bones. What windows were left in the small houses shattered with the vibration that the hum carried.

Before she could so much as blink, her father charged for the shadow beast, a beast easily ten times the size of the Shadow Hounds. But her father in his dragon form made the monstrosity look meek in comparison.

Kaster released a stream of flame that pooled into what looked like lava as it fell from his mouth. The Penumbra sidestepped the blast, snapping its teeth in response. The rows upon rows of its sharp gnashing teeth dripped with a slimy green ichor she had never seen the likes of.

The dragon and the beast circled each other. In a tangle of claws, teeth, and flame they fought and scrambled for control over the other.

Ash continued to scream, begging Asvin to bring her to her father. She knew he would never let go. She knew she could do nothing. The Penumbra may have looked small from her point of view above the mist but she knew by the sheer size of the monster next to the nearly demolished village houses that she was gravely mistaken.

Her focused fear was stolen by a scream, a scream of pain. A scream that didn't belong to her.

She looked back to the party. Blackwell and Nik were running to Lyra and Ori who were standing over who she assumed was Percy. The women blocked her line of sight, Ash could only make out Percy's blue robes draping the ground.

She desperately searched for the source of panic among her companions. Ash's eyes halted.

She didn't dare to blink when she locked in on Callan who was mere feet away from two Shadow hounds.

"We have to help him! He can take down one of them from a distance, but they are too close, there are two of them, Asvin!"

To her surprise, Asvin didn't argue. He dove down towards them, the speed at which they plummeted took the air from her lungs.

She couldn't watch her father fight the Penumbra; she couldn't bear to take in the terrifying and overwhelming scene for one more moment. But she wouldn't let Callan sacrifice himself.

When they were closer to the party, she saw the blood. Percy lay flat on his back, his arm... his right arm was *gone*.

One of the Shadow Hounds had blood caked into the fur around its maw, and it smiled.

The fucking dog smiled.

Its twin was prowling towards Callan who had nothing—his quiver was empty. He had no blade, nothing to defend himself yet he was standing before two of these hounds with nothing but his bravery.

His idiotic bravery.

All Ash could see in that moment was a Knight, a Knight ready to give up himself in the name of those he fought for.

Those that he would die for.

When they landed Ash bolted and ran as fast as her body would take her. Asvin flew up again and he landed behind the hound that was now only two feet from Callan. Asvin brandished the sword strapped down his back and with one magnificent, clean swing, the hound no longer had a head to smile with.

While the other Shadow Hound was distracted–preparing his attack on Asvin who was gloriously splattered in the creature's gore–Ash was able to reach it, just close enough to unleash the flames of her father. The flames she was proud to wield.

The beast was howling, the scent of burning hair hit her nose before the melting flesh did. She was disgusted and wickedly entertained by the power she felt coursing through her body.

When the hound no longer moved, its eviscerated body lying on the ground, she turned in search of Callan.

His face was streaked with tears but the genuine smile on his face made her heart break into two. This was her brother, for all intents and purposes, *he* was her family. The person who never left her, the person who was always there for her, the person whom she would never fail.

She ran again until she had her arms tightly around Callan's shaking torso. He held her just as tightly as he whispered into her hair, "I was so scared."

She almost didn't believe him, he had never admitted to being afraid of anything. Of all the ridiculous stunts they'd performed, of all the dangers they had faced in the last few days—Callan was never afraid. But he confessed this to her now and it only made her aching chest crumple. "It's okay. I was scared too."

Before Callan could respond to her own admission, a roar—a *cry*—rang out over the village. She broke her hold from Callan only to grab him to steady herself after seeing what she wished she never would.

Kaster had three large, gaping slices down his throat gushing shimmering blood, and oozing with the same slimy film she saw from the Penumbra's teeth only moments ago.

She knew she screamed but she didn't hear it. She heard nothing when her father's body, still in his dragon form, fell to the ground and shook the realms.

She couldn't hear Asvin or Callan speaking to her.

She could barely feel Asvin pick her up from the ground that she didn't know she had fallen to.

She was numb, empty.

The only thing that broke through her mind was her father's voice, "You *will* fly again."

And she would.

She looked to Asvin, whose eyes were filled with worry and sorrow, she could practically taste the emotions that he projected.

"Take me to him." Asvin didn't respond but he also didn't move. Hesitant to break her even further from the grief that threatened to drag her down.

"Lead it to the water!" Lyra shouted over the party. Asvin who moved quickly, placing her on the ground and flying towards the Penumbra. She felt the last pieces of her heart disintegrate as he flew away. She would not lose hi—

She stopped herself from that thought. She would not lose *anyone else* today. She would not let herself fail them. She would not leave them.

Ash ran. She knew that if her wings weren't littered with scars and tears that she would have been flying towards the body of water.

She ran as fast as her legs would let her, following Lyra to the small lake that lay just across the clearing and past a few scattered trees. Callan and Ori ran with her too.

Asvin was drawing the Penumbra closer to the water. She still wasn't sure why Lyra made the command, but they had followed it blindly.

She would not let the beast win.

Lyra reached the edge of the lake and placed her foot where the water touched the bank. Water flowed up her leg and over her body. A whirlpool spun around her causing Ash to stop in her tracks, Callan and Ori coming to a stop next to her.

The tsunami of water rose high into the skies, absorbing the mist that lingered in the air. All at once the water lost its cylindrical form and splashed onto the ground around them.

Lyra no longer standing at its center.

A dragon stood in her place–similar to the one her father took the form of, but its scales were various shades of blues and greens, and the arms and legs had webs between their joints, something that would help her to move through the waters.

A Seadragon.

Ash's mind immediately recalled the story that Ori had shared with her over a week ago, about the Lumi Faeries taking to the seas of Qoohr.

Lyra stooped, moving across the ground, slithering like a serpent until she was only feet from the Penumbra who was still distracted by Asvin flying above its head. The Penumbra was too late when it finally turned to see the Seadragon who would clamp down on its throat.

And that's exactly what Lyra did.

She locked her long jaw down around the Penumbra's neck, thrashing and jerking, sinking her sharp teeth deep.

With a snap, Lyra released and drew back, spitting the same slimy liquid that had oozed from her father's throat.

Ash didn't think.

She moved.

Ash bolted again, straight for the wounded beast. The beast who had hurt her friends, threatened her brother, and slain her father.

She thought she heard Asvin scream, she thought she may have heard someone running behind her, yelling for her to stop.

But she kept moving.

She slid to a stop when she was standing directly beneath the Penumbra, who was unaware of her small presence. The monster struggled to grasp its protruding throat. She pushed away the exhaustion, the trepidation, and her grief as released every ounce of flame that she had left.

She knew it wasn't enough.

She knew it would likely be her end.

But she knew she would not fail. She would not let anyone else die. She would not leave them.

Her flames crawled up the beast, growing, stretching higher and wider, an amount of flame she had never wielded before. She saw that the edges of her flames were glowing a soft white and the slightest tinge of that white outlined the fire that poured over the Penumbra.

Ash felt herself weakening. Her vision began to falter but instead of black encroaching her peripherals, all she could see was white. A white wall claimed her vision completely as she pushed with every ounce of her being.

Her body gave out and the ground claimed her. Soft and warm.

*****

Her head throbbed with a pain worse than any she had ever known in her life. When Ash shifted slightly, she could feel the tensing of muscle below her head. Muffled voices whispered around her.

She opened her eyes slowly, her vision adjusting to the darkness around her. Above, a thick mist covered the light of the moon, leafless trees sticking out through the wispy clouds.

When her blurry eyes cleared, she tried to sit up but felt a strong hand pull her back down. "You shouldn't move, at least not so quickly."

His voice. His voice warmed her mending heart, the heart she had forgotten about, left to the wind when she made the decision to risk everything.

Her memories before she blacked out returned like a tidal wave. She jerked up realizing that they were still in the forests of Qoohria. A fire had been started, and bedrolls were scattered about in the small clearing.

She felt an arm slide around her waist, slightly tugging her against a hard chest.

Her body calmed but her mind raced on. "Where is the Penumbra?"

She hadn't realized she asked that out loud until a low voice spoke behind her. "You took it down." Asvin's voice warmed her even more, she slowly became more aware of her surroundings.

She had been lying on Asvin, using his leg as a pillow. Callan was sitting diagonally from them but when Ash spoke he had crossed the few feet between them and knelt in front of her. Ori followed suit.

As if Asvin could hear the questions running through her mind, in a calm tone he said, "The Penumbra is gone, and the Shadow Hounds are gone. Lyra is resting. The beast had a poisonous fluid in its veins, and she took some in when she bit its throat out.

"Nik and Blackwell are fine and watching over Percy. He is stable but he hasn't woken since…" Asvin trailed off, but Ash filled in the missing words with the visceral image of Percy lying in a pool of his own blood… missing his arm.

Asvin pressed a soft kiss to the top of her head. She wasn't sure why, but the act felt so *normal*. It made her feel grounded and it restored some sense of calm in the storm.

Callan reached for her hand and when she placed it in his and met his eye she could feel the sorrow in his gaze. His eyes lined with tears when he spoke. "I'm so sorry Ash. You should've gone to help him, not me."

The realization hit her then. Her father was gone too. Tears blurred her vision and her lip quivered, but she never tore her eyes from Callan's.

"You do not need to apologize. I alone chose to come to you. If we wouldn't have flown to you when we did, I would've lost *you*, Callan." Ash placed her other hand on his cheek. "It's *you* who has been with me all these years. Not my father. You have been with me through the good times and the bad. You have never left me; you have never once let me down. You are my *brother*, Callan. I could never regret coming to your aid. You've always done so for me."

Callan turned his eyes to the ground and whispered, "The Flame will sacrifice the Sun to save the Knight."

Ash was astounded by her ability to keep her composure. She had been wrong when she first heard the prophecy. Her father was not the Flame, she was. But her father *was* the Sun.

She chose Callan over her father. As much as the loss of Kaster broke her spirit, she knew she would make the same choice again if given the chance. She had already lost her father long ago. She had already grieved, cried, and hurt over losing him.

But losing Callan, she knew even now, was something she would not survive.

Ash leaned forward towards Callan. Asvin loosened his arm and braced her hips to balance her as she wrapped her arms around Callan's neck and whispered back to him, "I lost him a long time ago. I am so so grateful that I had you with me then and I am so grateful to have you with me now."

Asvin had finally agreed to let Ash go, but only so she could take reprieve from the group. He truly only agreed because Ori volunteered to accompany her.

When Ash took care of her personal needs she reconvened with Ori again, still away from the camp. Ash knew she probably didn't have a lot of time before Asvin came looking for her like the mother-hen he was turning out to be. She could hardly blame him after the ordeal they'd just been through. The fact that he cared so much warmed her.

"How's Lyra doing?"

Ori gave Ash a half smile and nodded. "She's doing fine. I will admit I was losing my mind the moment I saw her shift into her Seadragon form and then again when she shifted back to her normal form and collapsed. That poison has to be lethal, but Lyra is strong, she will be fine."

Ash smiled at the thought of Lyra being so tenacious, but it quickly faded when her thoughts drifted to the fact that her father was not so resilient.

Ash figured that Ori noticed her change in demeanor when the silence bled into the air between them. Ori spoke softly, "I am truly sorry, Ash. From what I saw of your father, he was a great man."

Ash managed to give Ori the same half-smile she had given to her moments before. It hurt knowing that she truly would never see her father again. Before, she had the inkling of hope that they would be reunited, like a small ember floating around in her mind. Now, that ember had been snuffed out.

But Ash didn't regret her actions, she didn't find herself wishing she had run for her father instead of Callan. She knew through the thick weight of sorrow and grief that she had made the right choice.

She would miss her father just as she always had. She would always remember the way his voice calmed her as a child, she would always remember how he made her laugh, she would always remember the way he smelled of embers and sandalwood, and she would always remember the days before she lost *both* of the people who loved her endlessly.

She lost her parents on the same day in her mind, and she was beyond grateful that she had one last time to see her father, to hug him, to speak with him. A few blessed moments that she would never take for granted.

"I'm sorry." Ori's whispered apology pulled Ash from her thoughts. Ash's brows creased, she had no idea what Ori was apologizing for.

"I'm sorry that I didn't tell you… I wanted to tell you about my gift, but I was worried it would bring you into danger. The only person that knew of them was Lyra. When the Shadow Hounds attacked us after we left Keld, the shadow you saw pulling the hound from Callan was one of my own."

Ash hadn't put two and two together. She faintly remembered seeing the shadowy tendril pulling on the leg of the crazed hound that went after Callan, but she had forgotten its relevance over the past few days. That day was a haze in comparison to what they had just gone through.

After seeing the nightmarish creatures drenched in shadows she supposed she should be afraid of Ori's confession, but she knew Ori would never hurt her. Ori had been a friend since she climbed down from the tree Ash and Callan found her in.

"It's okay. In a way, I understand. I understand that knowing where your gift comes from would be scary. I know I would have done the same thing to protect those around me and those I care for."

Ori's eyes filled with tears but not a single drop fell. She took in a shuddering breath. "There's something else that I've never told anyone, something that I have a hard time admitting to myself at times. After today... someone should know. Just in case."

Ash braced herself. After the last week everyone had shared she wasn't sure what else could make their present situation worse.

Ori waited, it was like she wanted to tell Ash, if only to take the unbearable weight off her own shoulders but she was... afraid. Ash could see the emotion on Ori's face and how it stretched over her tense body.

"It's okay, Ori. It can't be that bad." Ash didn't understand what Ori meant by 'just in case'. In case of what? What was she planning to do?

Ori closed her eyes and took in three controlled breaths before she opened her eyes once more and met Ash's. "Lyra told everyone that the Shadow Hounds and the Penumbra were coming for me because I am to be Phyrus' celestial."

Ash nodded, remembering the concern in Lyra's voice when she shared this with the party on Blackwell's ship. It made sense to Ash at the time, but it still terrified her thinking that those creatures were out there searching for Ori, sent by The God of Oblivion and Souls no less.

"She was right, they are coming for me. But it's not because I am the child of a celestial and destined to follow in her stead." Ori paused again, the tears that had once maintained their station began to slide down her cheeks. "They are looking for the child of a *god*."

Chapter Twenty-Four

Callan

Callan sat, looking up at the stars through the mist that had thinned ever so slightly. According to Captain Blackwell, The Nameless was reportedly only a few hours south from where they now camped and would proceed there in the morning if Percy and Lyra were fit to travel.

Callan couldn't help but feel like their injuries were his fault. All of this was his fault. If he hadn't pushed so hard to become a White Knight he would have never approached Captain Blackwell, he would've never convinced Ash to go with him, and he wouldn't have met Ori, Nik, Percy, or Asvin. He wouldn't have put everyone's lives in danger.

He supposed that the prophecy would have come to fruition in its own way, but he still held the shame.

He took a deep breath in and pushed it out with a heavy sigh. Kaster said they had found each other. Wouldn't they have come together one way or another? Maybe it wasn't all on him. But the guilt lingered over him. Monsters were hunting Ori; Percy and Lyra had been injured and on the brink of death, and Ash's father had died. All for what?

What were they going to do with this celestial power?

Was there some greater purpose?

He really didn't think there was. No purpose was worth this much effort, this much loss. Was there?

He took a moment to check everything around their camp, standing and stretching before he began his walk-through. Ori was snuggled up to Lyra who was regaining the color back in her cheeks. For a few hours, she had taken on a sickly shade of green as the Penumbra's venom coursed through her body.

He took another glance at Ori. She seemed so fragile now compared to when he first saw her, when he thought she was a threat. He still didn't know if she had accepted his poor attempt at an apology, but he also wasn't sure if he wanted to know. He didn't think he could bear to hear his rather large mistake turned back on him.

Did that make him a coward? Most definitely, but he didn't care. Or rather, he only cared about her. He made Ori a promise and he didn't plan on breaking it. Not again.

He made himself move on. Nik and Blackwell weren't far from where Percy lay. They were able to staunch the bleeding wound that began at Percy's shoulder and ended a few inches from where his elbow should have been. They had wrapped the stub in the cleanest cloth they could find. Percy had only awoken once in the aftermath, long enough to take in some water and a few bites of bread. His brother hadn't left his side, not once.

Much to Callan's surprise, Asvin was actually asleep. He leaned against the base of a tree with one long leg crossed over the other and Ash was nestled beside him with her head on his chest, a feathered wing wrapped over her shoulder.

Callan felt like he'd missed something between them over the last few days. He had distanced himself from everyone, even Ash, so he didn't blame her for not explaining the close nature of this newfound relationship. He still didn't like Asvin, but he begrudgingly found himself trusting the odd-looking bird.

When Kaster told Asvin to get Ash away from the chaos he knew would ensue, Asvin didn't hesitate. Callan had thought that Kaster was referring to Ori with his command given what Lyra had told them about Ori being hunted by the Shadow Hounds, but his last wish was for his daughter to be protected.

An inkling of trust was cemented in him when Asvin tore into the Shadow Hound that had been mere inches from Callan and his perceived death. If it weren't for Asvin and Ash, he likely wouldn't have been standing there looking over the people he felt responsible for.

It wasn't long ago when he thought it would be he and Ash against the realms, responsible for only each other, but that had changed. He was placing hard-earned trust into people whom he'd known for all of a week or even a few days. Something he didn't freely give. They fought next to him, traveled by his side throughout the entirety of southern Baasaris and into Qoohria, and took care of him.

He wondered if this was what it felt like to have a family. A concept he had never truly understood.

Callan let his mind wander, rummaging through the last few days and where they left him. He didn't realize he had walked a short distance from the campsite until he felt the small vibration from the ring in his breast pocket.

His mother's ring glowed the most vibrant amethyst. He turned back towards camp and the glow dimmed.

This intrigued him, when he tested his theory and turned back towards the direction he had aimlessly begun to walk, the ring began to glow again. Was it taking him somewhere?

He didn't think it would do much harm to follow it. His mother was trying to tell him something; he could feel it.

So, he followed her light.

When the ring would dim, he would adjust his direction until it pulsed brightly once more. When he took in his surroundings he didn't see anything of significance, just more naked trees, moss-covered stones, and the muddy ground that squelched with each press of his boots.

The further he walked, the less he thought about going back. Callan hadn't even realized that his bow and half-filled quiver still lay back at the camp.

Maybe wherever his mother was pushing him to go would give him answers, maybe it would give everyone answers. Maybe they could all go home. He didn't know where that home would be, but he longed for it anyway.

He wasn't sure how long he had been walking, following the violet glow of the ring but his legs didn't tire.

He started to see what looked like the ruins of some place long abandoned scattered about. He stepped along broken and forgotten stone that had begun to resemble a pathway. His mother was guiding him through the ruins.

He stopped when he heard something behind him. He didn't know if it was the snap of a twig or another boot squishing onto the ground that pulled his attention from the path, but he scanned his surroundings and saw no one, not one living soul was around.

He continued on a few more feet and then felt the hard sudden blow of an object connecting with the side of his head.

His vision blacked out completely before he hit the cold, wet ground.

Chapter Twenty-Five

Asvin

When Asvin woke, he could no longer feel the soft weight of Ash's head on his chest. He did not wake to the warm smile that he wished to see at every waking minute of every day, and he did not wake to tears of grief and sorrow that he had prepared himself to quell in case she needed him.

Asvin woke to chaos.

Ash was up, pacing back and forth across the campsite. Ori was frantically searching through what Asvin believed was Callan's pack. Her head hung down in defeat as she stood and ceased her rummaging.

As his gaze panned his surroundings, he saw that everyone else was still snoozing peacefully in the early hours of the morning.

Asvin wasn't used to not rising with the sun, Qoohria's skies were constantly blanketed by thick clouds or heavy mists.

"Ash, what's wrong?" When he spoke Ash immediately stopped her pacing and practically ran to his side.

"Callan is missing." Her words carried a tremor. The usually harmonic lilt in her voice was empty. Her eyes were coated in pure fear, the likes of which he'd never seen from Ash. This was not like when the Penumbra attacked or when her father died. This was an unfettered torment that crawled up his spine as her silver eyes swirled.

"How do you know he is missing? What if he just took a walk around the camp and hasn't returned?"

Ash didn't answer him right away; he could see her searching for an answer and failing to do so. "I just know. I can feel that something isn't right."

Asvin reached out to place a loose strand of hair behind her ear and then held her cheek in his hand.

He could feel her worry; it was a weight that would've belonged to himself if it were Ash who was missing. He only knew it was her anxious emotions he felt because he couldn't bring himself to the same level of fear over Callan not being with everyone else. The Parastella having taken its place between them would be an adjustment to say the least. Sensing and feeling your partner's emotions like they were your own was not something he'd prepared for. Loving and being loved by another was not something he'd prepared for either.

Asvin looked Ash directly into her eyes and said, "If you know it, if you can feel it in your soul, then I believe you. That feeling brought me to you. I followed it and I will never regret it for as long as I live."

Ash managed to form a half smile and a small fraction of her fear slipped away but Asvin still felt it sitting on his chest like an anvil. And in its wake, that sliver of fear was replaced with determination and recklessness.

"Ori, I think we need to tell the others what's going on."

With a curt, focused nod, Ori followed Ash's suggestion and began waking those who had not yet left their dreaming. A small part of him hoped they weren't going to wake up in a living nightmare.

"The headquarters for The Nameless is rumored to not be very far from where we are now. It's likely that he could have gone there on his own." Captain Blackwell's observation did nothing to ease the tension that radiated through their campsite. But his suggestion was the least frightening of those that had been passed around like being taken by a Shadow Hound or stumbling through the path of a god. They were too close to their unknown destinies in the forests of Qoohria.

The party stood around the clearing and tried to formulate any ideas as to where Callan could be, but Asvin sensed that they all hoped Callan would simply waltz through the nearby trees unharmed and unscathed by the horrors that were being dredged up the more they spoke.

"I am not sure how it works but we may know someone that could find him. The sentinel of the trees." Percy's rough, weakened voice cut through the silence that sat heavy over them. He was met with confused faces, but he smiled, he genuinely smiled while everyone around him carried looks of anger and frustration. His hopeful eyes scanned the leafless trees around them. "Sakura."

Ash, Ori, and Nik all shifted from frustration to realization while Asvin, Blackwell, and Lyra looked at each of them, waiting for an explanation.

"We met Sakura while traveling from Keld to Midscar, right before the first Shadow Hound attack. She is the one who told us of the prophecy. She imparted the knowledge that she was one with the trees and that when you speak to the trees, you speak to her." Percy began to try and stand. Nik and Blackwell rushed to his side to assist him.

"So, do you just talk to a tree, or what?" Lyra's bitter tone reminded Asvin of the way Ori would typically speak. Direct, straight forward.

"Well, we haven't tried since we last saw her, but I suppose it could be that simple," Percy said as he shuffled to the nearest tree. Asvin couldn't help but raise a brow at the absurdity. He supposed that talking to trees wasn't the strangest thing he had seen over the passing days. With dragons and Penumbras at the top of his list.

Percy placed his wrinkled palm on the moss-covered bark and whispered, "Sakura. We need your help."

Asvin noted the way in which Percy spoke gently to the tree, with the respect one would show to a person who stood before them.

Seconds and then minutes passed. No one moved and Asvin was pretty sure no one breathed, holding their breath with anticipation. Those breaths slowly released to sighs and the stench of fear and annoyance crept back into the space.

"Long time, no see." A sweet, childlike voice flitted through the mists. Everyone froze and scanned the surrounding trees.

"Sakura?" Percy's voice was hopeful, longing.

In one swift movement, a creature lept from the mist-covered treetop that Percy had only pleaded with moments ago.

She was very strange to look upon. This creature had the form of a full woman, with perfectly placed curves and shapes that would turn heads in a crowded room. But her skin was a pale shade of green, not a sickly green, a green teeming with life. On the crown of her head were antlers that resembled tree branches, small leaves decorating the tips of them.

When she moved it was like she floated, dancing towards Percy, her eyes locked on him. "Sweet Percyful, I thought you'd never call on me."

With one line and a small giggle, Sakura had Percy's cheeks turning pink. Speechless Percy didn't–or rather he couldn't–seem to find a response. Percy was usually the first in the group to form words when they couldn't.

The rest of the party watched on, some, like Asvin, still airing on the side of caution over the stranger while others had wide grins plastered on their faces at Percy's bashful side.

"You are all seeking the chivalrous Callan, yes? Well, I did see him walking in the direction of The Nameless' base like the captain here has said, but that was hours ago."

"Hours? He left in the middle of the night and just... started walking? How would he even know where to go?" The frustration in Ori's words was clear. She tilted her head back exposing her throat and let out an exhausted moan. Normally Asvin would be annoyed by this, but this was a bitter slight that even he could understand. Especially when it came to the annoyances of *Callie*.

Sakura turned to face Ori. "I saw him walking in that direction, he had a small light with him but, I do not know how he would've known where he was going or why he would've gone on his own." Sakura shifted her gaze to her bare feet. "I am sorry that I do not know more."

Percy took a step towards Sakura, close enough for him to reach out and place a finger below her chin and lift her face to his. "You have given us more than enough. You have helped us in ways that we didn't know we needed. You are the reason we have ended up where we needed to be. Without you, we would be wandering aimlessly. Do not be sorry."

No one disagreed with Percy's heartfelt words.

Sakura's eyes were lined with a shade of watery blue when she responded to Percy. "I have something for you. I had to look really hard to find it but..." Sakura scrounged around in a pocket that had been sewn onto her tattered skirt and pulled out a small seed. "Here. This is a seed of restoration. I am not sure if it will work but I think it could heal your arm and possibly restore you to who you truly are. I was so afraid for you. When I knew you would live, I scoured every forest in the realms to find this."

She placed the small, iridescent seed in Percy's upturned palm. The seed reminded Asvin of a teardrop. It looked more like a shimmering jewel than something one would plant and expect to bloom.

Asvin was still trying to understand what was happening, from who–or rather what–Sakura was, to where the hell Callan was, and what this seed had to do with anything.

While Asvin's mind proceeded to do impressive flips and spins around the overload of information, he watched Percy who stared blankly at the seed in his hand. He said nothing and Asvin wasn't sure if Percy even breathed until he finally spoke. "A seed of restoration. I have read about this but… I thought it was a myth, a fairy tale." Percy broke his stare and looked back to Sakura who was practically beaming, the smile on her face was enough for Asvin to see there was more there than just a budding friendship between the odd pair. A shared compassion between two outcast creatures. "You found this for me?"

Sakura nodded in answer to Percy's heartbreaking tone. His eyes had begun to water, and it took only a few short seconds before Sakura placed her delicate hand on his shoulder and said, "You deserve to be happy, and you deserve to feel alive. I can see the real you hiding behind your eyes. He is a strong, intelligent man and deserves to be seen as such by everyone. You deserve far more than you let yourself realize, Percyful."

Tears poured down Percy's cheeks as Sakura spoke. Even though the party stood all around them, it was as if they were completely alone.

Sakura took Percy's face in her hands and used her thumbs to wipe the tears from his eyes. "All you have to do is swallow the seed, you may feel a little odd, but the effects should take pretty quick."

Sakura removed her hands and watched Percy intently as he lifted his hand to his thinned lips and knocked his head back, swallowing the tiny glittering stone.

Nothing happened at first, then Percy's eyes began to glow. In a matter of seconds, Percy's body was shrouded by a green-hued mist. When the cloud dissipated, a completely different man stood in his place.

A tall man with an angular structure and tanned skin now wore the blue robes that Percy had been wearing moments before. His oval-shaped face was framed by sandy blonde shoulder-length hair that fell in soft waves. The only reason Asvin knew that it was still Percy who stood before them were the same dark brown eyes that hastily scanned over his own features.

Percy shed the robes revealing a blue embroidered tunic that matched his robes, a white billowy shirt beneath, and a pair of dusty brown pants.

He ran his hands over his face, his hair, his chest, and his arms. His *arms*. Percy's right arm was there. The seed had not only restored his image but his aging body, his health, and an entire appendage. Before he could assess it further, Nik pulled Percy into a hug, holding him tightly like he had been missing all this time.

"It's really good to have my little brother back." One tear slipped free under Nik's glasses as he whispered these words to his brother. It felt like an eternity before they finally pulled away from each other.

Sakura walked up to Percy once more and placed her hand on his young face. "I knew you were a handsome one." She smiled deeply and Percy's cheeks were stained pink once more. The phrasing recalled to Asvin's mind the very same compliment Captain Blackwell had given to Percy back in Greenside. He must've known Percy before he'd cast the spell that aged him.

Sakura's focus darted behind her to the empty forest, though Asvin could see nothing in the direction of her gaze. When she turned back to Percy who was about to say something, she placed her finger on his lips and said, "I have been called. Go, find Callan, he may be in danger."

With one more quick smile, she dissipated into the same green mist that Percy had been engulfed by, and the strange, mysterious Sakura was gone once more.

Chapter Twenty-Six

Ori

Everyone packed the camp and their horses so fast that Ori had to question if it had all been a dream. Where was he? How could Callan just leave on his own? She'd give the *chivalrous* idiot a piece of her mind when they found him.

The party quickly decided that heading towards The Nameless' headquarters would be the best course of action. Blackwell and Lyra were fairly certain of the direction and led the party on its way. The former having been to Qoohria many times and the latter having lived in Qoohria throughout her childhood.

Behind Blackwell and Lyra, Ori rode next to Ash, who had been so quiet and focused since they'd left. Determination practically radiated from her as they moved through the forest. Ori felt comforted being next to Ash, she was the only being in all the realms that knew the burden she had carried for so long.

Phyrus, The God of Oblivion and Souls was not just the god she would soon be the celestial to; he was her father. Ori's mother had told her this only once. It was only a few short weeks after Cytheria's admission that her life was taken by the man in black, and Ori hadn't told a single soul since that day.

She chose to hide and in that time hidden away, she found a family. Lyra took care of her and Ash had proven on multiple occasions that she trusted Ori completely.

Ash didn't flinch; she didn't show one ounce of fear when Ori told her that Phyrus was sending the Shadow Hounds and the Penumbra to collect his *daughter*. Ori wasn't sure if Phyrus knew that she would be his celestial or not but... he had to.

In her dreams he had spoken directly to her and that voice had haunted her nearly every night since the first. She was glad to not relive the man in black coming to claim her but Phyrus calling her by her true name scared her far more.

Takara Orelia Keres.

Treasure. Infinite. Death.

Her mother never told her what her name meant, and she had never called her anything other than Ori which had been shortened from Orelia. She knew her name, something that was rare among all people–especially Draoi people–in The Five Realms, but she had never used it or even heard it spoken aloud until the dreams she had of Phyrus began.

Ori shook off the shiver that crawled up her spine. She centered herself once more and tried to bring her thoughts back to the present. Those thoughts were not very comforting in comparison. Ash was beside her, but Callan was not.

Ori blamed herself. Why didn't she stay awake with him? He had been so close to death and probably still reeling from what could have been, or rather what *would* have been if not for Ash and Asvin.

Asvin had proven to be far more helpful than Callan had predicted. Callan only looked at the surface of Asvin. Ori was glad to have him with the party, and she was far more glad to see Ash happy and content in the face of travesty and grief.

Ori had absolutely no idea how Ash was able to focus on anything after watching her father die. Ori herself had been spared of seeing her own mother's death but what Ash had witnessed? She watched as not only her father but her mother were brutally killed right before her eyes. For that reason alone, Ash had to be the strongest person Ori knew.

*****

Time passed painfully slow. They wove through more bare trees and mossy rocks. The only sounds were the moist ground below hooves, Asvin's wings beating above, and small chatter.

The chatter mostly came from Percy who was still amazed at his restoration. Ori didn't blame him for his distraction, seeing him transform from a fragile and frail elder to the now handsome young man who rode next to his brother was something she still couldn't quite piece together herself.

Ori was so grateful that Sakura answered Percy's call and that she knew where Callan had headed. It was more of a blessing that she was able to help Percy and ultimately heal him after his body had taken a tremendous toll.

He once again had both arms; after taking a few seconds to check himself over once more, the arm appeared somewhat mangled, scars covering him from his fingertips to the midpoint between his elbow and shoulder, where his arm had been severed. He wasn't sure what the lasting effects would be as he tried to recall what he knew of the seed of restoration, but he didn't have time to think about that.

None of them did.

The question occupied everyone's minds–whether it be a prodding fiend in the back of their mind or a tempest at the forefront–was where Callan could be.

Was he in trouble?

Was he with The Nameless?

Was The Nameless this big bad evil monster or was he just a simple Nondraoi?

No one knew what they were going into, but not one of them objected when Ash stated that she would be going to find her friend, her *brother*, alone if that's what it took. Everyone in the party made their own choice to set out to find the one who had brought them here, the one who had helped them find each other.

Ori had never known true fear, she thought. She felt fear when the man in black dragged his blade down her face, she felt fear when Lyra met with Captain Blackwell in that alley in Grimmstone, she felt fear when the Shadow Hounds came for her both times and when she learned about the prophecy.

But those instances of fear felt like nothing compared to when she told Callan about her shadows or when she told Ash about her father.

It didn't feel the same compared to watching Percy come so close to death or when Ash collapsed after incinerating the Penumbra.

That fear she thought she knew did not hold a candle to what she felt now. Ori now knew that this true fear was the cold, harsh fact that she could lose what she had come to *want* in her life. Family.

She couldn't, wouldn't imagine the worst had happened to Callan. She wouldn't let herself do that. Callan was smart, sure he was cocky, but it was backed by the intelligent mind that would weave in and out of conversations so easily. He could and would take care of himself long enough for her to find him. And she would find him. Ori made that promise to herself as the party came to a slow stop.

The rocks she had paid no mind to were not rocks. They were stones, ruins of something that she imagined used to stand proudly. Before them stood a massive archway of cobblestones that had etched symbols of onyx throughout, resembling black shimmering veins. The archway led to nothing on either side, just more forest.

"This is the temple of Qoohr." Lyra's somber tone made Ori break her attention from the archway and turn to her, but she didn't seem to be able to find the words she was looking for. Blackwell noticed this and picked up where she left off.

"The Nameless' headquarters is not far from Qoohr's temple based on our findings in Prism Shield. Now is the time to be incredibly vigilant and very quiet moving forward. We will be leaving our horses here; Lyra and I have the utmost faith that Qoohr will look after them."

Ori couldn't help but make a face, one that probably read "that sounds like bullshit" based on Blackwell's returned look of "do you have a better idea?".

As the party dismounted and gathered the bare minimum of what they felt they needed, Ori caught sight of Lyra walking around her horse, approaching Blackwell, and rising on her toes to place a kiss on his cheek. It was such a small gesture, a gesture of love. If Lyra had faith in Qoohr coming down from her godly post to watch over six horses, then Ori would believe in it too, with reservations of course. But it was the renowned Captain of the White Knights believing in Lyra that made Ori smile.

Blackwell addressed them all one more time, "We will continue on foot from here. Keep your eyes out for... well... anything."

Chapter Twenty-Seven

Callan

When he opened his eyes, he was surrounded by darkness. Callan blinked a few times in hopes of convincing himself that he wasn't somehow blind.

He couldn't see but he could tell that his hands were tied behind him, his left arm numb from the weight of his body lying on one side too long. The floor was cold and hard, and the air was stuffy enough to lead him to believe he was no longer outside.

He struggled, trying to wiggle his wrists enough to loosen the cord that bound them.

But then he heard light footsteps and murmured voices. He stopped, freezing in place he forced himself to slow his breathing and try to hear what the distant voices were saying.

At first, he thought that he must've had great hearing, but then he realized that both the voices and footsteps grew closer.

"We found him wandering around Qoohr's temple early this morning, before sunrise." The grumbled voice of a man that was too low in register to be quiet was speaking. "He has been knocked out cold for hours, sir."

Hours? I have been unconscious for that long? Oh gods, what do the others think?

Ash, Ori, everyone was probably losing their minds, all because he felt the urge to follow his possessed ring. He wanted to blame himself, but he knew he wouldn't have ignored the ring if given the chance again. He did, however, blame himself for ending up hand-bound, head-sacked, and writhing on a stone floor in unknown territory. A *true* White Knight wouldn't have ended up in this predicament. He wanted to kick himself; the irony was that he was already down. He was lost. drowning in his own pity before being snapped back to the reality of the situation by another voice.

"So you have no idea where he came from or who he is?" The male's voice was familiar, but Callan couldn't place where he'd heard it before.

"No, sir."

"Well, let's find out if he is a friend or foe."

Callan felt a whoosh of air from an opening door merely inches from his face, it startled him, but he lied still, pretending to still be unconscious. The new-yet-somehow-acquainted voice continued.

"Well, he doesn't wear clothes that the wealthy wear in Grimmstone, his boots are well worn and he wears no jewels. I do not see anything that leads me to believe he is Draoi or Corpoi. No wings, tails, claws… unless there are horns under this sack."

Without warning Callan felt a hand tug the itchy cloth from his face. Callan noticed three things:

One, the room he was in was clearly a cell.

Two, the man leaning over him was the same man from his most recent prophetic dream.

And three, he was in fact, not blind.

Callan was led down a long hallway. The stone floor and walls reminded him of the cobblestone streets in Atreyu, but far less dirty. The wall to his right had various paintings, sconces, and detailed decor, things that felt so extreme in comparison to the mostly barren walls he was used to.

He remembered the walls of The Phenomicron that held his sketches, the art that had taken him so long to complete. Callan wondered if his art would ever be something someone coveted enough to place on their own walls. Callan wasn't sure if his odd derailment of thoughts was brought on by the confusion of where he was or the sheer panic of what he had gotten himself into.

The female he followed was a Corpoi. She wore a dark-colored blouse with the sleeves rolled to her elbows revealing small patches of scales that mostly appeared in various shades of green but reflected in rainbows when they passed by the open windows that lined the opposite side of the hallway. The building they were in had to be high enough above the low-hanging clouds since the sun cast a few rays into the hall.

The woman wore leather pants that were also dark in color, but they were custom-made, leaving a space for her long, scaled tail that almost brushed the ground as she walked. Given that he could only see the back of her head, he wasn't sure what her face looked like, only getting a brief glimpse before she opened the door to his cell and motioned for him to get up and follow her. He mainly focused on not stepping on her tail as he followed her. He somehow knew stepping on it would grant him the sight of a violent face rather than a neutral one.

After the man from his dream–the dream that now felt fuzzy in his crowded mind–removed the sack from his head, the man looked to be in a state of shock. He stood completely still for a few breaths before quickly turning, shoving the sack into the hands of the man who had led him to the cell Callan had been placed in, and sternly whispered something that must've terrified the minion greatly.

The man strode off without looking back at Callan. The stout man who had been sweating so much he struggled with the ties on Callan's wrists and ankles, unbound him, stood him upright, and offered him a drink or a cloth to wash up. Callan politely declined his offers which only seemed to make the man sweat even more. Callan's confusion at the rapid change in his treatment was mind-boggling to say the least.

It was only a short time later that the scaled Corpoi woman retrieved him.

The end of the hall held two large wooden doors that had images of crescent moons and stars carved and shaved intricately among swirling patterns that reminded Callan of ocean waves. The woman knocked twice on the door, pushed it open, and stood aside for Callan to step through.

When she turned he could see that her orange eyes had small vertical pupils that made Callan think of a reptile. Her browline and the bridge of her nose had some of the same scales that were on her arms and tail, and her short black hair was pushed back by her ears which were long and slender and came to a sharp point just beyond the back of her head.

Callan hadn't realized he was staring until the reptilian woman nodded her head towards the open doorway, signaling for him to step inside so that she no longer had to hold the door. She didn't seem to be annoyed or impatient with him, but Callan felt intimidated by her presence anyway. He quickly inclined his head in apology and stepped through the doors.

The open room had cathedral-like windows that were perched just above the tree line and showed a view of Qoohria's misty lands. The room held a large table that Callan's wistful imagination pictured being used for detailed battle plans and heists. Or dinner.

Sitting at the head of the table was the man from his dream.

The man studied Callan before he rose and motioned for him to join, "Here, sit. I believe we have much to discuss."

"How can we have much to discuss if we don't even know each other? Not to mention the small fact that you've held me captive for hours." Callan was shocked by how steady his voice was. He may have sounded confident, but his sweating palms gave him away. He just had to wait long enough for the others to find him. All he had to do was keep this stranger talking.

The man cleared his throat, and Callan was sure he saw a small grin tug at the corner of the man's lips before he spoke again. "I can explain everything. Well, I can explain what *I* know."

Callan was intrigued by his words, but he was more afraid of what the henchman had been sweating over after one whisper from this man. He also didn't feel like crossing paths with the Corpoi woman if she happened to be as intimidating as Callan speculated, so he sat. The studious man *appeared* far less hazardous.

The man took the seat across from Callan and placed his folded hands on the table, fidgeting with them before he finally met Callan's eyes. The man had the same green eyes—his eyes—this was definitely the man from his dream.

But he couldn't just say that. He couldn't confront him about a dream. After all, confronting someone over one dream had placed him in the predicament he'd found himself with Ori only days ago.

This man had no idea who he was, even less so that he was the stranger in Callan's dream.

The man took in a deep breath. "What is your name?"

Callan could see longing swimming in his eyes, longing and a hint of trepidation. He wasn't sure why, but he didn't feel the need to lie to the man, at least not about his first name. "Callan."

Though he hadn't decided if he would take one of the last names he'd come to know belonged to him, he kept them to himself for the moment.

The man smiled deeply as his features brightened and chuckled. "She named you after her brother." He lifted a hand and rubbed the place that rested over his heart.

The smile slipped from his face and was replaced by a somber emotion, his brow creased, and his eyes emptied. Callan could sense the pain emanating from this man, but he didn't understand him.

Until he did.

It all clicked into place.

Every piece of the puzzle that he had collected was fitting into the places they were meant to be and then the name whispered in his sleep came back to him.

"Ezra. You're Ezra Ellis."

The man shifted his empty gaze back to Callan and nodded. "Yes, but, how did you know that?" Curiosity replaced some of the sadness that had clung to his strong face.

Callan didn't answer him, the realization that he was sitting across the table from his own father had him frozen in time.

How long had he wished for this moment, prayed for it? How long had he been deemed to live a life without the guidance he thought was only bestowed upon those who deserve it?

Ezra waited. He studied Callan before he spoke again. "I am sorry. As soon as I saw your face, I knew who you must be but it brought up so much from the past and now all I have are questions that even you may not have the answers to."

Callan took in a deep breath and slowly released it as he tried to bring his mind back from reeling. Ezra had as many questions as he did.

Like father, like son.

He understood how Ezra felt. Callan did not know this man, he did not know his story, and he couldn't imagine what it must be like to have his child just show up one day—

Callan knew what he wanted to say then, what he had to know.

"How do you know who I am? I only just learned who my mother was and that I have no way of ever meeting her. In the same breath I only just learned that I had a father but that he had disappeared from all the realms. I want to know why you gave me up, I want to know why I wasn't good enough for you." Callan shocked himself at the way his words hardly rose in volume. He did not yell, he simply stated what he needed to know but even he could feel the poison behind his words.

Ezra harbored no anger in his expression, but Callan couldn't quite determine what emotions were keeping Ezra from speaking. Callan did as Ezra had done for him, he waited. He wouldn't search for an answer, just as Ezra never searched for him.

Ezra, like Callan had before him, took in a deep breath before he broke his stare and returned to fidgeting with his intertwined fingers atop the table. "I'm sorry." The whispered apology was muddled but Ezra lifted his head before he continued. "I'm truly sorry for the life you have lived, and I am sorry to tell you that until I saw your face moments ago I had no inkling that you had lived at all.

"Hyacinth kept this from me. I didn't know." Callan held his breath as Ezra spoke. "One day she just left. She left me a note that told me not to follow her, but she knew that I would. I would have followed her into any oblivion she traveled; I would have followed her onto any plane of existence if that was where she would be. She was all I ever wanted. I was a young, foolish boy then."

The room was silent with the exception of a faint breeze that blew just beyond the great windows. Callan thought this was odd given he'd felt no wind or breeze since stepping foot into this realm. He–almost–imagined it may be his mother pushing them to speak further.

Callan gathered the courage to say something, anything. "I had the pleasure of meeting Kaster Tanwen, and he told me what he knew of you, that you used to work together in the peacekeepers union."

The sad smile returned to Ezra's face and maybe even a bit of excitement at the mention of Kaster's name.

"Kaster? How is he? Is he traveling with you?"

Callan couldn't bring himself to take that small bit of happiness that broke through the layers of pain that had cocooned this man, so he just shook his head.

The one person Ezra truly loved kept the knowledge of his own child from him. Callan thought that he would get some answers about his mother upon realizing that it was his father that sat across from him, but he could see that the same questions that ran through his own mind now were not so different than what had plagued the man he sat across from.

The breeze played with the thick hair atop Ezra's head.

"How did you know who I was?"

Callan still couldn't shake the instant recognition Ezra had upon seeing him. Sure, he had his eyes and his wavy brown hair, but that wasn't enough for Callan. It wasn't enough for someone who didn't know if he had a father and it certainly wasn't enough for a man to have no knowledge of fathering a son.

Ezra's reply was interrupted by the creak of a door across the room from where they sat. The door had a frame detailed with gold-foiled leaves and vines that flowed from the top of the archway to the floor. Callan stood when he saw his reflection. It was himself he saw standing in the doorway, but his eyes were not the same green, they were an intense violet.

"Son." Ezra's voice, which had hardly been above a whisper until then, made Callan jerk but he didn't break his stare as he looked into his own wild eyes. "Come meet your brother."

Chapter Twenty-Eight

Ash

Ash almost missed the dilapidated keep as they silently approached. The stone walls protruded from a rocky hillside that was covered in the same moss they had seen dispersed over Qoohria's landscape. The front gate was now only a few yards from where the party gathered behind an outcropping of stones and trees, still unseen by the two guards that occupied the entrance.

The gate wasn't so much a gate as it was two massive statues depicting The Goddess of Night herself, carved out in the same stone as the ruins and the castle.

The statues mirrored each other, depicting a beautiful Qoohr slightly bent backward at the waist, the tips of her mirrored fingers meeting each other in an archway, and poised above them was a slender crescent moon.

The guards standing below the twin Qoohrs were no match for her eternal beauty. In fact, Ash could see that they were both Corpoi, one of them had a long thin tail that reminded her of field mice, and the other had furry legs and hooves that resembled a farm goat.

She pondered their openness, how they let their differences out in the open. In and around Grimmstone they would've had their tail tucked or hooves covered but here they openly shared their true natures with anyone who would cross their paths.

Could they be a threat at all?

Before she could express her thoughts aloud, Ori and Lyra had already maneuvered away from the party. They snaked their way behind the guards and each simultaneously grabbed them by their necks and held them firm until the guards were rendered unconscious.

Ash sighed, thinking to herself that she hoped the Corpoi males didn't have the potential to be allies. If they were, they had just lost a smidgen of trust to the thieves in black. Ash wondered what kind of training they went through in the Celerity Channel. How deadly did thieves have to be?

Lyra waved the party towards the Qoohr gates, before they got to the opening Lyra splayed her fingers wide and her palm flat to stop them. Ash froze, not needing to hear the wet squelch of boots behind her, she knew the others had come to a halt as well. Lyra and Ori didn't move from the gateway, they only stood still, almost as still as the twin Qoohrs if not for their chests rising and falling with deep controlled breaths.

Ash knew that look—they were assessing a threat.

Ash snapped her head up to look for Asvin, to make sure he wasn't in the line of sight of... well, whatever stood in the direction Ori and Lyra now faced.

He wasn't there, she only dared to move her eyes, but he wasn't in her peripheral vision either. Before she broke to seek him out, she felt a cool breeze down the back of her neck, and it carried the scent of a summer storm. She knew then that Asvin was safe. She wasn't exactly sure how she knew, but she felt that comfort in her soul, the same comfort that his presence had brought her from the first time their eyes met. The very same overwhelming sense of safety his kiss brought her.

She also knew that Qoohria had not one inch of space that wasn't shrouded in humid mists with no trace of wind or breeze. The Parastella, it told her that he was safe, he was fine, and so was she.

She took a moment to ground herself and refocus on the situation at hand. She looked again at Lyra and Ori who had both brandished their matching daggers. Ash realized now that the two of them were so similar to herself and Callan. A sibling not of blood but by choice.

The thought of losing Callan disturbed her mental clarity for the hundredth time since Ori woke her that morning asking where he had gone, but she didn't know. She felt a strange mixture of worry and guilt. Worry for where he was and guilt for not knowing.

Callan had been distant over the past days, and she thought he needed space, but the overwhelming feeling spread its poison through her as she thought over and over again that she should've made him talk to her. She should've made him tell her what he was thinking, what he was worried over, what she could do to help. But it was too late.

"The Nameless is expecting you." The toneless voice of a female broke through her rampant thoughts. The voice didn't sound like a friendly one, nor did it sound like one that harbored ill-willed intentions.

Ash was pulling her flames to the surface in the span of a heartbeat—she would take down anyone that stood in the way of her reaching Callan.

If he was still somewhere she could reach.

"And why might he be expecting us?" Lyra's voice was clear and calm; she spoke with the control that Ash wished she had. She felt her hands tremor in anticipation.

The voice spoke again but it carried a lilt of charm this time. "We have an unexpected guest who informed The Nameless that a group of his... confidants would be arriving to find him. If you'll follow me, I'll take you to him."

"How do we know we can trust you?" Ori cut in.

Ash heard the sound of boots scuffing on stone as if in mid-turn, "I guess you'll find out when you see Mr.... Bram? Is it? Unharmed."

Ori's gaze immediately snapped to find Ash. She gave her a short nod in return; she would follow her. She would back Ori up no matter what was about to happen. Ori had already given so much of herself to help, and the secret she gave to Ash was one that she would never betray.

One that she knew carried the greatest trust one could give. And she would give that trust back in full.

Lyra and Ori moved in unison through the twin statues as Lyra motioned once more for the party to follow. When Ash and the others approached the arching statues, a set of stone stairs covered in the same putrid green moss lay ahead of them.

Ori and Lyra were already halfway up the steep incline and just above them, a Corpoi woman with the features of a snake stood waiting. She had scales in patches along her angular face. She wore battle leathers, the kind that Lyra and Ori wore, but they were a dark shade of green that could blend into the moss that surrounded them. A clever camouflage for Qoohria.

As the party began the climb up the stairway, the reptilian woman turned sharply and entered a half-open doorway that led into darkness. Lyra and Ori moved in a tight formation made for two as they cleared the entry of the castle. Ash and the others knew to follow when they continued to creep behind the woman who walked in long strides, not taking a second to look back to make sure her new *guests* followed.

Ash couldn't help but turn her neck ever so slightly to the right, just to make sure everyone was still with her. She counted.

Nik and Percy were directly behind her; she was still getting used to Percy's appearance which had admittedly startled her for a brief moment. Blackwell followed them closely, turning to close the door they had been led through. When she turned her head back to her left she saw only gray feathered wings. That was all she needed to keep moving forward.

They were all together and they would be reunited with the missing piece of their group soon. She hoped.

The hallways slowly began to lighten with lit sconces lining the walls. The hallway had dampened sunlight pouring through at the end revealing to Ash that there were windows open enough to bring an end to the perpetual darkness that likely filled the small castle throughout the night.

Qoohria didn't have long hours of sunlight, but Ash was grateful not to move around in the unfamiliar halls with only shadows in their corners.

At the end of the hall, the mysterious Corpoi woman led them to the right which opened to yet another hall. But this hall was decorated with paintings the likes of which Ash had never seen.

She had only ever seen the art that Callan had made for Phenom's advertisements; most art that was left in the realms was showcased at the Grimmstone Museum. The museum of death was what she and Callan lovingly referred to it as, given the amount of traumatic history stored in its walls of war and betrayal.

The other side of the hall had large open windows that were high enough to see a lake surrounded by the same leafless dark trees they had been traveling through.

Her wandering thoughts were cut short when she heard murmuring. The end of the hall was only a few feet away where two large wood-carved doors stood closed. The door had intricate patterns of swirls and stars that ran symmetrically over both doors with mirroring crescent moons on either side.

The Corpoi woman stopped and knocked twice on the door before opening it and stepping aside for the party to walk in.

Lyra only stared the woman down, unwilling to move until she knew where they were going. Ash knew that Ori would have been just as stubborn, but Ori's focus was no longer on the woman before them.

"Callan?" Ori's whisper was hushed, almost silent, but Ash heard it, and she knew that Ori's voice was choked up enough for it to accompany tears.

Ori moved forward like she was in a trance, but Ash still couldn't see what or who she was looking at beyond the doors from her position. She cursed herself for being so short.

Ash pushed past Lyra to come next to Ori but stopped dead in her tracks as she saw Callan sitting at a table in the center of the room. Ash blinked hard. She blinked again, confused at what her eyes beheld. Callan was right there, but across from him sat... Callan. But that couldn't be—

"Ori! Ash!" The Callan she knew—the *other* Callan looked... off somehow—pushed from the table and began to run towards them before he was fully out of his chair that swung back and clashed onto the stone floors.

Callan crashed into both Ash and Ori pulling them into an embrace that made her momentarily forget where she was.

The emotion she felt building inside of her was not the same one ridden with worry and guilt but with love. Ash still couldn't quite believe that it was Callan who held her and Ori against his chest. This was different. This was a man who had panic laced in his firm hold. When he pulled back, the same alarm swam in his green eyes but the toothy smile on his face was genuine. He looked between Ash and Ori in a panicked daze, possibly not believing himself that this was real. Yet another dream.

What had happened?

What had he gone through?

"Are you okay?" That was all she could bring herself to ask. It was the only important question that pulled itself to the forefront of her mangled disposition.

Callan took a deep, shaky breath. "Physically, I am fine. I am a little sore from sleeping on stone floors, but I'm fine. But I feel far from okay at the moment. In fact, I am not sure there is a word for how I'm feeling. I've just met my family."

As the last few words came from Callan, Ash looked around his arm towards the table once more.

The other Callan sat with wide eyes, confusion and amazement in his stare. Another man, older but still handsome for his age, stood only feet from them. He waited patiently with his hands clasped behind his back, but his face didn't have the same patience this body expressed. His face was tangled with a mixture of untrust, relief, and maybe regret? Ash wasn't entirely confident in her observation, but she knew those eyes.

They were the same eyes she had known most of her life, the eyes of her best friend.

As she opened her mouth, surely to throw aimless questions at the stranger, he spoke first. "Welcome, please come in and sit. I can have Vidhi bring us some refreshments."

The eerily familiar man paused as he surveyed them when he landed on Captain Blackwell he took in a sharp breath of surprise. "Edmund, it has been many many years since I saw you last, you were but a lad back then on your father's ship!"

Every head turned to face Blackwell, having never heard his first name used, it felt almost informal to Ash like this man truly knew Blackwell on a more intimate level, but the captain had no inkling of shame or surprise at the man's recognition.

"Ezra, it is good to see you well." Blackwell removed his black hat and inclined his head before crossing through the party and clasping arms with the man, Ezra.

She knew that name, it was the man who'd worked with her father, the one who had disappeared... Callan's father. The memory of Kaster's recollections flashed in her mind in rapid waves until she was able to piece it together. "You're The Nameless?"

Ezra turned his body to face hers and motioned towards the table. "I promise to explain everything. I know there's a lot that you all have processed recently and I am more than willing to tell you everything I know if it will help. Please, take a seat."

The party hesitantly made their way to the large wooden table that held enough seats for them all with excess space for more. There were even chairs to accommodate for Asvin's wings as he claimed the seat next to Ash's.

Once everyone was seated and Vidhi–the reptilian woman– brought in trays of water and tea, the room was quiet.

With Asvin on her right and Callan seated to her left, Ori occupying the seat on Callan's other side, Ash took in the faces that she didn't know–or rather the faces that reminded her so much of Callan it scared her a little.

Ezra cleared his throat and took in a short nervous breath before speaking to the room. "As you have likely put together, I am Ezra Ellis, otherwise known as The Nameless. When my..."

He choked on the word, the word that he chose to replace with another. "When my partner, Hyacinth, disappeared, I traveled throughout all of The Five Realms to find her. I even did some things that I am not proud of in hopes that someone could lead me to her. It drove me mad and sick with worry trying to find her. One day, I returned to Grimmstone only to learn from Captain Robert Blackwell, Edmund's father, that Hyacinth had been murdered in cold blood."

Ezra paused again, the emotion poured from his features, raw and unfiltered rage trembled over his body, but he took a few breaths to bring himself back to the present. His tone deepened.

"When I found out about Hyacinth's death, I didn't know what to do with myself. I couldn't figure out why anyone would want to hurt her or, more importantly to me, take her beautiful life. She was the most pure, unyielding, and the bravest person I have ever known. My soul was broken, my mate of the heart was gone, taken from this plane with no hesitation.

"So, I hid away and in the darkest parts of my days, I planned for revenge. At the time, I thought that the Grimms were to blame for her death. Having worked closely with them through my parents, I knew how slimy and vengeful they could be.

"I rallied every Draoi and Corpoi being that I could find in hopes of uniting them in a new world, a new way of life where they didn't have to hide. Being a Nondraoi myself, it was difficult to bring untrusting people together, and I don't blame them."

Ezra looked to the *other* Callan who was the only person at the table not looking at him, his head bowed looking at his hands under the table.

"When I was searching for Draoi people in hiding, it was in Estana that I found Baastian. There was a Corpoi family in Ironhaven, a town in the northeastern part of the realm, that had a small child who did not have their features. That child looked at me and I knew at that very moment; he was my son. He was… our son. I would know those eyes anywhere, his mother's eyes."

It was then that Ash saw why the other Callan looked odd to her. His eyes were not the same vibrant green that Callan and Ezra had, his eyes were a deep shade of violet.

"I brought him with me, and we traveled together until we came to Qoohria. When we got here the entire realm seemed to be abandoned. Not one living soul could be found. I assumed that much of Qoohria was ransacked and destroyed after the raids. This was the only place I felt no one would come looking for us, after all, this is the home of the most terrifying beasts in the seas. Not many people dare to make the trip. Though I have never laid eyes upon one myself." Nearly the whole table cast a glance towards Lyra. "So, we stayed and anyone who chose to join us has been here since."

Ash was reeling over the details of Ezra's story. Hyacinth and Ezra had two children. Callan had a brother, a *real* sibling. Baastian. It hurt her a little knowing that wouldn't need her to be that sibling for him anymore. Shame covered up her curiosity.

"I didn't know she was pregnant when she left," Ezra spoke a little softer, "she simply disappeared, and when I found Baastian it all made sense to me then. She left to protect him, to hide him away from the danger she felt was coming. I didn't know until today that she had not only had *a* child, but she'd had twins.

Chapter Twenty-Nine

Asvin

Asvin listened intently to the details of Ezra's side of the astounding tale he had only learned part of days ago. He was mildly distracted by the pounding emotions coming from Ash.

He placed his hand over hers, which had a white-knuckled grip on the arm of her chair. When their skin touched her body relaxed and she threaded her fingers through his. The emotions that had been stirring fervently, stilled to a slow churn. It was enough to know that he had helped her to calm a little. But he could still feel the heat of a flame through her hand.

Asvin watched as Ezra continuously looked between Callan and the young man who they now knew as Baastian, his twin.

Everyone was tense, no one spoke or interjected as Ezra spoke about his time searching for Draoi beings or learning of Hyacinth's plans and secrets. Ezra told them that Hyacinth placed Baastian with a Corpoi family she had come to know in Estana and Callan in the safe hands of Madame Loch in Baasaris. Ezra had of course known her through the union but couldn't bring himself to see his friends–Hyacinth's friend–until he found the justice for her that he sought. So, he never knew Callan was there.

"When I found Baastian, all thoughts of avenging Hyacinth's death and the deaths of the other celestials came to a halt. I was a father and that became more important to me than anything in all the realms. Hyacinth left the realms with a small piece of herself, and I knew that one day Baastian would take her place as the next celestial to Baasis, his namesake given to him by Hyacinth. I have spent much of my time hidden away here to help teach him what I remembered of Hyacinth's gifts. But we have stumbled upon some things that we can't quite figure out."

"Do you have a ring?" Callan was the first of the group outside of Ezra to speak up.

Ezra looked at Callan with confusion, and Baastian–the recipient of Callan's targeted questioning–had the same look, but he nodded. "Ye-yes, I have a silver ring with a stone in it."

Gods, even their voices were in the same pitch. Annoyingly so, Asvin concluded.

"I have the same one!" Callan reached into his breast pocket to retrieve the ring his mother had left with him. Baastian raised his left hand and showed the identical ring that decorated his index finger. "When we were in Midscar, Ash and I met an oracle, and he told me to remove the ring. He said that the ring has a protection charm on it and that it can stop our celestial gifts."

"*Our*? You have celestial gifts, Callan?" Ezra stared at Callan with a slack jaw.

Callan seemed to realize then that he would have to explain what he and the rest of them had gone through throughout their shared journey.

Asvin sat patiently as Callan started from the beginning. He talked about his young life at The Phenomicron with Ash and how they had learned everything they knew from the performers they'd met throughout their childhoods.

Then he talked about how he had always looked up to Captain Blackwell and wanted to be a White Knight of Knife's Edge, his greatest desire. Blackwell gave Callan a small nod of appreciation at this confession.

As Asvin listened to Callan's version of events he found himself relating to him for the first time since they'd encountered each other in the Bassarian forests.

When Asvin was young, he too sought after a greater purpose and often found himself stuck; ever searching for *something* rather than living as nothing. Only, Asvin didn't have a goal like being a White Knight to aspire towards nor did he have a friend to push him to achieve something greater.

Asvin was glad that Callan had Ash, although he still found himself jealous of not having Ash for himself. He reminded his envious mind that it was *he* who had part of her now, and she too had part of Asvin, always.

Callan continued on explaining the start of his journey with Ash to find information about the Draoi war cuff. He reminisced over their meeting Ori who had been tracking them for almost an entire day before Callan or Ash noticed her presence. Asvin noted to himself then that he had respect for Ori too; she was sneaky but in a way that he wished he could simulate on his own. He'd have to inquire about her skills learned from the den of thieves.

Callan went on to tell the story of meeting the Cromwell brothers and sharing the information that led them to their set destination of Qoohria. Then Asvin was able to relive the rest as

Callan told Ezra and Baastian of their first encounter with the Shadow Hounds. Ezra's face had slowly turned from shock to worry for his new son's past trials, but he didn't interrupt Callan, he absorbed every detail of his words.

When Callan shared the details of his reading with the oracle, Enoch, all Asvin could think of was what else Enoch had seen about Ash. She had shared with Asvin the small part about the Parastella and his blue eyes that Enoch saw, but she hadn't yet told him anything else.

He wondered if it was something that had stayed with her, something she hadn't had the time to process yet. He hated the idea of anything haunting her beautiful mind.

Asvin tuned back into the conversation as Callan was going over the second Shadow Hound attack and the tragic death of Ash's father to the Penumbra. He again felt the unmistakable sorrow and grief coming from Ash in waves. He squeezed her hand slightly to remind her that he was still there with her. Ash turned to him and gave Asvin that beautiful smile he loved so much. Pained as it was, it was still his favorite sight in the realms. An image that threatened the glory of every sunrise and every sunset.

He loved everything about her, the way she spoke, the way she looked at him, the way she demanded the eyes in a room.

He even loved the dark parts of her soul, the parts that were difficult for her to express in words, but he knew they were there, lingering behind the wall of light that she had built to protect herself. He loved her. He couldn't help but smile back at her knowing he would never outshine hers.

His heart forever belonged to the woman whose smile could bring him to his knees.

Callan spoke directly to Baastian again, pulling Asvin's wayward thinking back to the task at hand. "So, if you remove the ring you should be able to feel what I felt. I still haven't really experienced anything out of the ordinary other than the prophetic dreams. We have the same blood running through our veins, the same celestial power. But, if you do remove it now, you may black out like I did. I had my first dream when I removed my ring. My dream…" A sudden look of realization was plastered on Callan's face, "…you were in my dream. I thought I was seeing myself in a mirror, but it was… you. My reflection."

Basstian's cheeks were stained pink, his eyes wide searching Callan's face for any facade or lies. "I… I always thought this ring was from my—our mother. It would glow at seemingly random times, and I never knew what it meant. I think she was leading me to *you*, and you to *me*."

Callan slowly nodded in agreement, a small grin turning the corners of his lips. Asvin watched as the twins stared at each other, it was like they were speaking mind to mind. Everyone at the table only watched them in awe.

Ezra cleared his throat. "The war cuff." Callan turned back to Ezra, excitement altering his serene face. "I do have it. Of course, I knew it would be of no use, but I held onto it in case the celestial to Vytarr ever wanted to claim it."

Asvin turned his attention back to Ash whose face had gone slightly pale at the mention of her future calling.

"Based on Callan's story I am assuming that not only Baasis' celestials sit at my table but so do the celestials of all the Gods and Goddesses."

Asvin felt himself go rigid at the statement, remembering that they had no time left. Sakura told them before he arrived that the prophecy would come to pass on the summer solstice… which was today.

Asvin looked around the table and the same look of dread was on the faces of everyone who knew of the prophecy.

Callan was the only one brave enough to speak through the thick cloud of uneasiness. "Yes. Baastian and I would be the celestial heirs to Baasis, I don't know if there has ever been more than one celestial to a god but, I suppose we will find out one way or another.

"Ash is the celestial to Vytarr, Asvin to Estus, Lyra to Qoohr, and Ori to.. Phyrus." Callan gestured to each of them as he spoke of their soon-to-be-appointed Gods and Goddesses.

Asvin felt his throat knot up, he struggled to pass a breath— he felt a small tightening of the hand intertwined with his. He focused again on Ash whose presence brought him the clarity he needed. How had he ever lived without her? He never wanted to find out.

Callan spoke aloud the prophecy to Ezra and Baastian who had not heard it in full. "The Fallen Star will slay a shadow to claim the Flame. The Seadragon will tame the Red Phoenix. The Fox will step out from the darkness and see the light. The Flame will sacrifice the Sun to save the Knight, and the Knight will find himself In the mirror. The powers of The Five Realms will Unite as one and fulfill their Divine decree by joining life's essence into the Dyngheloi."

As if summoned by the words of the prophecy, Asvin heard the faint sound of voices singing in the distance.

The voices were ethereal in nature and echoed around him yet no one at the table uttered a single note. When he observed those around him, he saw that Callan, Baastian, Ori, Lyra, and Ash were all trying to find the voices as well, some of them looking frantically around the room.

"What? What's happening?" Nik's concerned tone broke through the locked-in focus of Asvin and those who were trying to locate the voices.

Ori answered, "I can hear singing."

"Did you say *Dyngheloi*? A crystal?" Ezra directed his question to Callan, but all of the celestial children nodded as they listened intently to the melodic voices that sang in a language Asvin did not recognize.

Ezra was silent for a moment as he watched them. "I have it here. I didn't know what it did or what it was, but I found it abandoned here in the keep when we came to Qoohria."

Ezra stood from his seat at the head of the table and began walking across the room to an open doorway with a frame decorated with golden leaves and vines.

They didn't hesitate, everyone moved from their seats and across the room to follow Ezra. Asvin held Ash's hand in his as he braced for whatever they would find beyond the golden archway.

The ethereal voices grew louder as they fled through two rooms, down another short hallway, and up a spiral set of stairs that led to a painted black door at the top of a tower.

When Ezra touched the door handle, the ghostly divine music came to a complete stop.

Chapter Thirty

Ori

Ori's hands shook as Ezra opened the ebony door and walked into the small room.

When she entered Ori was overwhelmed by the ornate boxes and items strewn about the room and piled in tall wavering stacks along the walls.

But her attention was drawn to the center of the cylindrical room where a black crystal orb was fixed on a gold pedestal that had three long claws wrapped around the crystal.

Ori wasn't aware of anyone else in the room as she and the others—Callan, Baastian, Ash, Asvin, and Lyra—approached the Dyngheloi in the same trance-like state she herself was in.

A small vibration ran from the tips of her toes, up her legs, through her spine, all the way to the top of her head. The sensation made her tremble with fear and the unnerving sense that only danger came from this mysterious stone her eyes were glued upon.

Ori felt something at her side. She didn't jump or move at all until a warm hand took hers. She broke her gaze only to see that Callan held her hand, not only as a sign of solidarity or comfort, but one that she sensed he needed too.

Ori held his hand tightly as apprehension alerted her to what could be the beginning or the end of her story coming into view.

"The prophecy said that we have to place life's essence into the Dyngheloi." Ash's voice was one that gave Ori the clarity she needed in that moment, a friend. She was with people who cared for her, people who wouldn't let anything harm her. They were in this together. A sliver of bravery fought back her dread.

She looked around the room then. The six children of the celestials were all standing closest to the crystal and Ezra, Nik, Percy, Blackwell, and Vidhi–the Corpoi woman who'd led them to The Nameless himself–all stood around them, watching and waiting.

"Life's essence is the very thing that gives you life, what keeps your body moving, what all living beings must have coursing through their veins. Your blood." Percy's statement was dark but each of them met his warm brown eyes and knew that he was right.

The crystal would need their blood, the blood of their parents, the blood that was forever changed by the gods and goddesses of The Five Realms to confirm that they were the ones to receive the gift they were promised.

Lyra unsheathed her dagger, the twin to Ori's own, from her thigh and sliced a thin cut through her palm and placed it over the onyx orb, small droplets of her ruby blood splashing onto its surface.

The crystal had been completely dark before but with Lyra's blood sliding down its spherical form, the crystal flashed once and then dimmed again.

Lyra passed the dagger to Ori and she repeated Lyra's movements, running the sharp blade across her palm and then adding her blood to the top of the crystal. It flashed again and then dimmed once more. That horrible nightmare of the man in black forced itself into her mind, but she shook it away.

Ori handed the blade to Callan who repeated the same process and the blade was passed all the way around until it sliced through the last hand belonging to Asvin.

Ori hadn't noticed that Callan had returned his bloodied hand to hers, bracing for what was to come. She thought it was odd that he chose to cut his dominant hand, the one that held her now wounded left hand.

Something about the action warmed her soul ever so slightly in the looming chill of the room. His life's essence forever intertwined with hers.

As Asvin handed Lyra's dagger back to her, he grunted suddenly in pain. His face was pinched, his eyes closed, his body seizing. When Asvin opened his eyes, Ori saw flashes of lightning coursing through the sky-blue irises. Then his veins lit up with the same intensity as a storm throwing lightning bolts through dark clouds.

Asvin raised his hand in front of his face, taking in what everyone else was watching with horror and bewilderment. Tiny bolts of lightning stretched past his fingertips and skittered up his arms. Ori saw that the crystal orb in the center looked to have the same bolts running over it.

Ori's focus was torn when she heard Lyra scream in pain. When Ori turned her body she noticed that the room had gone dark around them, the others who she could once see clearly were barely visible in the room of treasures.

Lyra, much like Asvin did, was convulsing but instead of electric bolts, she had small beads of water dancing along her skin.

When Lyra stilled and opened her eyes, Ori was looking into the deep waters of the ocean. The ocean that had the silver of the moon reflecting on green waters, and again, the orb mimicked the sloshing waves of the waters to match Lyra's change.

The sting of pain was abrupt, but Ori knew it was her turn.

Her mind was shrouded with the darkest shadows. But the shadows were her comfort, her safe place, they always had been.

She fought through the convulsions that took control of her body. When she was finally able to open her eyes she could see everything around her, but it was intensified. She could see every single hair follicle on Ash's head. She could see the red feather stirring on Blackwell's hat. She turned and could see every perfect detail on Callan's concerned face. He was more than handsome, he was beautiful. His strong jaw was prominent beneath the dark beard that matched the loose curls of his hair which stopped just above his rounded ears.

She tried to soak in every single inch of him. Her shadows had released themselves to caress his stoic face.

They were doing the very same things she had been, admiring him. Ori's shadows coated her arms like a loose fabric. When she looked down at her body, her shadows completely covered her. But that one tendril of dark smoky shadow was cradling Callan's cheek.

Her shadow snapped back to her in a swaddle of protection when Ash's cry echoed through the room.

Asvin caught her before she collapsed from the same pain Ori had just endured. As Ash willed her body to calm, she appeared the opposite of Ori. She was covered in a bright white light. Ori found it difficult for her new eyes to focus on what she was seeing. Ash's eyes were pure silver, gold streaks of sunbeams floating throughout them.

Ori forced herself to turn away, knowing that Callan had to be next. Before she broke her gaze from Ash, she could see the faint outline of scaled wings behind her, formed by the blinding light that poured from her body. When Ori looked down at the crystal, the image of a white dragon flew around the surface.

Ori felt the hand that held hers so firmly slip away. She flipped to Callan and grabbed his hand and arm to steady him through the pain she knew was coming for him now.

She saw that Baastian too was being inflicted alongside his twin. Their agony shared.

Their eyes snapped open at the same time, both laced with hues of purple and green that looked to be fighting to take over their irises, swirling in battle.

A purple haze clouded around them both, the smoky violet cloud brought with it luscious green vines that snaked around Callan and Baastian's arms and legs. Ori felt one of the vines brush past her fingertips that still clutched Callan's arm. The vines withered as quickly as they formed, fading into the purple smoke as they shifted from lively plants to dead waste.

The room was completely still, silent. The six of them looked over their bodies once more and then assessed at each other.

No one could find the words they searched for. Ori was in a state of shock and twisted euphoria simultaneously. She only assumed the others were frozen in the same turmoil of the new thriving power humming in their veins.

Ori turned to Callan whose eyes were locked on hers already. The swirling pools of his eyes had calmed but she could still see shadows of violet swimming through the green she'd come to know.

He took her face in his hands and rested his forehead to hers.

She thought she would've pulled away. She thought she would've run.

But she stayed.

She placed her hands—one bloodied and one teeming with shadow—on top of his and the room faded out of existence.

It was just the two of them.

They had survived what they both feared. The uneasiness and the angst of the unknown.

They'd survived it together.

Ezra's voice broke through her bubble of relief. "That was truly the most amazin—" Ezra stopped mid-sentence.

When Ori turned to look for him in the cramped room, reluctantly pulling her face from Callan's impassioned hands, Ezra wasn't where she had last seen him.

She and the others looked around the room, but Ezra wasn't there.

The panic returned and settled in, its presence too normal to be unknown.

Ori's heart began to race, her shadows racing along her body to shield her from the impending danger she felt. "Where did he go?" She forced the words out past the blockage of bundled air in her throat. No one answered. The unsettling weight in the pit of her stomach told her that no one had an answer to the question that they were all asking themselves already.

Callan reached for her hand again, but he didn't reach it in time.

Ori felt the wretched gloved hand slide over her mouth.

No.

She felt the blade press into her cheek.

No.

She heard the man in black whisper into her ear. "He's ready for you, Takara."

Shadows pressed in around her, but these were not *her* shadows.

This was not her comfort, her safe place. These were the shadows that came with the Shadow Hounds.

The shadows that followed the Penumbra.

The shadows that took her mother and the ones that claimed the lives of her friends' parents.

Then, she saw nothing.

The room faded into nothing, and the faces of her friends drifted out of view.

The last face she saw was Callan's as she held on to every detail she had memorized in those small moments.

The darkness had finally come for her.

Chapter Thirty-One

Callan

"ORI!" Callan could feel his voice break as he yelled, as he screamed in horror. He thought the cloud of shadows belonged to her—

They didn't feel the same.

He remembered too late that her shadows were warm, he could still feel the small tendril that caressed his cheek only moments ago. The shadows that pushed his hand away from Ori's were... cold, and evil in nature.

Ori's shadows had always been warm, a welcoming presence. The shadows he had just felt reminded him of the Shadow Hounds, but there was no Shadow Hound in the room with them. Only the people who had been in the room stood before him then with the exception of Ezra and Ori.

He had been looking for Ezra when Ori vanished, he was distracted. While he was searching the room he wasn't protecting *her*.

He had broken his promise. *Again.* He had made the promise to himself only days ago that he would never hurt her again. Now she was gone and Ezra with her.

"Wh-at's going on?" Baastian's voice startled Callan from his thoughts. But it wasn't the question that made him jump, it was hearing his own voice. Callan thought for a brief moment that he had been talking out loud.

"Where did they go?" Nik asked the same question in a different form but still, no one had the answer.

Callan shook his head and squeezed his eyes shut in an attempt to keep the tears of anger that rimmed his eyes from slipping. "I don't know where they are, but I will find them. I *just* found my family and I will not lose them, not again."

Everyone in the room looked to him then, each face filled with the same bewildered look of confusion and utter horror.

Callan tried to make sense of what had just happened. There was a sense of ultimate–godly–power flowing through the room. They had just gone through perhaps the most extreme change in their young lives and even those who'd only witnessed it surely felt the charge in the air.

In the midst of it all, something else happened. Something happened right under their noses, and he didn't know what to do.

Callan closed his eyes and took a deep breath. He could feel the essence of the gods thrumming through his veins, it felt like a great wave of growth and healing, but he could feel something darker, something… poisonous that sat heavy on his bones.

When he felt somewhat grounded, he opened his eyes and looked into the faces of his companions, his friends, his broken family. "The shadows I felt brush past me weren't Ori's. They felt like the Shadow Hounds'. I can remember the way they felt when I was bitten, they aren't like hers."

He scanned the room again looking for any sign of understanding. Ash was the only person with a look of recognition and fear in her eyes. "I know who it was. Well, I know why she was taken at least."

Taken.

That one word alone stirred the anger and the poison that had taken root in his very soul.

"What do you mean, *taken?*" Callan tried desperately to keep his voice calm even though his mind raged on imaging the absolute worst.

Ash looked away from him and down at her feet.

"Come on Ash, if you know something," his voice began to rise in volume, letting his anger slip through the too-thin wall he'd built, "you have to tell me. If something happens to her, it's on me."

Ash snapped her eyes back to his and in that moment it was as if they were the only ones in the room. It had always been the two of them against all of The Five Realms but... he'd never felt more distant from her.

She stood in silence for what felt like an eternity, contemplating whatever had been squirming around in her mind. Her own frustration was clear by opening and closing her mouth, searching for the right words. Callan could tell Ash had kept something from him.

She never kept anything from him.

Ash blew out a breath, giving up her need to not upset him further, and said in the softest voice, "Ori told me why the Shadow Hounds and the Penumbra were coming for her. When we learned of the prophecy I had assumed that Phyrus was sending them for his celestial. But..."

Ash trailed off. She looked again to her feet. She was nervous. In all their time together, Callan had hardly ever seen Ash nervous, she even radiated confidence when they were children in Phenomicron performances.

This nervousness was unique. It was laced with terror.

Whatever she knew had to be one of the bad scenarios that Callan had conjured up in his head. He braced himself. Anticipation overtaking his misplaced anger momentarily.

Ash looked up to him once more and she spoke more softly still. "Ori isn't who we know her to be exactly. Her name is Takara Orelia Keres. She is the daughter of Cytheria, Phyrus' former celestial." She paused again, her arrow of admission nocked, prepared for release. "But she is also the daughter of The God of Oblivion himself."

Her deadly arrow struck its intended target. His wounded heart was incinerated, like the ticket stub stuck to the walls of the Phenomicron arena. His heart no longer existed. The gaping hole in his chest was replaced with a rage he had never known. A venomous, toxic rage.

The room was so still, so silent that Callan couldn't hear anyone breathe. He turned to face Lyra who was on the other side of where Ori once stood. "Did you know this?" His tone was lethal.

It would have scared even himself if he weren't so blinded by his anger.

Lyra didn't move, didn't blink.

"Did you know this?" Callan repeated but she still didn't acknowledge him. Callan's blood boiled over as he yelled, "DID YOU KNOW OF THIS?"

As the words left his lips, so did a hazy violet cloud. The smoke billowed around Lyra's throat, and she began to choke.

Her eyes pleaded with him to stop but he only saw red.

"Callan! Stop this!" Ash's demand did nothing to soothe the violent rage that flowed throughout his system.

Then he felt a hand grip his shoulder and another on his arm, pulling him back. The jolt broke him from his actions, the cloud dissipated, and Lyra gagged with the air that pushed into her lungs as she collapsed onto her hands and knees, head bowed.

It was Baastian that held Callan by the arm but before he could turn to his twin Lyra had unsheathed her dagger and placed it at the base of his throat.

"The only reason my blade isn't carving through your neck right now," her whispered words escaped through a snarl, "is because I know what *you* mean to *her*." Her breath was mere inches from his own, both of them fighting for the air between them. A battle of indignation.

"I know nothing of this. I know she was alone most of her young life and she rarely spoke of her mother, much less, a father.

Don't for one second think that I would jeopardize her safety over a prick like you."

Lyra jerked the blade from his throat, nicking his skin with the movement, and sheathed it once more at her thigh. Callan didn't move an inch as he watched the same lashing anger that he felt running through himself whipping in Lyra's eyes like a storming sea.

He knew deep in his soul that she knew just as little as he had. "I'm sorry." The words came out of his mouth like a defeated croak, but Lyra nodded like a soldier in response, curt and precise. He knew by her firm stance that he would never live down that mistake.

Percy stepped forward, breaking Callan's concentration from the blade at Lyra's hip, Ori's blade. "We should move from this room. There are too many Draoi artifacts, too much power in this room and we don't know what else lies here."

Nik stepped to his brother's side. "That, and we need to have a conversation without blades at throats."

*****

The battle table felt so empty, not only without Ori by his side–whose chair sat empty–but Ezra was no longer at the head of the table, Baastian was.

Ash sat to his left, holding his forearm as the only sign of support in his clouded mind. Only moments ago Callan was pacing back and forth in the long room, his mind racing, unable to sit still long enough to think. It was Ash that eventually led him to the table.

Callan had a white-knuckled grip on the arm of the empty chair to his right. His broken promise sat in Ori's stead.

Across from him, Percy stood and addressed them all. "You have all just... *absorbed* an extreme amount of essence. You already had trace amounts of essence but now I can only imagine what you are all feeling. You even look different."

Callan was surprised at Percy's last words. He looked around the table at the new celestials.

Ash practically glowed; her hair was brighter, and her eyes were like looking straight into the sun but without the inevitable pain.

To Ash's left, Asvin looked like something from a child's fable. His gray wings were larger than Callan had initially thought, his skin no longer looked like a dead gray but slightly pinker, like he was truly alive.

Across from Asvin, Lyra was sitting next to the captain who held her reluctant hand in his. Likely to keep it from her dagger below the table. Callan hadn't taken note of Lyra's features much before, but he knew that she didn't have the silver streaks of hair that now framed her face. The rest of Lyra's pin-straight hair was as dark as the depths of the ocean and her eyes shone like the brightest moon.

He wondered if he looked any different. Callan knew he *felt* different but—

He looked to his twin, Baastian had his likeness in almost every way. His hair was a little shorter, the dark brown curls fell on his forehead. His face was clean-shaven, and his eyes were violet whereas Callan's were sea green.

Baastian looked regal. The sharp angles of his face were admittedly handsome, and Callan couldn't help but wonder if he'd changed too. He didn't think he could face his sad reflection anytime soon. Not without her.

Percy continued. "You will all have to learn what the essence of the gods has gifted you in time, but right now, we need to find Ori."

"And Ezra," Callan interrupted. He still didn't feel as if he could claim Ezra as his father, but he would never truly know him if they didn't find him first.

Baastian turned up the corner of his mouth ever so slightly at Callan before turning his attention back to Percy. Percy's wise voice was the only part of him that Callan recognized from the man he'd known before. Ash told him about Sakura and how she'd led them to his rescue. Not before she bestowed a seed of restoration to Percy, gifting him with the youth he once had.

"Yes, we need to find them both. We know that the shadow beings are from Phyrus' realm, and we know that it is Phyrus who sent them in search of Ori. But why would he send for Ezra too?"

Percy looked to Baastian for an answer.

Baastian raked his eyes over those who now faced him, and Callan couldn't help but feel like he had made this same face a million times when faced with a question he couldn't fully answer.

"My father has made enemies throughout his life. In his search for my mother's killer–the man in black as you call him–he learned many things that no one *should* know.

"As I grew older he told me some of what he knew after I practically begged him. He had locked himself in that damned tower searching through all of the artifacts he'd collected for an answer he would never find."

Baastian paused and Callan related to the frustration he saw strained on his twin's face. Callan wasn't sure what to do but when Baastian met his eyes he gave him a nod that he hoped reassured him in some way to continue. "My father told me of a man named The Necromancer."

"The Necromancer?" Asvin cut in, and Callan couldn't help but snap his head towards him with a menacing look that said he'd better have something good to contribute. "I've heard stories about him in my travels. Everyone said he was a Shadow Wielder who took the souls of those who wouldn't willingly enter Phyrus' realm. Souls who had done terrible things in their lifetimes; thieves, cheaters, murderers."

"Yes, my father said much of the same. He said that The Necromancer was once a man who'd challenged Phyrus when it was time for his soul to enter Phyrus' realm and the god found enjoyment in the challenge so much that he transformed the man into his soul-assassin. The Necromancer would travel through the portals of the gods and collect the souls who refused their inevitable destiny, wielding shadows and the Soul Blade crafted by the most evil souls in Phyrus' realm of oblivion."

Callan was captivated by Baastian's words. A man who challenged a god, wielding the power of shadows and a-a *blade*.

The scar on Ori's face flashed into his mind and the anger from before threatened to take him again.

He felt Ash tighten her grip on his arm with one quick pulse, reminding him to keep it reigned in. Callan took shallow breaths into his lungs as he thought of The Necromancer–the man in black–dragging his blade down Ori's beautiful, horrified face.

"The shadows that Callan felt are likely those of The Necromancer. He is Phyrus' collector, come to collect my father who knows far more than he should. Come to collect his celestial, his child." Baastian trailed off when he met Callan's eyes once more.

The sorrow pierced through his anger, pain-filled sorrow for the loss of a father and the loss of… something far more.

She was imprinted in his mind in a way that no other had managed. In his soul, if it was still there among the ruins.

Chapter Thirty-Two

Ash

Ash could feel her flames lapping beneath her skin.

Before the change, she could just feel the warmth of her flames, but the heat had intensified. She would've thought it was burning her from the inside if not for the absence of pain.

Ash tried very hard to listen to what everyone was saying around the table, but she found herself completely distracted by the way they had all changed.

Asvin was… well, she didn't know where her thoughts began and ended on how Asvin looked now. She could feel the electricity between them even more than before, she could sense his emotions entwined with hers, swirling around her mind, body, and soul. The Parastella was stronger somehow. Ash felt the jolt of life that he gave her simply by holding her heated hand in his.

She looked to her right where she still had her other hand resting on Callan's arm. He too had changed, she wasn't sure how, but he looked older. His beard looked more full, as if it had gone through a few days' growth in a matter of minutes, the dark coils matching his wavy brown hair that flowed just below his ears.

He'd truly frightened her when he unleashed what she believed was only a fraction of the power he possessed. Ash saw the ultraviolent cloud of poison take Lyra's breath as if she were being strangled, suffocated. If it weren't for Baastian, Callan's rage-filled power may have accomplished its hidden intention.

She looked past Callan to the head of the table where his twin sat, where his father had sat only a short while ago. His features were unbelievably similar to Callan. In every way his mirror reflection, but Ash could see the details of Baastian's face more without Callan's full beard. Baastian reminded Ash of a young Callan, one who hadn't yet learned what they knew now.

One who hadn't yet come to face something that none of them were prepared for.

Ash thought that it was cruel what they were tasked with, or rather what was placed upon them. They had no idea what tasks their respective god or goddess may require of them.

When would they call for them?

Would they have to do as they asked?

Would they have any choice in their futures?

Ash couldn't imagine a world where she didn't have Callan by her side. A world where she didn't have Asvin, her Parastella. A world where she didn't have Ori…

Her mind raced through all that had happened in that tower of terror.

She thought they were beginning anew. She thought they were going to receive a great gift. But instead, they faced a new dangerous path, one where their friend just vanished into thin air during the one moment when they were all distracted by the overwhelming changes.

This was planned. Phyrus had to know they'd be thwarted by godly essence in its full power.

Ash could even see in Nik, Percy, and Captain Blackwell that they too had changed. They had just witnessed something that no living being would likely see in a lifetime.

How had it been for her mother?

For the other former celestials?

Did they face the same treacherous path that lay before them now?

She shook her head in an attempt to refocus on the conversation at hand. Baastian had begun explaining the portals into the realms of the gods and goddesses.

Ash always believed that she would enter Vytarr's realm of endless sun when her time in the mortal realms came to pass, but she never imagined the possibility of easily stepping through a portal and into the realm of a god while still living and breathing.

Baastian feinted a calm aura as he spoke, "My father told me that the gods and goddesses place their portals at their temples. I imagine you saw Qoohr's temple on your journey here and perhaps the temples in the realms you hail from. Father believed that there was a spell that when spoken correctly, the portal would open to a traveler in need. But I don't think he ever figured out the correct wording for any of the portals."

"So, you're saying that one can walk into the realm of a god? That easily?" Ash thought Lyra sounded so much like Ori then. Maybe that's where Ori learned her overtly direct way of speaking.

Baastian nodded wearily towards the force that was Lyra. "Well, yes, but the hard part is learning what the spoken words are and if that would even open the portals. My father only came to this partial conclusion and stopped searching when he found me. For the past fifteen years, we have simply lived out our days here in Qoohria, unbothered by the outside world until we learned from our guards that they spotted Callan during their evening hunt."

Ash noticed from the corner of her vision that Callan bowed his head and closed his eyes while Baastian spoke. She could only imagine what it felt like to hear those words. To know that his father was alive and that he had a twin brother living life with one another, at peace, and happy. To know that he never had that opportunity and maybe never would now.

Ash didn't have a long time with her parents, but she still knew them, was guided by them, and was loved by them. Callan had gained all of the things one should have throughout life in a matter of days. And all of it was stripped away before his very eyes. She slid her hand from his arm and clasped his hand, squeezing just once to let him know that she was still there and that she always would be. Blood relation didn't matter when it came to their little family. The family that had unknowingly grown on this journey.

Ash knew they couldn't just sit there, they had to do something.

She took in a deep breath and stood from her chair to address the table, "We have to divide and conquer. Percy, Nik, could you look through your collection of legends back in Keld for anything about the temples? I'm sure if anyone can find something it would be you two."

Nik and Percy simply nodded, Nik gave Ash a proud grin that pushed his round frames up slightly. She didn't know how much she needed to see that jovial face.

"Captain Blackwell, as I understand it, the White Knights are under your command and not that of Art Grimm." Blackwell nodded and gave her a grin like Nik, but his grin was that of a challenge. "Would you be able to infiltrate Grimmstone for any hidden information? Maybe some of The Five Realms' history that they've kept locked away? I'm not sure that it exists but if it does, you would be the closest with access."

"Yes, incandescent one, I am sure I know of a few ways to sneak around Arthur Grimm's secret realm he keeps all to himself. I know of another who can assist in that endeavor." He turned his gaze to Lyra who was already fixated on him. "Lyra is the head commander in the Celerity Channel. Their lives are dedicated to finding what others don't want to be found. I'd say she is our best bet."

Ash returned Blackwell's gesture with a nod, challenge accepted. "Very well. The two of you can work together to find what you can about the portals in addition to anything about The Necromancer. If we know more about his past life, maybe we can get closer to Phyrus and in turn... Ori and Ezra."

She turned her attention to the winged man she would most certainly cut her heart out for. All he needed to do was ask. "Asvin, would you be willing to go to Titan's Terrain? Your mother is a powerful woman; I am sure she knows something?"

Asvin held her stare, his eyes told her that he was proud of her even though she felt nothing to be proud of in that moment. Then she sensed his nervousness, though everyone else wouldn't be able to see it. "I am not permitted entrance to Titan's Terrain." He lifted his hand and brushed his fingers over a small triangular cut in his left wing. "This is a marking given to cloud giants who have been banished from Titan's Terrain. I have never set foot in the haven of the Cloud Giants."

Ash sucked in a breath; she felt her heartbeats crawl to a stop as the words left his mouth. "My mother was told by her advisors that I was a demon, a parasite that should be 'taken care of'. Bronte freely put me in their hands, and they tagged my wing, placed me in a basket, and dropped me in the village of Bleakhollow where a small family took me in.

"I am here now because of you, Ash. It was your pull that brought me to you. Not some royal decree. I am sorry I lied to you before."

Ash felt tears slowly sliding down her cheeks, cold on her too-hot skin. Her heart hurt for him and by the look on his face, he felt her pain for him too. But he did not give that same sorrowful feeling in return, all she felt from him was the swelling pride mixed with relief from letting his tragic story out into the world.

"I am not allowed entrance as a half-Cloud Giant with a tagged wing. But... something tells me that they cannot say 'no' to the Celestial of Estus in the flesh." He flashed a wicked grin in her direction. "And I am also sure they will not feel the need to say 'no' to the beautiful Celestial of Vytarr."

337

He took her shaking hand in his and placed a soft kiss on her knuckles before shifting to face Percy directly in front of him. "Percy, I have heard tales of Titan's Terrain library. They are known to have their own version of history locked away for only their kind to learn and know. I am sure there are some things you'd find of interest."

Percy shook his head in joyful disbelief at Asvin's confident tone and smiled in agreement, his young face brimming with determination.

"I can try to find my grandfather, I think he may still be in Pyrecliff. My father..." Ash winced only once at the mention of Kaster from her own tongue, "he told me my grandfather was still at home. I can journey there to see if he remembers anything from my mother's time as Vytarr's celestial and if she traveled through his temple and—"

Asvin cut her off, "I will go with you to Vytarrion."

"But, you have to go to Estana—"

"We will go to Vytarrion and then to Estana, together. I will not live one more moment of my life away from you. In fact, I don't think that's even an option."

Ash didn't protest, she only hesitantly smiled knowing that she too didn't want one day, one hour, or one moment without him by her side.

She turned to Callan, who still had his head bowed but his eyes were open and fixated on the table where a cluster of scratches were burrowed into the dark wood. "Callan?"

He did not meet her eyes. She reached her hand out to cup his cheek and guide his green eyes that now showed tiny slivers of violet, to hers.

"Callan, go find her. I know you think you've lost her, but you haven't, not yet. Don't break the promise." She knew those words would wake him from the trance he was in. Ori shared with Ash the night after the Penumbra attack that Callan had apologized to her, he had promised her that he'd never hurt her again, that he would protect her. Ash thought back to the expression on Ori's face, one she had never seen until it was on Callan's face in the tower. She was shocked by their embrace, one that she realized was short lived for both Callan and Ori.

Callan's eyes lit up from the dark path he was undoubtedly traveling in his mind and nodded. He stood from his chair and wrapped Ash into a hug that only a brother would give his sister, a hug that meant he would find Ash again, that they would be reunited no matter the wrath that would come from standing up to The God of Oblivion and Souls.

"I'll go with you." Baastian stood up from his seat to stand next to his twin.

Callan turned to face Baastian assessing him and his words, his promise. "Are you sure you want to leave? You don't even know Ori, and you want to sacrifice your safety here to help me find her."

"No." Baastian's answer cut through the heat in Ash's soul leaving a trail of unease. "I don't want to sacrifice my safety or my life for someone I do not know."

The room was completely still, and Ash was reminded then that it was not just Ori they needed to find. The fate of Baastian and Callan's father rested in their hands as well.

"I want to sacrifice my safety and my life for the return of my father. I also want to sacrifice my life for the twin I didn't know I had, but *felt*. I knew our mother was guiding me to find you, but I never had the strength to leave my… *our* father here alone and I knew he wouldn't let me enter a world where hatred lies for those like *our* mother, for *us*. It is because of you that I know what my purpose now is. For the first time in my life, I know what I was meant to be, and I know that *our* purpose is to stand together, against all odds."

Chapter Thirty-Three

Ori

Her head was pounding.

Ori knew her headaches were only this bad when she suppressed her shadows for too long, but she had just used them only minutes ago.

Had it been minutes?

Her entire body ached as if she had been climbing cliffs like she did back in Coulteron as a child. Her muscles were sore, and her joints held a dull ache when she shifted on the cold floor.

Ori tried to recall the last thing she remembered but her mind was drenched in a thick fog. She could remember his face, imprinted there behind her eyes. The only wish she had was that when she opened them she would see Callan's face again.

When Ori opened her eyes, she was not greeted by the handsome face she'd come to… she couldn't even admit it to herself.

She was instead surrounded by perpetual darkness. She could see no further than the length of her arm that lay stretched out in front of her. The floor she laid upon was a black stone she didn't recognize.

It had webbed cracks stretching past her vision and into the unknown. Ori couldn't even tell how large the room was or if it was a *room* she resided in at all. She could feel a cool breeze brushing past her skin which also reminded her of her childhood home where the winters were longer than any other season and carried that infinitely chilled breeze even on the warmest days.

Ori's head surged again with the throbbing pain. She could barely see the tips of her fingers in the darkness, but she summoned her shadows, pulling the string to free them hoping to dilute the headache.

An intense, searing pain shot through her body forcing her to let out a grunt through her gritted teeth.

What the hell was that?

She'd never felt pain when summoning her gift before.

Ori stilled as the pain subsided, leaving the headache remaining in its wake. She realized that she could usually feel her shadows, they were a presence all on their own like an instinct or a gut feeling that had always followed her and protected her in times of trouble.

But now, she couldn't feel them at all.

She heard footsteps in the distance. The clacking sound of shoes hitting the stone floor reminded her of the wealthy Nondraoi in Grimmstone. Confident and cruel.

Ori couldn't determine if the footsteps were growing louder and closer due to the echoes and the relentless pounding in her head.

She closed her eyes and pictured Callan once more, trying to ground herself with the only image of peace she had. Their shared relief had been so brief. She longed to return to the shelter of his serenity.

Ori reached for her shadows again and the same shockwave of pain ripped through her body and left her writhing on the floor.

When the pain subsided this time, the footsteps were no longer sounding around her. The eerie silence had returned to the cavernous room.

She opened her eyes to see towering black stone walls cast aglow in a soft orange hue from flaming wall sconces. The room was oval in shape with cathedral ceilings of glass that revealed dark, starless skies. She then realized that she had been lying in the middle of this great room surrounded by plain black stone walls that matched the floors with only one open doorway.

There were no halls, there were no furnishings, and there was no one in the room with her.

She pushed herself up onto her hands and knees, wincing at the tension that radiated through her body as she moved.

When she raised her head and looked to the open doorway, she thought she saw a pair of glowing red eyes, eyes that she knew belonged to the Penumbra.

That wasn't possible. Ash had eviscerated the beast.

Ori squeezed her eyes shut; she had to be imagining things. She had no idea where she was and *that* was what she needed to focus on. Not demons lying in wait in dark corners. Something she was too familiar with.

If she lingered on fears that weren't possible she would get nowhere.

Before she could open her eyes again, she felt a warm sticky breath on her forehead. She knew if she opened her eyes that beast would be there. She still didn't feel her shadows moving to protect her, so she couldn't be in danger…

Or so she thought.

Ori couldn't bring herself to open her eyes for fear that her brain had produced an image so real that it would eat her alive.

She heard the clacking of shoes again and a voice that she knew all too well, "Now, now, Merikh, he would not be pleased if his *treasure* was dead before he arrived." The venom of his unmistakable voice sounded from all around her. Echoes bouncing off the black slate.

Ori opened one eye and saw the Penumbra lying on the stone floor only feet from her like a lion ready to pounce. Only if lions were the size of the townhouses in Grimmstone. The beast's stare bore into her with its teeth bared and claws digging into the floor.

She wouldn't have given it the satisfaction of turning away if it weren't for the presence she felt looming over her shoulder.

Ori turned slowly and looked up from her position on the floor to see the man in black.

"Takara, the quest to find you has been a long one. I've lost many of my beloved hounds to your *friends*." He said the word as if the thought of relationships disgusted him greatly.

He began to circle her as he continued speaking. "I even sent my brother to kill them all but you had not one, but two, dragon shifters with you. How did you manage to find such vile company? Who would find company in faeries? So beneath you."

Brother? He didn't mean... Ori snapped her head back to the Penumbra but in its place stood another man dressed in black from head to toe. All Ori could see were his piercing blood-red eyes through dark strands of hair. A cloth covered the lower half of his face.

"Oh, don't worry about Merikh. He is still a little sore from the regeneration process. He will be just fine in no time. That little *faerie* did a number on him. My brother isn't whom you should be worried about though." The man spat the word faerie out like bad wine, and it made Ori's anger shoot to the surface.

She stood too quickly, stumbling back and almost falling back to her knees, but she held herself up. She wouldn't let this man who'd taken so many lives already speak of her friend that way.

She reached for her dagger–it wasn't there. She'd always had it on her, nestled in the sheath it was gifted in. That sheath was empty.

As Ori began to speak she felt her mouth moving but no words sounded. She reached for her throat and found a loose collar; she ran her hands over the material but found no buckle or clip to take it off.

"Yes, you won't be talking back unless he decides to remove that fine piece of jewelry from your pretty neck." The man in black had his face covered as well but Ori could see the man's cheeks rise forming what she knew was a vulgar smile.

"Cain," Merikh called from his designated spot in the chamber, "He is coming."

Cain?

She rummaged through her mind for any answer to her thousands of questions, questions that she wouldn't be able to ask if she didn't get the dreaded collar off of her.

The man in black–Cain–turned to her again and stepped in close. Ori took a step back, but shadows wrapped around her waist and legs, holding her in place. She knew then who he was, The Necromancer. She recalled the story of the Shadow Wielder Asvin told them about.

Her eyes widened in fear as only inches separated her from the man–no, the *monster* that took countless souls from The Five Realms.

"You aren't the only one with your father's gift." He reached up and slid the silky black cloth down below his chin.

He had thin, pale lips that almost blended into his sickly white skin. His eyes stood out in stark comparison, they were wholly black, matching the dark hair she could see underneath his hood with the close proximity of his body to hers.

The Necromancer smiled as if he were looking at the prize he'd won for himself.

She was no prize.

Ori had never been the desire of anyone, and she wouldn't let the murderous creep that stood before her now see her as anything other than what she truly was, dangerous.

Ori drew her fist back in anger, thrusting it with enough power to break his nose. But before her knuckles made contact with his face, a tendril of cold shadow gripped her wrist which was frozen only an inch from his face.

"I always knew you'd be fun to play with." The Necromancer's obsidian stare drew down her body and then up again to meet her eyes. "This realm has been waiting for you entirely too long and he is most pleased that I have brought you home."

Home?

This was not her home. She wasn't sure she actually had a home, but she knew this was not one she would ever claim. She still had no idea where she was, to begin with. Her mind raced as she tried to piece together what she *did* know.

It was cold here, like Coulteron's frigid winters.

The night sky was darker than any she'd ever seen. Even in Grimmstone, one could still see faded stars and a gray moon through the smog of the city.

Asvin had told them about The Necromancer, he was... *Phyrus'* soul assassin.

Ori was in Phyrus' realm.

"Ahh, I see you've figured it out now. It took you long enough," The Necromancer turned and walked behind her with his back turned to Ori, the shadows still held her firmly in place.

"Welcome to the realm of Phyrus, The God of Oblivion and Souls. The place where the abominable and gruesome come to pay for the lives they've taken for granted. The place where you, The Treasure of Infinite Death, will come to know your place in the future of The Five Realms and beyond."

Ori felt her heart pick up in speed, she felt sweat beading down her spine.

She couldn't handle this.

Only moments ago, she was in the arms of the one person she felt she could have a future with. She didn't understand it fully, but she had found what she believed felt like *home*.

A place with friends and family. A place where she was accepted for who she was, not what she was capable of.

She didn't want the future this deeply disturbed man spoke of. She didn't want this; this is what she had run from her entire life. She ran, just like her mother told her to do.

But she hadn't run fast enough this time.

The Necromancer turned swiftly on his heels and bowed deeply. The shadows that held her fell away leaving Ori to fall right onto her knees.

She cried out at the pain, but no sound echoed through the room. The blinding pain ebbed and flowed through her entire body as she pushed up onto her feet and tried to stand.

When she looked down, the cracks in the stone floor were glowing. Deep shades of orange and red like liquid fire manifested through the spider-webbed pattern.

The sconces on the walls were burning brighter, casting a shadow where she weakly stood.

Ori lifted her head up to see what–or rather *who*–she knew would be standing there.

His boots were the deepest black, darker than the floors they stood upon, they stopped at the knee where black pants were tucked in.

He wore a black waistcoat made of silk with a matching long-sleeved shirt beneath.

She found herself not wanting to move her eyes up any further, but she forced herself to look into the eyes she *knew*.

The eyes she had avoided in the mirror, in every reflection she passed.

The eyes of her father.

Phyrus stood tall with his hands clasped behind his back. His pale, freckled skin matched hers but his hair, shaved down on the back and sides, was a brighter shade of red than her own. His hair looked like a dancing flame of deep orange that was encircled by a simple black crown holding one ruby stone in the center that lay on his forehead.

His golden eyes were dark, filled with an unmistakable malicious intent, the kind that made one fear for their lives without being given a reason.

Ori knew then that she likely wouldn't be leaving this realm in life–or in death.

"My treasure," The God of Oblivion and Souls chuckled, "you've made it just in time. Today is the day of a new beginning, one that will end with the other gods and goddesses bowing to *me*. And you," he looked at her intently, like The Necromancer had, like she was a gift, a prize that had been won, "*you* will be my weapon to unleash upon the realms of the gods, Takara Orelia Keres."

Epilogue
Percyful

He hadn't heard from anyone in the days after he and Nik arrived home in Keld. Percy was grateful to walk among the townspeople as himself again and not as his brother's grandfather; a weak old man shuffling through the dirt.

He was still amazed by the way his body didn't constantly ache. People no longer stopped in the street to aid him in carrying items or to help him cross a busy roadway.

Nik had even given him more space. But Percy was certain that had less to do with him and more to do with the fact that Nik had spent the majority of his time back home with Jo. Percy knew Nik had missed her and probably thought he'd never see her again after the journey to Qoohria.

The captain had brought what was left of the party, plus Baastian, to the seaport at Knife's Edge where they all parted ways. Lyra and Blackwell headed straight for the Celerity Channel, and Asvin and Ash took flight east to Vytarrion.

It was Callan that Percy had a difficult time leaving behind. He told Callan that he would search until they found an answer, though he didn't think that his words gave Callan much hope.

Callan assured Percy that he and Baastian wouldn't give up on finding Ori and Ezra, and their search would begin in Grimmstone alongside Blackwell and Lyra.

With a sorrowful parting, Percy embraced Callan and gave him a charm of good fortune that he'd always kept with him. He wasn't sure how well it worked given some of the unfortunate circumstances they'd encountered, but he figured Callan could use it more than he could. Perhaps the small silver token would benefit Callan far more than it did Percy.

Percy had done nothing but research the portals of the gods and goddesses. Though there were very few mentionings of them in his small collection of historical records, he had found some interesting passages that caught his attention.

The questions that formed from searching brought him to the woods that lay only a few miles inland from Keld.

He knew of only one person who might be able to answer his inquiries.

She happened to be the only person he wished to see at that moment.

Percy walked a few yards into the green trees, deep enough to no longer see the town from a distance.

His clothes soaked with sweat from the sweltering heat of summer in Keld. The humidity of home was something he didn't miss while they were in Qoohria. In fact, he almost wished he would've stayed in the abandoned castle surrounded by the cool mists.

Once Percy felt he was far enough away from civilization, he reverently whispered to the trees, just as he'd done before, "Sakura, are you there?"

Percy heard his voice tremble ever so slightly, remembering the last time he'd called for Sakura. He could recall the power of rejuvenation and healing that restored his youth and repaired his arm.

In the same breath he could still feel the teeth of the Shadow Hound ripping his flesh and snapping his bones.

The only physical reminder that the entire journey wasn't just a dream were the mangled scars on his arm and the nerves that hadn't completely regenerated.

He was about to call for Sakura again until he saw the pale green haze that gathered along the patches of grass and leaves near his feet.

When the mist built to the height of her tall frame and then dissipated, Percy was greeted with an overwhelming sense of relief at the sight of the enchanting Sakura.

Each time he saw her he was fully captivated by her; it was as if she had stepped right out of the pages of the legends he'd studied his entire life. This time was no different

But something was wrong.

The relief quickly spiraled into unease as he approached a Sakura who was not the bright, effervescent being she had always appeared as but something entirely different.

She was petrified.

Her hair was in a chaotic tangle, one of her branch-like antlers had been snapped at the midpoint, and her arms and legs with swirling leaves of green were splintered with cuts, scrapes, and bruises. But it was her eyes, the beautiful blue-green gems that still sparkled held a thousand emotions in them that Percy could not decipher.

Sakura didn't speak, she only stood before him with her hands clasped in front of her, fidgeting with her fingers restlessly.

Percy took another step forward and Sakura jumped, as if she was afraid... of him?

When he stepped back to give her space Sakura reached out and grabbed his hand, pulling him to her. Once they stood only inches apart she wrapped her arms over his shoulders, burying her face in his neck, and wept.

Percy just held her there, he didn't speak, he didn't rush her to move, he simply waited until she finally lifted her head.

With tears the color of the darkest oceans streaming down her face, Sakura looked deeply into Percy's eyes. She was searching for something, though he wasn't sure what she wanted or needed to see.

So, he simply smiled. Percy didn't know what had led Sakura to this extreme emotion, but he found himself wanting to take away some of the worry that undoubtedly rested on her shoulders.

Sakura attempted to return the well-meant gesture, but the forced lines of her lips faltered into a trembling frown. Percy desperately tried to read her mind but found no such power within him. He could, however, feel the overwhelming throb of essence that radiated from her. He noted that it was different from the times before when she had been near, this was almost frantic in nature compared to the calm waves that he remembered.

"Sakura," he spoke her name softly, using a crooked finger under her chin to pull her eyes to his, "please tell me what's wrong."

Percy ran through the other thousand questions he wished to ask first like "who did this to you?" and "where are they?" but his conscience decided that there would be time for those questions later.

Sakura looked deeply into his eyes once more and took in a shuddering breath, "Percy, I tried."

Tears slid down her cheeks one after another. "I tried to help. I heard what happened to the Shadow Wielder, Ori. I went to Baasis, and I asked her to help the celestials but she…"

Sakura didn't have to finish her explanation for Percy to know that it was no mere mortal who did this to her.

She suffered this brutal beating from a god, a god that many saw as the supreme leader of all the gods. The Goddess of the Hunt.

His overprotective side—a side of him that had only been reserved for his brother until Sakura—dwindled down to the size of a field mouse under the growing fear that crept like up his spine.

"Baasis said that I had no right to ask that of her considering who Ori *belongs* to. It upset me to hear her say that any creature could *belong* to another, even a god. She didn't like it when I challenged her and told her that she was the bringer of peace and beauty in the realms, the provider, the *mother* of all the realm-walkers, Draoi or no."

Percy saw that Sakura was no longer crying, her cheeks marked by dried blue tears. Instead, Sakura's eyes were blank, there was no sparkle, there was no endless searching or curiosity, just a blank stare.

Percy couldn't quite place the emotion behind her eyes as she continued to speak. "The gods and goddesses of the realms have not been friendly in a very long time. In fact, over the last century, they have been at each other's throats. And..." Sakura trailed off.

It was then that Percy knew the emotion that stirred behind Sakura's dull, beautiful eyes. It was the same emotion that he felt suffocating him in that very moment.

Sakura placed her cold hands on either side of Percy's face. He wanted to smile for her again but felt every muscle in his face and body locked into place rendering his efforts useless.

As Sakura brushed a single free tear from Percy's cheek, she whispered to him in a tone he knew was meant to bring comfort, though her words did not evoke the same. "The gods are preparing for war."

Pronunciation Guide

Draoi: dray-OY

Nondraoi: Non-dray-OY

Xestoral: zest-OR-all

Corpoi: korp-OY

Dyngheloi: din-geh-LOY

Malachi: mah-LUH-key

Places

Baasaris: BAH-sar-iss

Vytarion: vuh-TAR-ee-on

Qoohria: quh-or-EE-uh

Estana: eh-STON-uh

Phyruh: fai-RUH

Atreyu: ah-TRAY-uu

Keld: kehld

Midscar: MID-skar

Tregaron: TRAY-gar-on

Pyrecliff: PIRE-klif

Coulteron: KOAL-ter-on

Names

Callan Bram: KAL-lan bruh-AM

Ashlun "Ash" Tanwen: ASH-lun TAN-wen

Ori: ORH-ee

Asvin Falak: AZ-vin fah-LAK

Lyra Nocte: leye-RUH NOK-tay

Percyful "Percy" Cromwell: PUR-sea-full KROM-well

Nikolai "Nik" Cromwell: NIK-o-leye KROM-well

Sakura: saa-KOR-uh

Enoch Ferraille: ee-NOK FAIR-uh-lee

Enid: ee-NID

Varis: VAR-iss

Rohan: ROW-haan

Kaster Tanwen: KAS-ter TAN-wen

Reya Tanwen: ray-UH TAN-wen

Hyacinth Baas: hi-YUH-sinth

Ezra Ellis: ehz-RUH eh-liss

Cytheria Keres: Seye-THEAR-ee-UH kair-ES

Bronte Falak: BRON-tay fah-LAK

Myrsky Falak: meer-skee fah-LAK

Cordelia Nocte: kor-DEAL-ee-UH NOK-tay

Jaxe Nocte: JAX NOK-tay

Takara Orelia Keres: tuh-KAR-uh OHR-eh-LEE-uh kair-ES

Baastian Ellis: BASH-tee-AN eh-liss

Vidhi: VEE-dee

Cain: KAIN

Merikh: mair-ICK

Baasis: baa-seess

Vytarr: vuh-TAR

Qoohr: quh-or

Estsus: es-TUSS

Phyrus: fai-RUSS

About the Author

M.M. Bartlett, otherwise known as Madi to her loved ones, is a North Carolina based fantasy author. She resides in NC with her husband and three cats. She enjoys the little things in life most days, good company, a good drink, and a good book.

Madi grew up immersed in books like Harry Potter, Percy Jackson, Goosebumps, and many more that influenced her to dream about her own worlds and their heroes. As her reading evolved into a love for medieval literature, dystopian fiction, biographies, horror, non-fiction (usually about space), and even true crime; her relentless love for fantasy continued in worlds conjured from J.R.R. Tolkien, Holly Black, Brandon Sanderson, Sarah J. Maas, and many others.

Madi has been writing stories since she was very young and with the support of her friends and family, she has had the opportunity to finally bring together the colorful worlds and captivating characters that have occupied her mind for many years.

Madi plans to write a continuing series after The Way of the Nameless following the remaining characters and their interweaved lives in The Five Realms.

Madi loves the fantasy genre, but she has hopes to eventually take leaps into Science-Fiction and Horror.

www.ingramcontent.com/pod-product-compliance
Lightning Source LLC
Chambersburg PA
CBHW030234120726
47903CB00005B/1485